ICE CUBES ON DESERT SANDS

Sandeep Dahiya

Invincible Publishers

First published in India in 2018

ISBN: 978-93-88333-17-7

Invincible Publishers

G-120, Sushant Lok III, Sector 57, Gurgaon-122002

Registered Address: Opposite Kasturba Ashram,

Radaur, Haryana - 135133

O mother,

My first footstep

lies in thy womb,

From such a start

how can I go wrong?

In the loving memories of my

grandfather Master Pohkar Singh,

father Shri Ran Singh Dahiya,

uncle Satbir Singh Dahiya.

Preface

There is no separate story. Stories weave into each other like a well-spun fabric. Stories are rivers, ever flowing, existing yet not existing, shifting still static, different and similar at the same time.

The pieces. The patchwork. The story.

And different parts define the whole. Let's pick up little-little dust specks scattered over the anonymous path and weave a Story out of the Stories.

The little sparrow takes its first flight. A purchased bride fights back. A woman rises higher with love than the biggest work on theology by her husband. A porn star crosses the barbed fence to enter the mainstream society. The monk returns to keep his promise to a courtesan. Someone swipes the platforms to write his name under the stampeding feet. The tree decides to tell her murder story. Two hearts accomplish what many swords cannot. In a thorny bush, a flower blossoms to melt a cursing heart. The old sparrow reveals that happiness is a precondition to fly meaningfully in life. A young monk puts down the woman he carried; the older one still carries her whom he never touched. Someone has seen too much of death, now death itself shuns him. The moonlit landscape won't be there to see another season. Ice cubes melt on desert sands to leave a miniature oasis. Holi robs the woman of all smiles and colours, only to give it back as the last smile on her deathbed. There are ensnaring ropes in the mind stronger than anything external. A warrior returns from a point where duty turns into hate. A mouse casts a lion's shadow in the mind. The hangman pulls the death's handle with ease, but then his soul's questions cast a deadly noose. The boy on a devastated coast looks for hope, holding his little sister's hand. The young man brings bad luck all the time, except when his body is protecting his lover. She dances and raises flowers in the dust. A woman emerges from brothels to see the light finally.

Contents

to save it from the storms. Her love shines brighter than the masterwork of theology.

She has perfect figure, finest curves, very charming features and flawless skin. But she has a past to wipe out. A famous porn star, she is fighting to enter the mainstream of the so called decent corridors of film-making with routine roles. She has tired herself out on her acting skills. The world but doesn't want to forget. It's addicted to her past. She but is even more determined to cross the barbed-wire fencing around her.

On a beautiful spring day, a famous courtesan feels the pangs of passion for a handsome monk. He feels her pain and suffering but assures her that he will be there when she will need him the most. She cannot believe that her invitation can be spurned by a man. Years later, the middle-aged monk returns to complete his journey in self-realisation and be with her when she needs him the most.

He survived partition-time slaughter in Pakistan and lives like a faceless, nameless entity on a railway platform. The bigger world hurtles past him. With his unassuming, rested self he picks up the broom to gather the scattered pieces of his broken, dusted identity to collect and piece together a shape, a name-able entity on the fringes of the bigger world.

The mankind is at war with the nature and is mercilessly swiping away all natural boundaries without any resistance. The decades-old huge eucalyptus but decides to call a murderer a murderer. As the saws cut across its bloodless guts, the tree bears witness to its own murder, while still doing its duty to give oxygen to the murderous lungs. It continues on its duty till the last snapping sound deprives it of its small hold of land.

Only love has the potential of performing alchemy, capable of turning rusty iron of hate into the gleaming gold of humanity. The princess is famous for her beauty. The prince is from an enemy kingdom. Drawn by her fabled beauty, he comes to her kingdom, gets caught and is condemned to be beheaded. He is saved by the ray of love in the princess's heart. The peace that could not have been ensured by thousands of swords is effectuated by two loving hearts.

The seasons change but the meditating sage hasn't moved. Driven by a lovely mischief, a fairy plays a prank and pays by turning into a thorny bush by his curse. Years later, he comes with his enlightened self, and prays at the altar of the lone flower among the thorns in that very bush. They meet as a man and a woman, of course, bonded by love.

The parrot is young but tired and dispirited. The sparrow is old but happy and contended. They spend a night together in the sparrow's wooden hole. The parrot is told the wisdom of the ages to make happiness a precondition for one's doings, not a poor outcome of efforts. Happiness is a state of ***being so***, not the specific result of some hot pursuit. On a bright sunny morning, the parrot flies away, just being happy, not in pursuit of happiness.

1. A Ladleful of Lilting Memories

Cooling in the elixir of postmodernist afterglow? There are deft strokes, steely lines and spools of songs about our achievements. But there are shadowy poles which beat the fog with their pale, penetrating light, sending some feeble messages concerning our follies. The angelic, sacred balance and equipoise has been disturbed. The natural laws have been violated and warped. Something basically wrong has happened with nature during the present scandalous times. The odds were never so much staked against life and living. The push for survival is hurtling down too rapidly, crashing through the naturally set fence of checks and balances, taking us towards the precipice overlooking the valley of death and destruction.

Have you ever seen a sparrow couple fighting out with another one, the latter having set up its nest, mated, laid eggs and waiting for hatching under the mother's warm fur and father's protective watch? It does happen now. The force of human touch is too strong on nature. Everything is getting humanised. And with due respect to the pardonable—beyond the realm of sin and piety—non-judgemental fights among the innocent, instinct-led lives in the animal and bird kingdoms, we can still brand this particular attack as the most gruesome one on somebody's home and hearth to fulfil the basest of a selfish motive.

They were furiously screeching, twittering, hen-pecking their beaks into the rivals' fur like the men-of-swords at war; their little claws trying to gouge out the opponents' eyes. Mind you, it had all human connotations. Their rumpled feathers and crumpled fur had all the elements of a bloody street fight among the humans. And what was it for? To grab the nest! On the path of short-cutting greed, the predatory couple, eying someone's cosy home, had ditched the fundamental principle of the species: make a new nest before you taste the freedom of love and mating leading to the duties of parenthood.

Possibly the fact that the nest possessed the smell of human hand in making it had something to do with the things going nasty like among the supreme species of the earth. It was a barn roof made of wooden rafters and stone slabs. The box made of plywood was attached to one of the rafters. It hung there with a broad look of *TO LET for free* over the uncemented, brick-laid floor below.

Earlier, this transgressing couple never ever cared to look at the abandoned nest, vacant after the previous hatching, waiting for some laborious sparrow couple to sort out things for another cycle of home-making by the new entrants. Then a diligent couple arrived looking for a secure home. Finding the odour of long-left nestlings inimical to their pure, non-short-cutting instinct to procreate and preserve, they worked to bring it into order for a new homely start. Old bird-drops smitten sinews were thrown down piece by piece and new ones fixed for a brand new cosy interior. Then the eggs were laid and the expectant moments for hatching started.

Now there was a fight at hand. Perhaps, it's the modern day norm to destroy before getting on to the next step in the journey. The way they—the attacking couple, led by their hissing instinct which easily overpowered the much mellowed down parental defence—beat out the parents waiting for the fluid in their tiny eggs to form and shape into nestlings, made them condemnable as the rogue, brutish couple. Broken shells and spattered fluid on the ground for ant-feed provided testimony to the charge against them.

The winners knew that the mourning couple will take one more day to keep fussing around the site, so unashamedly they mated on a nearby tree, fully sure of their possession of the nest. The next day, they started flitting in and out of the sinewed shelter, with spring in their flight and much mirth in their dives; making minor adjustments to the grabbed property to satisfy that primordial birdy instinct to make a new nest before drawing out procreative self's best. Very cleverly they made those minor adjustments; gave themselves a clean chit and life started again in the nest.

Why have even birds started taking short-cuts like the humans, stepping over others' toes in the selfish stampede, crushing others' dreams to fulfil personal motives? Very intelligently the birds around the human world have also picked out a few paying lessons from our book of practicality. Kudos to the humanity!

******

I, a little sparrow, just out of the nest, and not even baptised, have been a witness to this happening which took place in the neighbouring man-made nest-box attached to the wood and stone-slab ceiling. Quite surprisingly, I've a wonderful memory to narrate the sayings of Mother almost as she did.

Now, since I'm sitting freely on a branch, I can narrate the whole story without being constantly chirp-sermonised, pecked and haggled to take first lessons in a birdie flight. Mama and Papa aren't with me for the simple reason that both of them couldn't withstand that hit by the ceiling fan (within a couple of days—Papa on the previous day and Mama the following day, that is yesterday) circling in air to make air out of air—and draw blood as well, if chance suited it—over, above, around, beneath the buffalos and calves in this rectangular barn with three wall sides and one side open fronting the courtyard.

Well, as soon as we were hatched and could make out the meaning of her chirping, many nestling anecdotes started. For a couple of week, we were just parting our tiny, yellow beaks to this someone who was funnily so kind and loving to these—I mean me and my sibling—ugly, hairless, soft, purplish balls. Amidst intervals in their frantic, beakful cargoeing to cater to our unceasing hunger she—Mama, I came to know—had some moments of respite:

"Your Papa and I were one day frantically scratching our beaks against the plastered walls and the ceiling of this open-fronted barn. Nowadays, it's rare to have unplastered walls having nooks, holes and crevices for us to sneak in and make nest. It's after all a sound, solid, smooth world of the modern-day man.

"And there are still lesser trees with holes in their trunks. You rarely find big, old, grandmotherly trees with crooked trunks these days. Ah, what a loss! The story of huge, centuries old trees was told by my mother who heard it from her mother and so on. I can spare your little head with those details. This is no longer the world for fairy tales.

"So coming back to our story, we were desperately trying to undo the smooth plasterwork with our little beaks. But beaks are no chisels. How I wish that we also develop iron in our beaks to cope with the changing times. After all, everything is changing so fast. So we just tried as hard as possible. And by the look of it, we felt sure to do with a hole in the walls just below the ceiling, around the rafter-ends.

"It is, as you can see with some care not to fall down, a stone-slab and wood-beamed roof, so we smelt our chance here. There are two iron cross-beams. The one that you see just ahead and the other you can't—but will see later as you come out to enjoy this big world. These run along the width and the small wooden rafters supported on the beams along the length across the three sections bearing the stone-slabs make our roof. Well, that's our roof. It's better to know one's roof. It's as good as knowing the roots.

"All of us need the hole of our size. But just for utilitarian purpose, we can't become ants to lay eggs. Harder and harder we worked for a fitting hole. I even envied the ants on the barn floor for having to bore tiny holes. But then they are themselves too small and must be having their own set of problems which we cannot see from a distance. The small must also be having their set of big problems. Our wings smeared with sweat. We could disturb spider-webs, plaster and lime whitewash only. There was little to show, except some dents in the lime-wash, in lieu of our efforts. It's so hard to make a home inside some bigger one's home!

"This farmer that you can steal a glance from above, tending the buffalos, cutting the grass, working on the chaff-cutter over there, and grinding wheat in that *chakki*—the way I do for you in my beak on a tiny scale—in that flour machine there in the opposite left hand corner, is very kind and understanding. We birds tend to make a bigger noise our little demands. It's disproportionate to our worth and feathery stature. But quite paradoxically our noise does appear a song to the bigger world having bigger brains. So most often, even our mourning for the dead goes on to be interpreted as a song of celebration, as if in some nest the prince of the whole birdie kingdom has been born.

"There are good people, simply like there are bad people. Are they really good, or they have to put up the pretention of being good through supposedly good acts, we don't know. Is goodness the first flash received in reaction to circumstances; or they have to labour for it? Well, these questions shouldn't rob us of our thankfulness we should feel for this farmer boy. God bless him with all good things in life, a nice harvest, good wife and long life and a longer trail of children! He knew it was no song of ecstasy and love. It was a noise of desperation. So he thought of helping us.

"Then there are various categories of people. Some don't listen even if they see it; some listen but don't act; some act in a bad way; and some act positively. And God bless him with more happiness than any other human being. He not only listened but acted well also. He nailed plywood boards into this beam here in the safe corner. He fixed this box to the wood rafter away from all storms and dangers.

"There are but many takers for such safe house-letting. So a rival couple, in the same position as we, arrived just as we had staked our claim to the wooden little box by ferrying the foundational sinews. To defend this fact and to save a position of being held culpable on account of not defending our right, and thus add to the lawlessness, we maintained and secured our foothold. It was tough though!

"Now there are some people who can repeat an act of kindness even twice: who don't turn their ears deaf and eyes blind, hands crippled and legs numb; whose mind is not seized with clapping for the already opened account of goodness; and heart is not basking and drawing moral solace from that sole deed for days on end. Defying all these simply affordable luxuries, he took another bitter swig of practicality (or maybe it was really a sweet pill to him), he made another one over there just to the other side of the iron cross-beam, where you can see the lower ends of the dangling grass sinews from its opening. Ours, however, is more favourably placed. Here you have this big swing they playfully turn on, and sometimes it gets turned off by itself; sometimes it starts again by itself and sometimes they have to put their index finger over that board!"

Well, you might complain that I, a young sparrow just out of the nest for the first time, my funny purplish body bearing a funny coat of grey-brown tufts yet to cover the whole of me, have ended up telling a whole epical story from the book of birdie mythology. But it isn't so. It's a simple narrative Mother told me and my little sister.

I take the onus and burden of being the elder sibling for the mere fact of my male gender, her relatively slow development, pathetic shrill cries as well as my outmanoeuvring her to grab most of the beakfuls Mama and Papa managed to get from somewhere. Where did they go, I was never able to know. To me the world meant this roof and the barn floor below; and for society, it just means the vague indication of hustling and bustling in the neighbouring nest.

I don't know why there are so many different types of birds. Well, there must have been some pattern and reason behind all this; otherwise all bird parents will make their offsprings look the same. And Moms and Dads will have problems in recognising their children. In that case, it will turn really funny. Elders would feed wrong kids, mistaking others' children for their own.

To some people physical requirements and convenience come first and the moral, material duties required to support the former come later. I don't exactly understand the real meaning of it. I've sort of crammed it up for the sake of my all-knowing Papa, as he told me on that stormy night while the big noise from where my parents fetched grains kept we nestlings awake. It was scary!

With a mischievous glint of pride, Mama and Papa bragged that day that the other couple was just the same; while they were the opposite. Here again I just reproduce the words—for I've been born with a wonderful memory—chirped by Mama about the meaning of 'opposite':

"To us the duty comes first. The duty to support the pleasure; otherwise today's pleasure becomes tomorrow's pain. So before deciding to bring you two to this nest, we worked on this opening in the box. It was a bit big and risky for you little ones. We almost sewed up the opening with grass sinews to avoid a fall, leaving this nice peephole for you and a door for us. It took us weeks before we finally entered the marital life. But she, the lady in that other couple, already had eggs in her furred belly when they came to fight us.

"Hadn't it been for the farmer boy, she would have been forced to lay eggs in open, much to the shame of birdie motherhood! So they had no time to secure their box's opening. While the nature's call or miscall struck at her belly and father's head, they scampered for a couple of days to get a famished bed for the eggs and the flimsiest of a grass wall around the opening.

"Thank God, you didn't see the consequences to the nestlings because then you were mere eggs! The day their scurrying for food started to shake the nest's sinew wall, their future seemed almost lost. More so because the farmer's son has a domesticated cat. A cat eats the likes of us! So always be scared of them. Now we hate cats for this fact. But we can pity her as well for we have wings. A cat can't fly. So unless and until we become too careless to allow the cat's earthly crawling beat our sky-high winged flight, we need not have fear at the cat front. So as youngsters, I'll not teach you both to get crazy about the cat's claws and make little, ineffective, hateful noises about the predator. Strengthen your wings. That is my advice.

"Now, before you both start hating this farmer boy for petting a cat, let me tell you that there are rats as well. And rats do a great harm to a farmer's harvest and interests. So they have to bear with the nuisance of even a cat. You must have seen her prowling below from the strong parapet of your nest, gazing with the patience of a sage at our box. Whenever the cat had time from the rats and its mean mewing at the stray ones of her type, it stood below our neighbouring nest. It saw a chance there. The opening was too big. Its mouth brimming with water as it listened to the meaty sounds coming from behind that thin curtain of sinews and grass at the box's opening. The nestlings were growing rapidly, as you were very slowly coming into shape inside your shells. The farmer boy knew the cat's intentions, so not to rob him of the credit for his good deed, many a time he shooed her away from the spot. But he couldn't beat her out of the house for the simple reason that there were many rats.

"The nestlings—three of them—had grown fat as the parents had been feeding them quite well. In this at least they were not idlers. Whimpering to eat more and more, they now hit against the grassy protection around the opening. It finally gave away and the two of them dropped like little meaty dumplings in the form of reward for the cat's patience. Before the farmer boy could run to their help, she, more agile, gathered up the freebies and ran towards the courtyard wall. She wouldn't let go off the prize even as a stick landed on its back while it cleared the fence. Now, you might say that he must have forsaken the criminal. To be fair to him, he must have even thought about doing the same, for I saw him chasing the offender for a couple of days. He must have started to become oblivious to the fact that there are rats if not for his mother's scolding. Even the rats came out of their holes. Since there were rats, so there had to be a cat. They are still hidden around. Beware of them! Rats are even bigger enemies because they cause the cat to exist in the house.

"Well, to leave the cat and return to the tragedy-stricken parents, we can't add wordings to their grief. The grassy facade had fallen. It now appeared a gaping hole of death in the far corner of which cowered the lone survivor. I saw it in the maker's eyes as he pitifully looked at the nest from below. We don't speak but our tweets make us understand our own chirping—it helps in telling you the story. But for the unspoken feelings of the humans! They are strange, so I cannot tell you anything about them. But I found him full of guilt for his design. His eyes conveyed that feeling to me. O yes, humans' eyes tell a lot about the things that aren't spoken. 'I should have put up a support along the opening,' I guessed him to rue sullenly. But somebody's good intentions can't match the perfection of design required to bring the full fructification of those kind wishes..."

Here again I'm just repeating the words, for the meaning gets lost to me. I must reproduce the crammed words. I feel more confident of my memory than of my wings. Anyway to carry on with my mother's story:

"So as a result of the bird couple's mismanagement, the boy's deficiency of design and the cat's simple validation of the fact that 'cats not only eat rats, they eat birds with even more relish' he blamed himself.

"After mourning the loss of two hatchlings, they had to still work for the sole survivor. As we birds forget easily, the task at hand becomes the real cause for flying, chirping, tweeting, pecking, peeking, etc., etc. They showered all paternal and maternal love upon the lone hatchling. The farmer boy knew that the last one was also doomed to fall, so he tried as many times to forget that there are rats and kicked the cat, followed by more and more lingering moments below the nest to catch the victim mid air.

"He is a very learned fellow, knows that a nestling—as soon as it gets onto its feet—tries to follow the parents after they have emptied their beaks into its greedy pout. So the moment he heard the little one's shriek of joy announcing the parent bird's arrival, he rushed to the scene to avoid repetition of the gory incident of the past.

"The young bird flapped its yellowish wings, pecked with its yellow-cornered beak at the saggy, scattered tufts of feathering. Many a time, it came almost toppling down as it continued on its repetitive haggling for food as the parents left the nest. Finally, one day its childish greed found it toppling down. However thanks to its good stars, there was no cat but the boy who had forgotten or trying to forget that there are rats. He plays the game of ball really well. I've seen him catching the ball over there in the playground where we get the grains and grass seeds outside the village. He caught the terrified thing midair. The screechy little drop almost choked itself to death with fear.

"Its unthankful parents, quite ignorant of the home-maker's latest deed of kindness, tweeted obscenities from the branches of the *neem* tree swaying to gentle breeze in the courtyard. He knew that any effort to play the role of father-mother by him would still fall way short of the mark to save the little nestling—so repressing the urge to keep it—he flew it or rather threw up towards the hanging branches. It flapped its feathery resistance against a fall, thus fell less painfully, but cried as if had been shot. Anger and blame game touched a new high from the parents.

"However, a tree is a tree because it gives air, shadow and shelter to anyone looking for these. The fact that it was a tree was proved by another fact that there was another bird in it. It was but a crow! On the second throw, the wily crow plucked away the offering mid air and flew away with a thanksgiving cawing. In desperation the boy hit himself on the head and stoically bore all humiliations heaped by the stolen kid's parents screeching, squeaking in pain.

"As penance, he boarded up half of the opening for a better future and clearer conscience. He came to our nest as well with the same suspicion about safety and the same set of resolution. However, both we parents chirped very confidently from our grassy fortress. He had to convince himself that at least we won't add to his score of self-reproach. You were only eggs then dears; and he left us as we were!"

Then we were hatched and grew at the cost of their parental labour. Then one day, I witnessed that genocide of egg-breaking by the rogue couple who sneaked into the other nest to set up their home by force. If not for that foul-smelling oddity, the life seemed birdie-small and infinitely enjoyable.

Mama and Papa were feverishly bent upon bringing each and everything available there in the outer world. The things and stuff cut by their beaks were easily lost in my gut. We thus grew bigger. I myself had a vague notion of this fact of growing stronger because now we made louder noise and ate more. But more was the look of desperation on the faces of Mama and Papa.

We thought we did them a favour by nibbling down everything they brought. So in order to make them happy in their occupation, we continued making noises even while our little bellies were full. Getting irritated, Papa sometimes gave us punishing pecks and chiding preens. He always talked of future...when you will grow up...when you will catch a worm yourself...when you'll fly. And we siblings wondered why he talked so much about something we didn't even know about.

Papa would have been really happy to see a day when his inexplicable and unmeaningful words dawned on us with their clear meaning. But then something happened and he was no longer able to repeat those words during the resting spells amidst his food-carrying duty. He had a scruffy look and spoke matter-of-factly in a serious tone.

But then one day he bore an extra serious expression, his beak open with a wearied thirsty look. His deep, kind eyes glazed to a frigid point somewhere far into the distances. Something had changed forever. It also meant that he no longer had to labour to and fro for the beakfuls of cargo to feed us.

The stoppages and pluggings born of the change meant that Mama now had to work doubly hard and mould her soft molly-coddling words to take the shape of his guiding phrases. 'The balance' she said. The toy which produces air out of air had mothered all these new meanings of a changed reality.

We birds have this faculty of minding only the business we are engaged in. However, it is a handicap as well. Handicap—faculty...faculty—handicap...advantages—disadvantages...profit—loss...loss—profit...paradoxically, these seem to have a peculiarly perverted, juxtaposed, interposed meaning to me. I can just draw a hazy meaning of what I just ended up telling you. Haa, haa but that makes me a bird philosopher.

From the grassy parapet we had a nice view of the swirling circle. We enjoyed its circular antics. It was so funny. Mama and Papa but warned each other while going out, looking at it apprehensively. However, coming in with a full beak is a totally different ball game. At that time possibly their mind doesn't mind too much about the funny thing. And darting in with proud air, Papa was hit by the air-producing toy. His skull smattered; beak offloaded for the last time. Air catapulted him against the wall and then he slumped without air in his wings down the wall. For a few moments the air still seemed wobbling inside him at the foot of the wall, as if to play with the air from the airy toy.

He seemed all the same except airless, flightless and a tiny patch of blood on the skull tufts and loss of few feathers. I wondered why Mama was making such a huge roar over such a minor difference in Papa's status. Then I grew anxious. Perhaps the difference was bigger than I had initially presumed because he didn't move. I got worried that the cat will arrive, but perhaps all rats had gone out of the house that day, so the cat luckily didn't reach the spot. It must have gone where all the rats had gone, perhaps on some vacation.

I learnt a new thing that day: if a cat isn't around then it gives enough time for the snaily ants to creep up in swarms up to the one who is at risk at the hands of a cat. And I wondered and tried to calculate their number; whether they will be able to carry him or not. Before a cat he seemed so small, but before these ants he looked huge. However, someone still bigger came to lift him.

Seeing my Papa on his palm, I wondered whether this change of status had brought a new friendship between the boy and him. It taught me a lesson that if you are a bird but don't fly due to change of status, you then become friend to a boy. Mama was in crying fits and we too imitated her; grew hungry in the process and opened our pleading beaks to her. Forgetting all her drift of mood due to Papa's change of status, she started with larger beakfuls more frequently.

During resting intervals, she sat in the nest and looked sadly at the changed status of the airy toy; which perhaps had been punished for blowing out airs from Papa's lungs. The boy also looked accusatively at it. However, there were mosquitoes and flies below and there was a buffalo as well who was being tormented by them. The insects, in dangerous droves, loved its blood. When the insects injected out the blood, it reacted furiously and that affected the milking process. So it was necessary to run the airy toy at least during the milking time for the black beauty, who had put so much of airs herself just because she gave milk to them to become fatter.

The next evening, when the barn was buzzing with so much of air, Mama shrieked painfully and got her status changed exactly like that of father, except the presence of the milking boy on the scene. He ran and stopped the airing toy and picked up Mama with even sadder face.

The air slowly went out of the toy. Mama also appeared to have lost her air. The toy and Mama went airless, but the buffalo had again too much airs about it. It kicked the bucket as a drone-fly penetrated its skin. In place of the cat and the ants, it was milk all over. I also came to know that if milk is not in the basket, but on the ground, then a beating follows, for the boy's mother beat him away from the place. He had my Mama in his hand. I couldn't see further where did they go, but I could hear his mother's shouting.

Me and my sister were thus left alone. And how wonderful being left alone is! One can either choose to cry his guts out or chirp to the happiest hilt. However, we had our bellies empty so we chose the first option. Our new neighbours in the other nest suspiciously looked, lest our constant noise portended something accusatory against their transgression.

The grown-up brown-white bully, with a patch of black fur on its throat, even pecked at the grass protection about our nest's opening to silence us. I remember Ma telling me that it was a male who looked like that and I instantly matched it with Pa.

We cried louder with wider beaks, thinking the good neighbour had come to feed us. But they had already split the future's shapes in present's semi-fluid, so expecting any help from them would have been asking too much. Still a kid sparrow doesn't know the nitty-gritty of others' and their own parents, so we cried to get some food, taking their reprimands for some caring, kind signals. Since I was bigger than my sis sparrow and ate more than her, I made more noise.

Our noise got the farmer boy's attention. Since he was aware of the status of Mama and Papa, he must have derived our status as well from their status. I with my funny pale brown head gloated at him as the saviour. Though he had all the looks in his eyes of Mama and Papa, he couldn't become Mama and Papa, because he had no wings to fly to the far place they visited and no beak to carry the food. So I forgave him on that account.

'You have a big noisy head. Necessity will force you to come out of the nest and become a sparrow from an orphan nestling!' he must have calculated in his big head, after all they seem to run this world with their big head buzzing with God knows what type of ideas.

I knew he had in all his kindness thought of saving us by playing a hardy role. But we were just nestlings. And he won't be able to grow wings and beak to become Mama and Papa two-in-one. So it was hopeless from the beginning. He thus left us to face our lonely orphaned night.

If I could break these shells—I looked at the egg-shell fragments lying crushed around the grassy interior—while I was the tiniest of a thing to come out, I can still do the same. I tried to brace myself up quite funnily.

All the day's bulbs dangling unseen outside were put out by turns and darkness crept up in the barn below. Though the boy lit up a feeble reddish thing on the wall opposite, perhaps to remove darkness from our scared minds and nest, in addition to the daily purpose of helping the buffalo see what was what and save her from conjecturing phantoms. But this was the darkest night we had ever faced. Nothing can be darker than being parentless. We both kept crying late into the night and when sleep could no longer wait for the stoppage of our sad songs, it somehow smothered us down.

When our eyes opened, the light bulb in the barn had been turned off and the bigger one somewhere outside had been turned on. Right from the word go, we started our day with a spell of fearful and heart-rending chirping in all its suffering connotations. Somebody must have said it pretty well that we must not cry out our sorrows too loudly, for in that case these tend to perpetuate themselves.

A sparrow sat to our side of the iron cross-beam and looked attentively, hopefully into the nest. I thought it was Mama who on account of her changed status now looked a bit different. But these little shards of hope were dispelled when she suddenly darted into the opening. Shorn of all our past sorrows, we gave a shrill cry of triumph, gave her a happy look for her new smarter, sleeker appearance—for Mama had pretty worn-out herself before her last status—and parted our beaks a bit accusatively and complainingly.

However, instead of love-cuddling pecks, she gave a painful bite at the soft yellow point of my beak. Still hopeful, I thought maybe she is reprimanding me for some silly mistake I might have committed during her absence. But a harsher peck at little sis's softer and almost tuftless purple body convinced me that either it wasn't Mama or if it was she indeed, then in this new avatar as the beholder of a new status she didn't need us or at least won't feed and love us.

She was later joined by another one. It was a young, strong male. I couldn't help appreciating this new look of Papa. However, he was even harsher in his mistreatment. Maybe, he was angry that we hadn't changed like them. But then I became sure they were not Mama and Papa, but some nest-grabbers like I had seen in my neighbourhood.

As the stronger elder sibling, I tried to protect the property, lest Mama and Papa returned to scold me for not protecting the home and hearth properly in their absence. Little sis cowered in a corner, while I fought them peck for peck. But I was just a kid sparrow who hadn't taken a single flight, hadn't taken a single beakful of his own. So inevitably I was finally dislodged from my precarious perch on the grassy rampart.

I knew there are rats, so making the presence of a cat quite logical. The floor below seemed an open jaw of a cat. So I flapped my wings with all my hungry belly's might. I just beat them like I had been flapping inside the nest purposelessly. But then there was ground beneath my little paws and now I needed to avoid getting grounded. So naturally my feeble, famished flapping was bound to follow. To my surprise, it came naturally. A sparrow is destined to fly some day, I think. But then flying isn't the only thing in life.

Life stuck up in my chirpy throat, I just flapped dizzily without knowing the path or direction. Much to my first shriek of joy for the last many-many hours—now it had started to appear like I hadn't chirped happily even once since that doomed rupture in the shell brought me into this world of sorrows—I found myself landing on the wings of the air-maker which fortunately wasn't making air at that time. Perhaps it had stopped to witness my first flight—otherwise my status too would have changed like that of my parents.

Now I cried for my little sis to come out. They were having a good time pecking at her soft, scantily furred body. I myself was disappointed at my own appearance in the new light. I appeared quite funny. A muddy greyish cast. My relatively better furred body carried the striking vulgarity of a yet-to-take-flight nestling. But then I remembered I had taken my first flight and that too quite successfully. So I convinced myself that in the department of looks also I will perform better after my consequent flights.

They then threw out my little sis also. From the first moment, I cried words of encouragement. But she was too small, soft and feeble. Her first flight was surely going to be a failure. She wasn't that mature to know that she had wings with a purpose to fly.

However, knowing the wings and putting desperate efforts to use them doesn't mean a successful first flight, which in majority of the cases robs further chances of a retry. Why? Because there are rats and that means there are cats also. She struggled harder than I could have ever expected. Just a few more morsels daily for the last week and she definitely would have made it with her will power!

Now I held myself guilty for eating her share and thus robbing her of that extra ounce of power which would have ensured success in the first flight itself. That is, in reaching a destination, safe from the cat, even if it means to land on this airy toy that takes air out of sparrows to give air to the buffalo.

Alas, she fell! Not vertically straight, which would have been an utter humiliation. She flew slantingly, plummeting down dangerously, out of the barn's all-open front except for the two supporting columns across the length. She almost hit the middle of the *neem* trunk in the courtyard.

"Clutch at the bark...clutch at the bark...dig your little claws into it!" I cried at the top of my voice.

However, it required a few more ounces of strength. But her long flight, longer than mine and I felt beaten on this account even though she ate lesser, had sapped her of the tiny reservoir of power.

She just slumped along the rough, dark-brown surface of the main trunk. There she sat on the ground by the trunk; her beak panting like the world outside was airless.

Some rat must have played truant in some corner of the house for it created ripples in the cat's catty self and she ran towards the scene. Screeching a warning, I threw myself out from my perch. But instead of landing on the cat's cursed head, I found myself clinging from the upper part of the trunk, where it branched off into many other parts to allow we birds some shelter and airy swings.

She proved that she was a true, unerring and unsparing cat. Much to my consternation even the farmer boy wasn't there to punish the culprit with a hit at its bum while it leapt over the fence. Enjoying the regal spectacle of the cat hunting a prey, my neighbours were chirping meticulously from the branches above. I don't know whether they were throwing obscenities or were just playfully chirping.

My initiation into the outer world was thus quite an ordeal. I knew this new world required one more effort to reach higher in the foliage and from there watch out for the new prospects that might exist for a tiny sparrow like me. So drawing out the last ounces of strength from my hungry belly and bracing up my aching wings, I put up my third effort.

This time but I almost failed. I came hurtling and crashing down the branches to anchor my little paws into some support. I had almost given up but then luckily found myself clinging from a low hanging branch. After panting and resting for long minutes, I decided to give another try. This time I was satisfied as I found myself perched on a bough in the middle of the canopy. And from my dear place, away from the cat's reach, I gathered my wits to collect some thoughts about this new world.

'So this is the new world Mama and Papa ferried food from!' I thought about their trials and tribulations.

The tree wasn't as big as I had supposed it to be. It didn't look as interesting and mysterious as I had imagined it. The *neem* just appeared a bigger nest on a larger scale. There were high-low zigzagging walls of the houses, where there were more people like our own farmer boy. Maybe, there were rats and many more cats also. And there was this dull-bluish ceiling—like our very own roof—seemingly very high overhead. I suppose it wasn't as high as it seemed, for it appeared to be supported by the upper edges of the walls at the farthest corner this bigger nest.

I mustered up my wings, thinking that maybe I'll be able to take flights long enough to take a peek around this larger—though not as big as I had thought earlier—nest to find Mama and Papa in their changed status. But the earlier efforts had been too daunting and tiresome. So I completely abandoned the idea and put all my faith in my vocal cords. Quite surprisingly, even with my hungry belly, I could cry quite noisily. This I banked upon to carry my chirping message to my parents. Sitting there in the branches of the *neem* tree I cried:

"Mama and Papa, do you hear? I have successfully taken my first flight as you wished me to. But the bad thing is that the little sis failed. Weak and small as she was. Her failure meant that the cat took flight with her!"

I was loudly chirping all that had happened in the course of the time since their change of status.

I was fully confident that this newer bigger world wasn't big enough to stop my voice from reaching their ears. But it didn't change my status or position in any way. Quite unlike the bulb on the barn wall, this bigger bluish roof had its bigger, far brighter bulb.

Quite surprisingly, it changed its position since the time I had started to cry my guts out. Still more interestingly, the shades of its light also changed colours.

My constant screaming did invite some attention. The way they were cawing they must be crows, I thought. I recalled a story Mama had told me one day about them. I immediately knew it didn't portend well, for like cats they too are enemies with the added faculty of flying. A sparrow has to outmanoeuvre them in variously agile flying pattern. However, my options were so few that I decided to wait and watch.

The crows then started quarrelling for me, as if none of them had a son of theirs and they wanted to adopt me. The black monsters made it a virtual battlefield on the tree. Now I realised that there still was a bigger world beyond what I saw, for the farmer boy surely must not have been there because he didn't rush to the noisy scene in his courtyard. Had he been somewhere in the bigger nest, he was sure to come out to inquire. And that would have helped me.

'Maybe he is chasing the cat—completely forgetting that there are rats—with little sis in its mouth!' I thought.

'Am I so dear to these darkies that they are fighting it out among themselves to lay claim on me?' now I got some little traces of pride.

Then a bigger claimant with a larger instinct to patronise me hovered above the tree. In contrast to the blacks, its colour was brown-greyish. Its size was also bigger than the crows. But those murderously searing, searching eyes looked at me with such force that I felt attracted, exalted and scared at the same time.

One more thing, it also made me sure that it wasn't just a rogue, outcaste crow painted differently as a punishment and given bloodied eyes also due to beatings. It had razor-sharp, pointed, hooked beak. The closer it hovered, more differences struck me and my fear plummeted high into the blue roof. It had deadly claws which far out-sharpened the crows. Now I realised that its claim on me was the strongest. What made the claim strongest? There was no likewise rival to blunt the sharp edges of its hooked beak and talons. I knew it had all the power to mould my status the way it wanted. I felt a strong surge of nostalgia about my parents' memories.

"If he takes me then my status as my Mama's and Papa's kid will be changed!" I cried attention to all the cawing and fighting darkies.

My warning little tweets, but, went in vain. They, after all, were so busy in fighting it out among themselves. Their love for me was forcing them to give each other bloodied noses. And then, before I could vent out my next warning, those strong talons just snatched me away. It happened so swiftly that my little eyes couldn't even smack their lids.

As he rose higher, with me squeezed in his talons, I cried *fools* at the blacks. My sound must have been stronger this time, for they got the message and followed us almost crying with tears in their eyes. They made all types of threatening cawing, flew swiftly with menacing agility. Even the great fiery bulb—it had changed its position, I got to know while squeezed in those claws—seemed cheering the new claimant's ownership of me.

One of the sharp talons was curled around my neck restricting my verbosity; others were dug feebly but still tightly in my feathering, giving sharp pain. However, that thrill of bigger, longer flight was giving me such pleasure that I forgot even the pain. The passing cool air, cooler than I had ever felt it, sang in my ears. Clutched topsy-turvy, I had a madly exciting view of the fleeting panorama of this still bigger nest spread far and wide.

There was also that exalted feeling about beating the blacks with the help of this mighty bird. They were left behind and retreated to their smaller world. While travelling trapped in those claws, I imagined all types of fanciful things about the world he was taking me into. Although this world we were flying through seemed limited always up to that line of tree-tops with the blue roof supported on top of the branches. But surprisingly, we were never able to reach the end, so I just waited patiently to come to the front of a newer world.

But all my hopes were dashed as—even before crossing the threshold of this bigger (but not that big) world which seemed just a few paces away by that line of trees across the fields—he stopped in this very world. I was disappointed about the landing place as well. It was a huge strange tree. A dry, leafless tree of this new world, as if my carrier-friend had eaten away all the foliage. At its top was a thick nest of prickly twigs, rags and wood pieces. And mind you, it was stinking like hell. Into this he dumped me. I fell on a dried piece of meat and a little bone which hurt me.

Aawo...now I realised that the big bird needed a playmate for his lonesome, brooding nestling put up so high at this solitary place on this charmless tree. Instantly my new friend, almost as big as a crow but looking so funny in his shabby feathering, came to play with me. I also reciprocated his friendly welcoming leap of joy at me. However, his pecking was severe in comparison to my own caressing and harmless one. I but forgave him just on account of his inability to play softer, given his bigger size and sharp talons making it difficult for him to keep the welcome hug down to my sparrow level.

He was really eager to play with me. His father—or was it mother, I doubted while playing—looked with parental glint of satisfaction from a nearby dead branch. Then I began to bleed at various points of my first coat of feathering. Still I tried to play, though with time, it became a struggle to defend myself from further cuts and bruises. My playmate was too big and almost toyed with me. I kept on complaining noisily. But he was all eager to play and didn't listen to me at all.

Here we have to stop our narrative for I'm on the verge of fainting due to this bloody game of his...aye...aye...I am perhaps losing in the game!

***

2. She is Cheaper than a Buffalo

The summer is at its peak. Hot loo vaporises the beads of sweat before they trickle down. It's almost noontime, and the sun is moving to its tortuous pinnacle. A little sand-swirl swings in its tiny typhoon-trajectory. It is shifting towards her. She moves away, but then forgetting herself runs towards the infant asleep among the crumpled soiled clothes put in a broad wicker-basket under a tree. She has to take up the little one before the sand-swirl passes over it. She stalls the ill omen by a whisker. The baby is safe, she smiles at it.

Her already fatigued body groans with pain as a result of the effort. The child whimpers, she gets a frown, the littlest trace of it, but then effortlessly turns it into a smile. She is a mother after all. No child exists to make a mother perfectly angry. Under the shade of the mulberry tree, at the corner of the tiny agricultural plot of land, she sings a lullaby. Her song spreads over the red hot, yellowish tomatoes baking under the sun.

She sings well. It sounds like an oddity against the background of rough Haryanvi outpours of farming retorts, abuses and crude diction, the famed ruff and gruff of the peasant dialect in this part of northern India. Their behaviour beats even their diction, by the way. The musicality gives a clue that she might not be a Haryanvi. Her looks stamp the truth even further. She is petite, dusky, round faced with delicate features. She has come from far, from a different world altogether.

The child is asleep again after suckling at the drops of her maternal affection. Nothing satisfies a mother more than giving something extra to her child. She now shades her eyes with the palm of her hand to look into the distance. The sandy path leading out of the village lying in the silvery blue distance is forlorn. The heat rising from the sand shakes the horizon like—she recalls it in a flash—the steam swaying over the cauldron on the fire-pit at home.

He is nowhere to be seen, her husband, who is expected to bring her food. It was supposed to be a breakfast, but it's now almost lunch time. She has worked on empty stomach for around five hours, taking just waters to subdue the guttural complaints of her empty stomach.

She isn't feeling as bad as she should, given her position overall and particularly today. Her five-month-old son is around, almost as a saviour, casting a lifeful shadow like a tiny fluke of cloud, sheltering her from the fire of hunger, loneliness and self-pity. The breaks from work, to hold him, to sing songs, to breast feed him, to change his cloth diapers, are more comforting than even the rest under the mulberry's dense shade.

She takes her dose of energy by looking at the sleeping child's serene face. It's as happy and calm as the face of the wealthiest person on the earth. After all, all of us are born with the same share of happiness. It's another matter that it gets robbed off as we grow old, making most of us poor and leaving just a few of us rich in the end.

She takes a few swigs of water. Immediately she feels fresh to start again. The sun is almost firing over the summer tomatoes. She is worried about the loo. It gives sunstrokes. If that happens, it will be worse for her child. She wants to keep herself safe, for it means keeping the child safe. Mother's feverish milk isn't good for the child's health. But then she has to work, there is no option. After all, the daily outputs of 30-40 kg help her in running the household.

It does serve another purpose also. Her husband beats her a bit less. It often is like this. Whenever she doesn't bother him with money to buy the daily necessities to pull the rickety cart of their humble home, he sobers down so much as to only throw abuses, instead of the kicks he delivers in the other scenario. To avoid bothering him, and be lucky with abuses only without the bonus of kicks, she home delivers tomatoes within the village, at a price suitably lesser than the street hawkers, to tilt the deal in her favour.

Despite fighting it out day and night, with sweat, kicks and social scorn, she feels like she doesn't exist at all. Not here at least. She is invisible, casteless and exists like a dirtpath-side bush whom nobody sees particularly. But she exists in memories. Vivid memories of her small hamlet in Jharkhand flash over her lone self. That was the time when she lived. Now she just survives. Somehow.

She remembers that world. Its flashes help her in meeting a present which is completely devoid of her past, and more poignantly, where she can't think of future beyond the grasp of another day with her infant in her arms and the toddler holding her hand. It's like dragging an ungrateful life like a stone tied to your foot. You are secretly eager to leave it behind and move on to get better luck in the next birth. Well, belief in rebirth is a big invisible blank cheque. It helps, guys! You fill up your figure as you deem fit.

She works for some more time. The hunger has returned. The baby is scowling again. She offers the remaining drops in her bosom. It is pacified. Again the flashes from the world that was! They reach her to provide solace, a replacement for bread: the greenery, the huts, the small hamlet, the stream nearby, the pond, and the tree. The big banyan in particular. She had grown playing hide and seek in its leafy green mess and aerial roots.

That was the world where she really lived. Here it is no life; in fact, there are so many occasions when she even wishes to be dead. But then even death repels those who look forward to it as a benefactor. It prefers to play cruel and barge in as an unwanted encroacher into destinies. That's what makes death what it is.

She recalls her mother's wails as they brought the father's body. He had died in a coal mine collapse. To keep the day's white for his brood of children, he worked in coal mines near Rajhara town. *Sakhui village, Padwa block, Palamu district, Jharkhand*, she reads the line in her mind as many times as possible, regularly, lest she forget it.

It contains her roots. One shouldn't forget one's roots. She knows it well. That will be even worse than dying and make this living meaningless. She has written it on a piece of paper and put it next to the silver earrings, her most valuable item on her bridal self. She gets worried about it. Has she lost it? It's her back-up because she doesn't trust her mind now because it's plagued with so many worries. After all, it's her domicile, her certificate of identity. She will write one more copy, she decides. It's better to have two. It's safe.

A quaint hamlet of 600 or so souls. Their faces loom large over her father's body. Tribals, scheduled castes and Muslims, surviving at the fringes, in blackness, in soot, and die a black death. They had to put a lot of effort to wash the black from the corpse but finally gave up, hoping that mother earth won't differentiate among white, black, yellow or brown in offering sleep in its sandy womb. The burial had to be postponed for a few hours. The village-head had gone to Daltonganj, the district city about 13 Km away. The coalmine labourer was buried outside the hamlet among the cluster of tiny earth-mounds which served as the cemetery.

She sees her world, vividly, as if she has hyperopia, disabling her to focus on the world nearby and taking her far-seeing eyes to peek into distances.

There is a solitary mango tree in the distance. There were so many around their village. She recalls the huge one by the pond. She had jumped from an overhanging branch into a group of frogs. She chuckles as the scene strikes with playful vivacity.

The cool breeze blowing through *Mahua* trees sashays over hundreds of kilometres and calms her down and comforts her, listens to her plight, feels her loneliness. She laughs loudly as she recalls a drunken melee at a marriage in the village. The drink made of *Mahua* flowers is the poor villagers' companion in celebration, just as are its wood, flowers and seeds. She closes her eyes and inhales the typical smell of *Mahua*. She isn't that far from her home, she feels. The distance though is more than 1,000 km.

Apart from tomatoes, she has picked up some lady-fingers today to sell in the neighbourhood. *Ramtorai,* she picks up one and holds it. She says it loudly. They call it *bhindi* here. People cackle with laughter when she calls these *ramtorai*. It's a big time entertainment to them. Pumpkin is *konhra* there. But it's *Kaddu* here. Cucumber is *Kundri* there. But it's *Kheera* here. She has been learning fast. She wants them to laugh a bit less at her.

There were oranges and melons along the stream; at least, a thing of delight for the eyes, if not for the stomach. She finds the treeless monotony here intimidating. It's an agricultural monolith propelled by mechanisation. It's in the grasp of paddy and wheat ennui. Her husband owns just a little bit of land, so they are into vegetables to survive.

The hunger is terrible now. All efforts to not think of it are futile. Her mouth waters as she recalls the instrument of beating hunger back home. It strikes her imagination: the corolla of *Mahua* flowers, a fleshy blossom, pale yellow coloured saviour when they hadn't almost anything at home. So delicious, fresh, exciting, disagreeable, pungent and sweetish! A riot of sensations, a poor man's delicacy.

The blossoms are dried under the sun to turn brown to be used later. It gives her goose-bumps as she recalls the blossoms springing from the ends of the smaller tree branches, in bunches from 20 to 30, approaching ripeness, swelling with juice, falling to the ground. And she and other children laying the first claim. She is smiling. The memory has driven away all the pains of life. The gathering of *Mahua* windfalls. Drying of the flowers on dung-coated earth. Gossips under *Mahua* tree. The oil-fried *Mahua* blossoms. The distillation of spirits from the dried blossoms. Well, that was life. None of it exists here.

Remembering the past means remembering herself. Although physically present here, nobody seems to bother that she exists. So she captures a piece of that world in her memory.

Mahua *blossoms fall till June when the fruits ripe. We don't shake the trees or break the fruits. It will not bear fruits if these are plucked by hand. We wait for their natural fall. The ripe fruit is about the size of a peach. It has three different skins and has a white nut or kernel inside. The fruit is used in three ways. The two outer skins are both eaten raw and cooked as vegetables. The dried inner skin is ground up into flour. Oil is extracted from the kernel which is used for cooking purposes and for fake-mixing with ghee.*

The trail of thought comes clearly. It feels triumphant like a lesson crammed to the hilt in a nursery class. She is thankful to the God that despite the hard living, she has retained the memories of her land.

She recalls the pleasant, acidic taste of hair plum and the pinch of its thorny thicket. They used to jest that it was their apple, the poor man's apple.

She isn't new to agriculture. They had a little plot of arable land. *Sanai* was grown as green manure. The goats really liked it. She remembers the robust crops of maize and *bora* paddy. She helped her mother in her backbreaking toil in the tiny field. That world in the memories is more substantial than the one around her.

Then there was the storm which blew her away from the land of her dreams.

Her mother found it impossible to feed the multiple hungry mouths around her. Her sister's husband stayed in Delhi, a fact of high esteem for anybody in that part. It doesn't matter if that person spent nights on the pavement, and worked as a labourer during the day or even begged.

He was visiting their place and offered to help the widow by getting a job for her eldest daughter in Delhi.

"I will make her life," he proffered with a glint of hope in his yellowish eyes.

So she travelled with him to Delhi, the land of dreams, where everybody had money, even the poorest had big bucks in their wallet. She was scared of the bigness of things around her. Everything was in a mad rush. It was so noisy that she stated crying. The craziness of hurtling things and rushing people held her in a tight grip.

It was a world squeezed in a tight fist by the railway line, between the railway stations of Azadpur and Subzi Mandi. It was so close to the railway line that the stinking air pushed by the trains left a clanking, steely storm day and night. Honking trains and clattering rails were the biggest facts of life, the facts which defined the world itself. These were tiny hutments and hovels, piled one upon another, encroaching by millimetres into each other, to leave no privacy, no space for anything you can relate to a human being. Illegally constructed on the railway's land, it stuck to the polluted, dirty neighbourhood like a leech that won't go even if crushed to bloodied death. And there it drew the feeble chances of survival for countless unfortunates hiding there.

Everything related to life was in a miniature, except the human misery, which was bigger than the trains passing by. It was a black hole which had sucked the whole world into itself. A human swarm which buzzed mindlessly. There was everything, but it was squeezed so tight that it felt like you are standing in a crowd with no space even to scratch your bum. On top of that the incessant clatter of rails bore into your bones as the vibrations crept into your spine as you lay on the wood board to get what they mean by sleep.

From this hovel, he ran a business of arranging purchased brides, a business born of the ill-famed practice of female infanticide in north India, particularly in Haryana, where patriarchy demands a male heir, even from those who have hardly inherited anything and possess no education and skills of any kind to make a living themselves.

There is a significant chunk of marriageable vagabonds in Haryana who are not eligible bachelors from any angle. They are from poor families, are almost illiterate, have low or no land-holding, and don't exist anywhere in social standing. They come with the added qualifications of chronic drinking and smoking. But they need to have a bride and a male heir from her; otherwise, their souls won't rest in peace after death. And here comes the business of selling and purchasing brides.

The unfortunate girl is taken as a sex slave cum servant by the incompetent drunkard, her best utility being an instrument of giving birth to a male heir so that the father can get *moksha* or liberation after his death.

She was bought for INR 75,000. A bit overpaid, many said.

That very day, someone in the neighbourhood bought a buffalo for INR 82,000. Quite underpaid, still many more said.

So she is the unpaid servant. About sex we need not say anything. About heirs, she has already started the prospects. But to fulfil the role of a mother to her children, who will have almost no inheritance except poverty and misery, she has to kill her present to salvage another day. Her partner, after all, spoils more than he earns in their shared life.

The baby is crying. She comes back to the present world. The shadows have lengthened. The memories have served like a feisty lunch.

She sees two figures on the sandy path coming from the neighbouring village on the other side. So she had been looking in the wrong direction. He is coming from the other way. And lunch? Forget about that. She looks agitated. Even anger creeps in, strange though, given her petite, humbled, unassuming persona.

Her heart starts beating faster. Her breathing is more laboured. The hours-long toil on an empty stomach hasn't been able to break her proud spirit. But the visuals, turning from vague signals to specific outlines, leave her jolted. Something seems to have snapped suddenly. She gasps for breath and almost falls down. Taking the baby in her arms she cries.

"It's that accursed woman. O he the filthy bag has...how can he?" she wipes her tear tears with the corner of her headcloth.

All the hard work in the field seems wasted. She has been fighting to make a home and he kicks it with such impunity. Repeatedly. Not that she minds too much about the kicks he gives her after getting drunk. That doesn't appear more than anything beyond the normal, acceptable routine of life. Even the talks and gossips of him having an affair with this woman is tolerable. But to be seen with her, his little sense of worth gets torn away.

She has been just a plaything to her husband. A purchased bride is more of a servant. Even with his low social standing and almost no reputation, he has been able to lord over her. After all, she is just a purchased bride, bought from the hut of misery like farmers trade in cattle. Her price is lower than a good, rotund, glossy black buffalo. No surprise that she occupies almost no place, no name, no dignity in the village. Hers is just an invisible, see-through existence.

Even the street urchins take her in casual stride like they do with the beggars roaming around. She moves around imperceptibly, like a ghost. People just see through her. The only fact known about her is that she is a lowly-placed Muslim from the poorest of a poor family and has been bought at a price lower than an average buffalo.

He is drunk and walks with swag: an arrogance which seems to be drawn out of the purpose to insult and wound his wife by taking the torture one notch higher, to a point where any woman, no matter whether she is the gentlest or most aggressive, will feel the brutal pain of it. He seems to have run out of kicks and abuses. So here is the new method to torture his wife, to give her deeper cuts and injuries.

The two of them are walking on the field divide now, having left the sandy countryside path to reach their patch of land. She can now see the face of her husband's companion. She feels something more painful than slaps and abuses. The other woman is hardly attractive in appearance. She is in fact obese. Somebody's wife from the so called *low caste* in the social hierarchy, she walks proudly with a Jat farmer, even though he is haggard, famished, hawkish, and even qualifies below many men from her own community. But then in a caste society, being born into the dominant caste takes precedence over most of the deficits own is born with and equips himself with after birth through his deeds or rather misdeeds.

The other woman in her husband's life!

Her soul burns. It's more insulting than the barrage of nasty legs and hands, and still fouler tongue. The other woman has a better social standing than hers in being a caste born Hindu. More importantly, she is not a purchased bride, bought like a buffalo at some cattle fair. The distance between them decreases. It arrives with more visuals now. The other woman has a proud, jibing, mocking look on her face. The confidence born of stealing a man from under his wife's nose can sometimes propel the evil version of femininity in some women.

A storm is building up in the otherwise unmoving waters of the little lake of her being. He has already started abusing her even before entering their field of tomatoes. Choicest abuses, redder, hotter than any tomato around. From the heap of rotten tomatoes, sorted out while packing in wicker baskets for selling, he picks up a handful and hurls at her. She turns around and crouches down to save her child from getting hit by the slimy, smelly projectiles. She can feel the rotten juice sticking to her *kurta*, the soft plops and hard hits.

She runs to lay the child at a safe distance. He expects her to take to her heels and is mocking, shouting at the top of his voice.

"Go and run to the hell hole you came from, you filthy bitch!"

She has already given him a male heir, two in fact, the other one, almost three now, is with her forever prone to faint mother-in-law at their small, misery-personifying house back in the village. So he feels free. If she vanishes in thin air right now, he will be the happiest person for the riddance.

To his mild surprise, he sees her coming to them now. "Bah, so she seems eager to get introduced to you."

The other woman shamelessly titters. There have been historical injustices to her and her community. Any chance to humiliate a Jat's wife is most welcome.

Her husband and the other woman are standing side by side. She forms the triangle at a distance. The man moves forward, raises his hand and slaps hard. It happens with effortless ease, no cause, no effect. She just stiffens her face, not showing any trace of pain. No tears, no howling. Perhaps this boldness is meant for the other woman, her way of dissent, her small effort in not showing them the effect they want to see. After all, a man strikes a woman to see basically the tell-tale effect of his brutish aggression.

He strikes on the other cheek. The strike is followed by perfect silence. The hard skin of his fingers goes plop on the soft skin of her cheek. She is unmoved. He is feeling ravaged by anger. This rebelliousness is worse that she hitting back. In the grip of cheap liquor, he pauses as if thinking of devising some newer way to insult and humiliate her.

It fuels the mocking spirits in the other woman. She takes it on from the point her surprised lover has left. She catches the mutineer, who has rebelled not to cry, by her hair and raises the other one to smack her hard on the face. The uprooted girl's small hand comes to life. Before the plumpy hand adds to her insult, her finger catches the soft, wavy wrist. The attacker's bangles get crushed, puncturing her skin. There is blood. The injured woman shrieks with disbelieving anger and attacks with full force.

To him it's comical, the heavy woman attacking the small one. The uprooted woman defends well. He is enjoying the show from a distance.

"Fight, fight you bitches, give each other the taste of nice blood," he hollers and claps in enjoyment.

It's a full on cat fight. They roll among tomatoes, crush many and get all earth smitten.

"I am his wife you slut!" her hair tangled, tomatoes crushed on her face, she yells with such force that the drunk man loses his disgusting sense of entertainment.

She has pinned down the woman who is almost double her size. The latter is panting, out of breath, her massive breasts heaving with the propensity to topple the small woman off her, beads of sweat surfacing profusely on the coarse dark skin of her face.

She raises her hand to strike, but it doesn't come down. Hurting doesn't come naturally to her. She has just defended herself.

Far away from her native place, with almost no possibility of ever meeting any of her relatives, she knows it takes a bit more to survive apart from the uncomplaining hard work and unquestioning acceptance of slaps and kicks by her husband.

She feels survival needs more. And survive she has to for her children. Perhaps survival requires a bit of honour as well. And honour she has salvaged. It feels better than having a bumper crop and a day without violence at home.

She lets go off the beaten opponent and walks up to her child. The moment she turns her face, tears burst out. She but doesn't want to be seen weak and crying. She wipes her tears, making it look like she is cleaning her face of the mess it is in. She picks a sickle lying in a furrow on the way. Holding it in her hand she stands by the child.

"More than with you, your husband lies in my cot!" the other woman is heard yelling, the words meant to hurt her, to salvage some victory from the defeat.

"How many of your children are sired by him? He has two with me. If it's three with you, go and tell your husband of your achievement!" she waves the sickle.

They are moving back to the village they have come from. She knows he won't be back at least today.

Far away from her village, with no chances of ever going back, and almost nonexistent chances of earning some honour in the society she has been cast into, she feels totally lost. There is a vacuum around. Her head is buzzing.

The child is crying. She offers it her empty breasts to suckle for satisfaction. She can barely walk, so cannot afford to waste the last ounces of her remaining strength. She has to wind up things. She has to collect the uncrushed tomatoes, then she has to walk back home. She has to see how is her other son. It has to be done as soon as possible.

***

3. All that Woman is

It's 819 AD. The classical Indian thought is handsomely ashore. It has been a long and arduous journey starting from the savagely unsystematic outpours driven primarily by fear. We have now reached the airy overbearance of spacious logic and busy realism. Indian mystics have laid firm foundations for the systematization of thought about the unknown.

With open arms, texts and commentaries on the Vedas welcome the infinite manifestations of the universal goodwill. Human thought has beaten the limits of awe, wonder, obedience, surrender and love for the unknown. It is looking beyond now, further into the mind to dive into the luminous whirlpool of the human brain.

Human mind is fertile with logical imagination. One more step has been taken. Vedanta literature has shown man the next step in Indian philosophical thought. It's no longer about the ideas shaped by plain conjecture. Now it's not just bare surrender to the gaping unknowns. There is an effort to interpret the forces of nature. There is cultivation of thought and logic. There is an effort to understand the process of the humans grasping the reality.

Brahma Sutras of Sage Badarayana Vyasa have set up a platform for human thought and logic to take the next stride. Human mind looks within to understand the ways and means of interpreting the messages sent by our sense organs.

Philosopher and theologian Adi Shankara is plodding and pushing across the vast Indian expanses to take the human mind's reach further by integrating the diverse thoughts in Hinduism. He has a huge collection of commentaries on Vedic texts. The pioneer sage has thrown further light on the Upanishads. Calmly commanding, he is slaying scores of blindfolding rituals to lay down the concepts of Advaita Vedanta, i.e., unity of the soul and the attributelesss supreme identity.

Ritualism has eaten the vitality of Indian thought and philosophy. He is travelling across India to revive the spirit of Hinduism to establish it as the instrument of self realization; to be a master of one's own destiny, not just a helpless beggar before the deities. Wherever he goes, he challenges those who oppose him, hammers down their shaky superstitions to overpower them with his logical interpretations of our thought processes and natural phenomena around. It's a blizzard of logic sweeping the length and breadth of India. Neatly accustomed to his efficiency by now, he arrives in Mithila state in the northern Gangetic plains, near the frontier between modern day India and Nepal.

The great scholar has reached Tharhi village. A gently gay autumn welcomes him. There is mystique restfulness spread around. A perfectly pensive evening is building up. The great thatched hall in the hermitage premises is softly abuzz with scholarly excitement. The forces of dark which put shadows in minds seem to peer grimly over the wooden fences around the place. The scholars wait with their vigorous jealousies. The Shankaracharya has arrived only a couple of hours ago and is ready to take logical pot-shots at the rival theologians.

His shaven head and calm eyes don't give any sign of the long, arduous journey. But he has much ground to cover. India is a huge landmass. The differences are numerous in nature and categories. They start immediately. Adi is on a spiritual rollercoaster and easily prevails upon daunting bearded *rishis* and feckless, incompetent scholars who make much noise like empty vessels.

A young student, a string of holy thread worn diagonally across his torso and wearing white cotton dhoti, is lost in the great philosopher's persuasive logic. He has big gentle eyes but still can manage a pensive look. He has a question.

"*Swamiji*, the words of your logic fail to take me to the exact picture of reality. Does it mean there is no specific plane of reality? And we just reach a level, given our understanding of the words involved in the sentences, where we infer as per our own convenience and limitations? Is it like a person with good eyesight can watch distant objects in comparison to somebody with a bad one?"

Adi smiles at the question. His calm eyes bore straight into the young student's handsome face. The penetrating focus in those eyes is very striking.

"Study hard for each word in the books of theology. Work for the meaning of each and every word. Focus your senses to grasp the maximum a word has to offer. You will see the farthest one can see!" it sounds like a blessing.

Time seems lost in some splendorous assumption.

There is something extraordinary about this boy. Next morning, before setting out on his mission again, the Shankaracharya calls the boy. He again looks into the deep, reflective pools of his eyes. The great philosopher smiles. There is the stability of an undisturbed ocean in the young student's eyes.

"He can take very deep dives to carry the gems of reality from the mysterious depths," the sage softly tells himself.

Adi gives the young student a palm leaf compilation of the Brahma Sutra of Badarayana. The text is a famous systematization of the philosophical ideas piled up layer after layer in the

Upanishads. The Brahma Sutras explore the nature of the human existence and absolute reality. They emphasise the importance and need of attaining spiritually liberating knowledge.

It is a reward and blessing beyond words. Just the ownership of the text containing the apex of the Indian philosophical thought is a matter of pride. The young disciple walks back to his house, holding the cloth bag containing the precious text like it is hiding the most precious jewels on the earth. He has been exceptionally hungry for the knowledge and words of holy Sanskrit texts. In fact this is what hunger means to him. He has mastered Vedas, Upvedas and Upanishads. Now he possesses the cream of all that knowledge, the gist. He wants to go further, see beyond, break the frontier of all human thought reached so far. He is holding the text even more dearly than his life.

"Vachaspati, Vachaspati come out. O God what has possessed this boy! That book has a magic spell. I have to call *babaji* to break it!" Vatsala, his mother, is very anxious.

Her neighbours are standing around her in front of the hut he has locked himself in. She is a widow and he the only son. They have sympathy for her.

"He hasn't come out for the last two days. These books can turn a young man mad," she is sobbing.

There is more sympathy for the widow struggling to raise her son, who is all concerned about Vedic knowledge and now this book. There are driblets of resentment against his lack of understanding for his widow mother's position.

With exaggerated indisposition, they raise a chorus. There is a pandemonium. He is drawn out of his moon-washed eerie. He hasn't opened the book even once. It is precious. It has priceless meaning to each and every word written in it. He has been looking at it and taken away into the sublime stillness of a mystifying trance.

He can hear his mother's lamentation outside and the words of sympathy floating around. He opens the grass and reed thatch door of the hut and steps out. The sun is too bright and blinds him with its garish luxury of sunrays. He squints and looks deep into the blue sky. There is musty silence. A cool breeze is blowing carrying malleable sensitivity in its gentle drifts. A flock of sparrows raises a ruckus and the noise goes unruly, whirlpooling over the huts. They hold him with empathy taking him to be sick.

The proximity of the precious manuscript carries the effect of a thunderbolt strike. He is lost in the yeasty aroma of the parchment paper. It is almost being in a delirium. The young man gets fever. He mumbles strange meaningless words about the ultimate reality. His mother gets scared and even thinks of throwing the book away. But then stops from doing this, herself being scared of its powers.

Vachaspati regains his footing from the jolt after a week. He carefully starts touching the book, almost cautious like touching fire. He familiarizes himself with the ecstatic swoop, smell and feel of the palm leaves and the Sanskrit words. He is vigilant as if he is walking on a rope with fire burning below. He has miles to go on the rope to reach the destination. The Brahma Sutras are the bamboo, supporting him, balancing him, preventing his fall into the sweeping pungency of illogical, straying thoughts and disbelief.

Away from the wrecking turmoil of mundane existence, the world then ceases to exist for him. It is just the Brahma Sutras, the beginning. And the end? He wants his awakened self to be that end. *Aham Brahmasmi*. I am the all potent supreme entity. But he has to prove it to himself. He has to break that delusional veil that filters the supreme knowledge from barging fully into the compartment of our being, leaving us angry, ignorant and frustrated. He has to understand why and how we see the perceived reality. Can the reality be changed for the better? Is it fixed? Is it pliable, to be moulded into better shape by our heightened awareness? There are endless questions. He has long left the path paved with well-tailored simplicities. This path is prickly, gives bloodied feet, but then which real path isn't?

There is an all-fired urgency for the cause. The intricate extravagance of his brain has sucked him into a world of its own. He has now cut himself off from the society. A secluded grove is the safe house with the precious book. Here he spends the time from dawn to dusk, pondering thousand times over the meaning of each word, phrase and sentence, and then looks ahead with the torchlight of his boosted reason.

With its sweeping scope, the time sees effortless change of seasons carrying hopes and heartbreaks in their overburdened carriage. The humanity heaves on, ladenly slogging with its load of miseries interjected off and on with flashes of happiness. With expertly manoeuvring conscience, he is engaged in his fight against his perennial foes, the unremitting doubts and questions.

It has been eight years since the book landed in his hands. There has been just one routine. Carried by early morning's verve, he reaches the grove with a time's meal and some water. The trees look down at him in astonishment and awe. And further upward, the sky seems lost in the quagmire of this pleasant absurdity. Away from the hoot and holler of the fight for survival on the familiarly well-worn path, here the stakes are etched into the infinite distances of the mysteries of the mind and the unknown.

He goes back to his hut late at night. Slowly opens his hut's door, finds the rice and cooked lentils on his bed, eats slowly and silently, and goes to sleep. The night closes over him with the same resigned, time-worn expression carried through its bluish dark shadows. Mournful starlight bearing a voluminous testimony to the extent a human mind can go within to seek the greatest mysteries exploding in the farthest corners of the universe.

His mother's tears have dried up. She has accepted her fate.

He has forgotten the number of times he has read the book. Each time he reads it, there is a new meaning to it. Each and every word appears to carry layers after layers of hidden meanings. He is peeling off the layers to reach the kernel of truth. It but is endless. There are foggy meanderings and he has to beat the teasing fatality yawning from side to side. He rises higher with each jump into the air to see beyond the fence. He just cannot overcome this feeling that there is limitless joy to be harnessed through the path of learning.

On the surface, it is acerbic and acrimonious. His mother is not keeping well these days. She struggles to catch her breath while toiling hard to earn two meals a day for herself and her son. She is worried what would happen to him after she is gone. Marriage as an institution is supposed to guarantee hope and care in future. She has been thinking of getting him married. But who would give his daughter to somebody who doesn't seem to act and behave like a common householder? A prospective groom should at least appear likely to stay yoked in domesticities. From that angle he appears feckless and incompetent.

Individual destinies are but battered and buffeted in varied ways. The world is full of people bound by conditions which force them to settle for the minimum. Like while most of the parents try to ensure a life-long security for their daughter, looking at the groom's prospects from multiple angles, there are still some who are placed so tightly that just getting their daughter married somehow to anybody gives them the satisfaction of fulfilling a duty. There is one such family in a neighbouring village. The father consents to Vachaspati's mother's proposal. Her maternal spirit hurriedly shambles off to take some solace for being saved from total disaster.

"It is our good luck to get our daughter married to such an avid scholar!" the girl's father even smiles.

Vachaspati is so lost in the questions raised by reading and rereading of the Brahma Sutra that he hardly knows what goes on in the world around him. He is so full of the ever-persistent questions about the finality, the ultimate reality that there is hardly any scope for the sense organs to do their work and break his spell. To him the extravagant green of the rainy season is no different from the death throes of the pale autumn windfalls.

He is in a reverie, like he is most of the time, when his mother informs him about his marriage. He doesn't seem to react in any way. His nonchalance is taken as his consent and the marriage is fixed. With overriding benevolence, slumberous sunrays change her world almost instantly. He is married to Bhamti on Guru Purnima (Vyasa Purnima) in the month of Asadha. It is an auspicious conjugal day when many couples start their marital innings. For him but it is the night to start on his real quest.

His hut is decorated for the bridal night. A full moon has lit up the stage outside. There is chirrupy laughter among the relatives. The nature is lost in effusive dreaminess. Shyly his bride is ushered in with a big tumbler of hot milk, the auspicious memento of libido, in her hand. She raises her eyes to sneak a look at him. In the light of the oil lamp a new world opens.

Vachaspati is sitting erect on a reed mattress on the floor. A sheaf of clean palm leaves by his side. On the small wooden writing desk, a palm leaf is waiting for the first word. His hand is on the feather quill still in the brass inkpot. Time seems to have been suspended. The lamp is burning almost steadily. It's a frozen moment, like it will remain for the next 12 years.

She moves slowly and sits on the edge of the bridal bed. There are flowers on the clean white cotton sheet. The sheet will remain as such. Undisturbed. Clean. Time has stopped. It's not before the dawn that he slowly opens his eyes. His hand frozen on the writing quill moves and the first Sanskrit word of his historical commentary on Brahma Sutra is written. There is a force. She can feel it. She knows she has no choice other than being a part in this creative stillness. She has to be present, but like there is nobody around except him. She gets housewifely busy, without been seen or heard.

And the days pass, as easily as the weeks, which roll like months, which in turn swagger with the ease of years. There is no distraction even for some odd, lean and lonely moment.

He is in a cocoon. He is breaking the walls of disillusions to see the light of logic to take the Indian metaphysical thought to a new level after the Brahma Sutras. The Brahma Sutras have given him the tools to dig the mammoth mountain of mysteries. Stoutly assured, he is busy with his spadework.

Bhamti knows the classical duties of a wife to her husband. She lives her duties. This is what marriage means to her. She has to keep his cocoon safe for him to continue working. She is the silent nurturer of his world. She is invisible but manages everything. She is like the air which you cannot see but one will die if not for its presence. It's her duty to help him stay on his chosen path and she abides to it without fail.

Subtle, lithe and statuesque, she moves so slowly as if afraid to shift even the air particles while she cleans the floor, puts food plate in front of him, takes it away, fills the ink pot, gets fresh pair of writing quills, safely stashes the worked upon sheaves of palm leaves, arranges new palm leaves, lights the lamp as it starts getting dark, pours oil in the lamp through the night, takes his dhoti to wash and put fresh one nearby. In between she lovingly looks at his picture, for he is just a picture, unchanging except the quill moving on the parchment paper.

The picture is broken only twice or thrice a day when he gets up for bathing and toilet. But this also is merely an extension of the picture. Stillness is layered around, its kind and condescending touch hush down any ruffled feather in any corner.

Initially, during the long drawn out spells of the lonely nights, she would feel cravings for his touch as she watched him from the corner of the hut, where she sleeps on the ground on a simple grass mattress. Then she felt guilty even in this much transgression for polluting the air with desire. Now just looking at his pensive, absorbed face gives her all the gratification she needs as a woman from her man.

She is a mother now. There is a child in the womb of her love and care. She has to nurture it at the cost of the major portion of her own life, her own share in this world. Her pregnancy has lasted years and she is the same smiling, uncomplaining mother, keeping her hands safely around her bulging tummy as the world moves on. In the cloaking silence, a divine acceptance is precariously eked out to hold onto the moments frozen to redefine time itself. Her soft self is saturated with a merry and mellow contentment. She carries a smile on her lips, while his face is drawn into a firm, unmoving expression.

Well that's what basically a woman is, a mother. A man is just the instrument of her reaching her status of being a mother. To be a mother she has to cut a major portion of her own self to help life thrive in a new unit, in a new human being to scale new heights and meet fresh dreams.

It has been twelve years since their marriage and twelve years of his working on his commentary on Brahma Sutras. It is a stormy night. Squalls of rain beat on the thatched hut. Wind plummets down hard. There is no risk to this hut at least. She has been working on making it sturdier and stronger over the years during her spare time. It's exactly this type of weather she has had in mind while working on it.

His face bears a strange expression, like you have been running for a long time, and then you see the destination, you want to run harder but the body is keeping you within limits. During the latter half of the night the storm starts to abate. His face also eases up, springing a surprise by getting a faint smile at the corner of his lips. It makes her world, that smile. He seems to be walking slowly now, with destination just nearby. And then he stops.

It's a bright dawn. Robust trajectories of a new day arrive with exuberant spirits. The storm has spent its fury. Calmness, as it's supposed to, has spread its resilient aura. He has written the concluding word. A journey has been accomplished. He stands up and stretches his arms. It's like a stone statue coming to life. He looks around and sees the world after so many years. There is a woman in the hut. Her uncared and untended beauty shines like moon's corner over the edge of a dark cloud. A sombre solemnity lingers over her gentle features. There is quintessential look of grandeur in her eyes.

The mother, the donator, the giver! Her pregnancy has lasted all storms. The delivery has been painful. She is shy again. She melts under his gaze. He is curious.

"Who are you and what are you doing in my hut?" he asks politely, words coming with huge effort after such a long spell of silence.

She smiles, in an unobtrusive way, like a mother listening to the first words of her child.

"I'm your wife. We were married 12 years back," she tries to remind him very delicately as if afraid to break his poise.

He has been on some other plane of reality, so doesn't remember anything. He looks at her hands and realization strikes him. He remembers these. Even in that astral plane, these hands have been the root of his support. These hands which bathed him, fed him, kept everything away that might have broken his mystical spell. He has been feeling that the task at hand has been as much of these hands as his own. This pair of hands has melted into his veritable being. His quest has been with four hands. He always had this feeling, but had taken it as some divine support.

But can there be a bigger divinity than a mother's efforts?

"You have been serving me for 12 years and never told me!" he has tears in his eyes.

She just smiles and her eyes melt under the faint warmth of an emotion. Unable to speak, she just looks at him.

"Why didn't you tell me earlier? I had taken a vow that I will renounce this world after completing this work!" tears are streaming down his bearded face.

"I always knew the importance of your cause, so just served you. It's my wifely duty," she speaks very sweetly, as if it was never about her, like her life did not and doesn't matter.

"But this is injustice to you. All this service and pain. With my vow, I have to leave for the Himalayas for penance. What becomes of your efforts? Where is the fruit of all that you did?" he is agonized.

There is a flood of tears. A sage who has busted the secrets of reality to make human thought further capable of deciphering more about the ultimate is crying.

She comes closer and again assuages his pain, frees him of his guilt.

Wiping his tears she says with a calm smile, "Your tears, your acceptance, your realization, this work, all these are my rewards. Like I didn't stop you earlier, even in your vow of penance, I will not be a hindrance. It will give me happiness if I still help you in seeking further truth as a recluse by allowing you to go. By freeing you of any duty that you may think as a husband might prevent you from your mission. Please go guilt-free."

He hasn't yet given a title to his commentary.

"What is your name?" he asks almost bowed before her generosity.

"Bhamti," she just drops the word softly to be picked by the invisible eddies of air and carried to his ears.

Wiping his tears, he moves towards the collection, picks out a fresh palm leaf and writes Bhamti on it. The title. And puts it on top of the work.

"You are the love and guiding spirit behind all this. You are the soul of this work, I'm just the body. This world may forget me but not you," he prepares to leave.

Bhamti.

She watches him go to the hills. Bhamti, the masterwork, is there for the world to dive into to fetch out more gems of metaphysical thoughts.

A man might take multiple rounds of earth to search his destiny; a woman realizes hers just by being there with her love and care.

A man might break mountains with the raw power of hammer; a woman is the air that fills his lungs to fuel his determination.

A man might aim to crack the ultimate secret; a woman normally does it just by being a mother, by allowing a life to thrive parasitically inside her, at her cost, gobbling her share of food, blood and flesh.

And no thought can be beyond love. And nobody is more suitable in manifesting love than a woman.

***

4. Virtue in the Womb of Vice

The new item number is just too crunchy and juicy. Voluptuous moves. Raunchy notes. Suggestive lyrics. It grips the audience in the slanting ambience of throbbing sensuality. The choreographer, the lyricist and the music director have done full justice to the edifying undercurrents of her mystical curves. They have had their own set of imagination about her while working on their respective parts in the musical number. She gyrates in thigh-length, tight, gold-threaded dhoti and beaded *choli*.

She has perfect figure, finest curves, very charming features and flawless skin. She flaunts her sexuality with cast-iron certainty. And millions gasp for breath. She carries the aura of a goddess around her: the queen of the forbidden--but most sought after--kingdom of sex. They make as much noise as they do in religious processions with cheering conches and clapping cymbals.

One thing, but, goes missing in all this glamorous show. There is a shadowy dot in the incessant bustle of revealing anecdotes. It's her innocent laughter and child-like simplicity of mind. When she smiles, it's a pure, soft outburst of merriment untouched by any trace of malice and shrewdness. When she laughs, it also is pure like a child does when amused at a small, simple thing. But this unsophisticated self is covered up by her dazzling sex appeal. Even if it shines at all, people prefer to ignore it. They have more important things to gloat over, to quench the hunger of mind, the famed Indian hunger of the opposite sex in the head, beyond all outside taboos and evil talk of dirty acts like sex and all.

She has left swerving trailblazers among young adults. She has earned quite a bit of name in the industry. She gets interviews now and then in the mainstream media. On such occasions, she is her usual unsophisticated self. However, the person on the other end seems on a watch, like peeping over a fence, guarding himself from some strange reaction inside. And all, the audience knows and understands the inhibitions running inside the anchor's head. They hardly seem to listen to her for their minds are somewhere else.

The skimpiest dress covering the barest minimum fuels the fire of repressed passion among the masses. For each artwork of dance by her watched on the YouTube, they go back to the gray zone on the Internet and draw out ghosts from her past. Yes, it satisfies the hungry, invisible ghosts inside the well-behaved, civilised self. They repeatedly prey upon those video clips where they can see all of her. Not even a shred of clothing intervening. They gloat over her curves, the act, the ejaculations, have theirs and come back to watch her feisty item numbers again. Her visuals in the song and dance videos serving as a mass foreplay to rouse the heaving humanity to take refuge in the purplish corridors of virtual sex. The storm over, all is well in the civilised lanes of society. Everybody is clean and upright. Only she carries the stigma permanently.

The ink of her past appears too dense. More than the ink's density, the people seem to just hold onto their lusty fancy for that particular image. It's their pride possession. They simply don't want to forego the dustbin to dump the ejaculations of their hungry passion. It gratifies the most overpowering sense, sex. Her item numbers just fan the fire even more.

It has been a massive effort: the journey from hard porn to soft porn.

The roles she gets, apart from the item numbers, involve sex, glamour, sensuous intrigues and extramarital affairs: the sociable, bridgeable sexuality unlike the unchecked rampancy of outright naked game.

She knows hers is a humongous task. The road from being a porn star to the so called normal film star is riddled with countless obstacles. Sexual zealots fire bullets from both sides. She exists in the chambers of lust in their ever-greedy minds, so she just cannot escape like this. They have to hunt her down. They have tunnel-vision about her and don't want to see beyond.

Only she knows the amount of effort she has put in moving from full porn to semi porn. It is like traversing poles at the opposite ends. From being a naked mannequin in full public glare, you walk down as they run after you, and you struggle to cover yourself with normal human sensitivities of respect and being treated like anyone around. People somehow resent it, throw jibes and try their best to keep their goods to gratify their lust. So the demonic retinue of the ghosts from her past follows her like a shadow clings to a person walking in the open on a sunny noon.

She is struggling to come out of the cloistered corridors, but the path ahead is nothing short of an ominous labyrinth. She has to dilute the dark ink of the past. Wipe it altogether and write a new identity, to feel normal like any other actor in the industry. It is like bringing night and day together: from soft porn to normal roles.

She wants to go further. She is an artist and works on her acting skills to the last ounce of her perseverance. She wants the regular roles like any other actress around. But she cannot enter each and every brain to wipe the pieces of her past lying there, allowing them to see her present and appreciate her art. The directors who approach her have ready-made, predetermined formula of a feisty woman, the woman for whom men fall, creating ripples around. These are feisty tales of sex, murder, extramarital relations and scores of lusty intrigues. All this but seems to set up a prelude to the same urge to see her porn movies.

There are trolls as well, the social media crusaders, who yank reputations to shreds, pour their boiling scorn and burn the images from safe heavens. There are abuses, lewd remarks, copy-pasted links of her online porn clips, gross invitations and still more. She no longer takes them head on and simply blocks them. But the words haunt her for long hours during the nights when she is practicing her acting skills.

With the big, bossy, disparaging world buzzing around, she sometimes gets judgmental on her own self, and finds herself at fault for getting into the porn industry to begin with. But wasn't that the launch-pad for crossing the jarring atmospherics of anonymity, escaping her adolescent nightmare of just getting sold by life without leaving any mark, and that too with such flawless skin, exotic features and dreamy contours? It was a search for embryonic possibilities, to give life to her dreams, to make a mark, to become **something** from *nothing*. And with her inexperienced self, she jumped into the pool with incisive sincerity. The towering grandeur of success bathed her flawless skin with pointed flashlights of riotous recognition. She wrote towering tales of her feats on millions of craving hearts.

The art of sex! It was a wild river toppling the mountains, eating the slopes and breaking boulders. Ruthless. Like it will never stop. But beyond the fury, after falling over a huge cliff face, in the slow-swirling waters of the after-fall majesty, the man lying sprawled, spent under her, she laughed so innocently, with such unassuming vivacity that it instantly changed her persona from an unsparing manhood-slayer to a simple vulnerable girl.

Even in her movies now one can hear that innocent trill, like a little bell softly chiming around the neck of a mountain sheep. A little jaunt on the green slope. And the whiffs of tinkling bell carried by the gentle air down the valley. It's but lost in bigger noises. This little insignia of her vulnerability, this tiny pause in the journey of the stormy mountain river, this interlude amidst crazily heaving waves is missed by almost all the spectators.

Most of the men, who comprise the audience of her current movies, have masturbated some time or the other while watching the porn clips portraying her as the temptress sucking away all the lust from the planet. Her super-feminine force raises tornados of infatuation, obsession and excitement. They own her in that part of their brain which stimulates desire. They want the sensation to remain stuck in their groins. They fight to stop it from sneaking into the aesthetic corridors of art and beauty.

The image, with its customary stimulation, is too big and overpowering. It keeps flashing in their minds as they watch her in the movies now. They expect the same gratification. While they ogle at the character in the movie, a different scene is playing in their minds. Parallel stories interlope: the one on the screen playing the part of foreplay, and the one in the mind catching up on the more concrete, luscious, lusty practicality.

The more she tries to prove her acting credentials, the more they delve deeper into the spools of the Internet to grab handfuls of lusty morsels to satisfy their hunger. With the scenes from hard-porn blazing in their minds, they are mildly comfortable as long as her roles are on the margin of soft-porn.

She is in the office of a famous director today. There is a word that he is finalising the cast for his upcoming pot-boiler. For the last two months she has been working on her acting skills in a famous acting school.

"Well, it will be too revolutionary to put you in the cast. The role is too, too....," he hesitates, rolls his eyes and draws his fingers over his bald pate.

His office is ensconced in luxury. There is private grandeur and imposing ambience well managed by a famous interior designer. She shifts uncomfortably in her chair. In the palpable silence, she can literally feel his chain of thoughts at the time. Her past and that iron-cast image seem to have seeped and submerged with the pulse of the ongoing time. Its magnetic force is too strong for her to completely escape out of its orbit.

He is in the pink of health for a man in mid-fifties. His eyes are assured like they have the fully authorised assessment of any situation related to film-making.

"The role is too mainstream for you," he says firmly and winks as if to convince himself of his logic.

She gets a pinprick and avoids a visible shudder. It is a fight to maintain her dignity in the halls of fame glittering with virtuous testimonies on the walls around.

"I have been working very hard for this role. Please take an audition, of any duration, of whatever intensity required for the character," she tries to stay normal.

"Oh, audition. You know, umn, it's more about suitability for the character. Like, all actors have certain affinity for the role they are most suitable. We simply spot that suitability," he is driving it hard.

"But it's not fair. I deserve a chance to be tested. I, I...," her determination is melting, the typecast of her past is too bold.

She avoids his gaze and is drawn to the reticent muse of a famous heroine looking at her from some framed portrait on the wall. Oh, that was the unhurried old world. Times have changed now. Her brief eerie is broken by his drooling words.

“Why work so hard to bruise your beautiful skin on a path that is new to you. By doing the kind of roles which you have done so far, you have earned name, fame and money! You rule their hearts like none of the actresses around,” he laughs and looks lividly.

“But, you know…,” he cuts her mid sentence.

He seems to have set up his mind into the pursuit of a fancy which lies inside all successful men. They have elastic interpretations of the situation of a woman who wants a part in their success story. They are naturally inclined to pull it for their advantage. He is no exception.

“Ok, you can spread more pleasure than you think. Let’s have an audition,” he leans back in his chair and his eyes bore into her bosom.

He appears perfectly at ease with himself, undaunted and untroubled by any doubt about the success of the project at hand.

“You know, it’s a huge budget film. A make or break for many. It’s not that easy as you think,” he knits his brows and appears damn serious.

She takes his serious expression even more seriously.

“Yaa, I understand. But at least accept me as one of the competitors. I can prove myself. Hope you watched my last movie,” she sits erect in her chair like a thorough professional.

He doesn’t remember anything except the feisty dance on a raunchy number. Her curves swirl around in his imagination. He closes his eyes and takes his memory still further, away to the fantasy world of naked, unprohibited revelry. He recalls the minutest details of her anatomy. The shade of pubic hair, the genitalia, like so many others, still different, her rampant foray into sucking out all pleasure and spit triumphantly, and that innocent trill of laughter.

She is surprised, watching him with eyes closed for a long pause. She breaks the reverie.

"Sir, you know...," she draws him out of that other worldly charm.

"Hmmm!" he appears a bit irritated like someone shaken out of deep sleep midway through a heavenly dream. "You know it will be too revolutionary," his eyebrows are drawn taught.

She doesn't say anything. For his age he is a strong, fit, confident man. He gets up to take out a file from the rack by the wall. He is aroused. Possibly he has got up in that state to show what is going inside him. She can see it. It's protruding. He doesn't want to hide it even, as if wanting to convey the message. She feels insecure, even sad and looks resignedly. On an instinct, she adjusts her knee-length skirt as if to protect herself.

The office air hangs in suspension as if jolted out of its senses by a startling, telling remark.

He gets back into his chair, more relaxed now, sure that his arousal has been seen. The message is directly passed. His bald head is glowing purple red.

"You know, it's a fight. This world of actors and actresses. Specially for the big banner movies. It requires talent, skills, luck as well, connections, image and even personal inclinations and choices," he stops for her to absorb the bitter truth.

She feels saliva in her mouth and swallows it nervously. The deep hum of sadness surfaces in her big eyes.

"You know ambitious young actresses go to any length to grab the top spot. And of course there are gentlemen who welcome such dedication," he smiles, staring deep into her bluish-brown eyes.

"Well! I, I am ready for ...audition," she mumbles.

She is losing confidence rapidly.

"Then go for the audition," he stands up.

He has already unzipped himself and the audition phallus is out. It's an open invitation. A simple give and take. A short audition and the role for her.

He seems helpless. He is shivering out of sheer excitement forced by the raw, scandalous adventure of transgression into her modesty, of being able to propel his naked instinct beyond the fence of law and decorum. He has transposed the dream onto the plain of reality. It's like grafting himself as the male character in all those plays of naked flesh.

Just the mere sight of it fills her mouth with the typical taste of it. She has done it many times in the past, with such gripping greed and madness that it felt like she was out there to drain all masculinity of its coffers of thirst forever.

He is shaking and imploring her to drain him out of his misery, of his frustration born of unquenchable thirst.

"Come on! After this there is no stopping for you. You will choose your roles," he is gasping for breath.

There is a chance for her to be an actress, a real actress like anyone around. It's tempting. She is holding the chair armrests very tightly. But something holds her back. She has been working too hard, late into the nights to push herself further to come out of this soft-porn mould. And the deal seems like going back again into the past to redeem future.

She has a struggle ahead she knows it. She is determined to face it. She is not ready to go into the future with the life-support of the past she is cutting from her life. It seems unjustified, even unethical to both the past and the future.

She gets up and turns around the table to approach him. He is on the verge of fainting, with all those wildest fancies just about to clutch him into the heavens of ecstasy. He feels her touch on the protruding phallus of his life-long hunger. Helpless he surrenders and closes his eyes.

He wakes up to the taut sound of his trouser-zip. She has safely put his strayed self into the safety of his pants and closed the doors on it. He cannot believe it.

"Do you even know what are you doing! It's over for you!" he flies into a blinding rage.

"Yes sir, this project might be over. But not all is lost for me. I have a struggle ahead and would prefer to work over months, even years, instead of taking five-minute short-cuts to reach there. That will take me back to where I started from," she is very calm, and looks at him with unoffended, sad eyes.

She comes forward again and shakes his hand very politely and professionally and backs out. With even more politeness she closes the door behind her. There are tears of pride in her eyes as she crosses the floor. And a new wave of determination pervades her beautiful curves.

***

5. Lip-kissed Lies and Soul-kissed Love

It is springtime in ancient India. Contended air goes swirling and sniffing around fresh blossoms. Snow is melting in the mountains. Flowers smile and let out perfume that is picked up by the cool air to be scattered around in love drops. This town in the Gangetic plains is awash with fresh hopes. The butterflies dart around in gay, colourful abandon. The air is full of love and procreation.

The breeze is blowing with a seductive message. A young, handsome monk is moving through the streets. His steps are slow and face has a faint smile. He has a begging bowl in his right hand. A cloth bag hangs from his left shoulder. The spring air is redolent with both giving and receiving. This saffron clad man but has just the goal of having one time's meal.

He is passing in front of a luxurious small palace. It's decorated for love, luxury and enjoyment. It seems like a place where one can just surrender the self to quench all possible thirsts for a human being. He is but moving completely unconcerned and detached from all worldly splendour.

A pair of beautiful eyes looks at him from the ornate balcony. Her heart stops for a moment. If she is the ever restless river, he appears like the calmest sea having the immensity to swallow her thirst, her restlessness, her quest for destination, her final fulfilment. She realises her hunger. It is plain desire. He is so handsome and so aloof from all worldly charms.

She has the world at her feet. But the innards of a woman's well of secrecy are beyond any attempt at measurement. The most beautiful and coveted woman of the state, she holds the title of *nagar vadhu*. Her life stands for love, opulence and luxury. Wealthiest traders, strongest noblemen and most creative artists kiss her feet to appease her and take a sip from the fountain of her beauty. Any man feels lucky if she holds her look on his face for more than a second.

The young monk with the begging bowl moves with perfect ease. Spools of meditative chants permeate his being. All restfulness. It's a calm, unperturbed lake. It doesn't happen that she is still holding her look on a man's face and the man's eyes move on. Her charms are so spell-binding. She is proud of this power, this feminine avatar of the instrument of control over others. With a faint smile, he just moves on. There is not the slightest change in his demeanour.

The hard shell of her ego cracks. It disturbs her. She even gets angry. With a frown on her luscious lips, she stares at his back. Her eyes glitter with a sparkling vivacity. He is now moving slowly down the street. The buds of anger inside her again blossom to plain desire.

Till now men have desired her, and confessed it as loudly and extravagantly as possible. This has been the norm with as much routine normalcy as you have a morning after the night. This loveful spring morning has but turned the tables. She desires this calm sea. She needs some rest. The spiteful torrents of her youth want to submerge and take shelter in his silent depths. It just attracts her senses like anything. She feels helpless.

She sends her maid to call the monk. Her heart is pounding against her breast. She is gasping for breath and at loss of words. Her hold over masculinity is giving in. She feels like a helpless, fragile woman. And finds it such a jolting emotion, a rare occasion when she is in the pursuit instead of being chased.

Her reverie is broken. The monk is standing in front of her door again.

"What do you want?" she asks, shyly, dropping her gaze around his feet.

She appears melted by some opulently warm emotion.

Where is that domination of men? Her servant girl wonders.

"Gracious lady, I just want one time's meal," the monk tells her in a pious tone.

He is as calm as ever, like a pond whose waters have stayed unperturbed for years. He has crossed over the storms. It offends her; after all, she is the thunderbolt which shakes up males without fail.

She laughs in a mocking way. "You should ask as per the status of the person. Even a farmer can give you that much," she is hurt that he isn't taking notice of her beauty, as if she is just like any other woman around.

The monk smiles. Vibrating, invigorating sunrays light up his aura and present him as some mythologized persona from still ancient India.

"Well young lady, this is all I need. It doesn't change with people," very softly his words pass out without any disturbance of any sort.

But his softness has disturbed her deeply in her heart. His unseeking, peaceful demeanour is pelting the waters of her desire-swaddled lake with stones of stoicism.

"You can have me, my palace and my luxury if you stay with me," she sounds desperate.

She doesn't remember the last time she had to pamper a man to get his favours. It is just a one-sided game, all high and mighty literally cringe before her to kiss her feet.

He is as cool as before, as if nothing has happened. "This world is my house. I take the minimum as charity to survive, just one time's meal. I am looking out over the path to take me further. I am searching for the destination where each particle of my being will be ready to give selflessly."

He closes his eyes. A smile surfaces on his shapely lips. He is mumbling a prayer.

"I am also ready to give all I have, including myself and my palace and wealth. Isn't it the same?" she stoops a bit towards him, straightens her bejewelled hands, presses her slanderous fingers into her palms, like she is holding herself back from some unseemly outpour.

"But you want to give only with the ambition of getting something back for your ego. You want the price of a monk abandoning his path for your beauty. There cannot be a bigger ambition, a bigger tool to pacify the ego," his soft words hit her hard.

Truth, even in its delicate most avatar, becomes more effective than a rant, barrage and fusillade of hypocrisy.

The monk is an unchanging picture of calmness. She is shaking with rage over the denial and feels worthless as if she doesn't carry any price now for the males' part of the world.

"At least stay with me for a night!" she is helpless and looks almost pleading.

"Do you really need my help? I can see the wealthiest to the strongest ready to help your needs," he gives her a kind look.

"Please, please..." she is imploring. "I really, really need you. If you spend the night with me, I will forsake all men. Believe me!" she is folding her hands in agony.

She has forgotten what it means to be defeated and overlooked by a man's passion. And she is searching for the traces of passion where it's all compassion; looking for physical cravings where there is just kindness; looking for a stormy rendezvous where all we have is the calm, unruffled sea of being one with the self.

The young man gives a pitying smile. He can feel her agony. "I will come and stay when you really need me."

She is tearful over the denial of her boundless desire. The monk takes onto his path. She watches him till the far end of the street. It is like a spiteful mountain river is looking for some rest in the cool embrace of a lake. Well, maybe there are longer journeys to reach such rest and redemption.

Life then moves on, like it was before. She gets more wealth, more men falling at her feet, while the young monk is moving slowly on his path of selfless realisation.

It has been two decades since that spring morning in front of her palace. The same monk is walking towards the city, the very same city. Years of penance has taken him miles up his path of selfless seeking. He is greying but looks wiser, calmer and even stronger. It's dark and he can see the lights of the city from a distance. It's just nearby.

He stops to hear pitiable moans by the dusty road. He walks to the bushy ditch by the path. A woman is crying in pain and agony. He sits by the bundle of misery. She is in terrible suffering. Wasted by leprosy, her open sores are oozing with stanching fluid. It's as bad as it can be. So much of pain. He isn't repulsed by the stench. He gets tears of sympathy. The calm surface of his being is jolted by emotions.

He lifts her in his hands and carries her to a nearby inn. They refuse to let him in with the foul-smelling creature. He decides to set up a hut outside the city to look after her. The rest of the night he spends under a tree, she lying by his side, moaning less now after the touch of affection and care. The human touch is a remedy in itself after all.

The spring sun rises in all freshness. The nature is abloom with sparkling green and laden with colourful, surprising nuances. He has been sleeping for the last couple of hours. The woman is also asleep. He opens his eyes and looks at her face. The evil-work of the disease has failed to completely destroy the vestiges of her former beauty. He recognises her. From there to here! What a chasm! What a trail of misery! More tears drip down his cheeks. He meets the destination of his selfless giving. She was lying there in the dark night to test the validity of his selfless love. And he has passed.

She opens her eyes and is surprised to find somebody crying for her.

"You said you needed me and I said I will come when you will really need me. See I have come. And you are the destination of my penance. Of selfless giving. Of loving from the core of my selfless being. I was not sure of myself till I found you. Now I realise it has been worth it. All this search," tears are dropping in a blizzard of compassion and sympathy.

So the monk takes care of her. Helps her in easing all her miseries. Stays with her when no other man would even come near her.

She needs him now. And he is there at a stage in his monkhood when he is all there to give. Just give. Without taking or expecting anything in return.

***

6. Nameless Graffiti on the Wall

Platforms—they are somebody's destination, someone's starting point. Many people depart, and many arrive. On the parallel rails of departures and arrivals, life chugs ahead with a determined unmindfulness.

Squeezed between arrivals and departures, there is a different type of life at the platforms. It is almost a secondary world. Right in the shadows of the bigger world hurtling with an exalted impulse, this secondary world carries limitless desolation.

Severely crushed, trampled and trodden under the furtively commuting and journeying larger mainstream world, it's a smaller world on the fringe. It involves beggars, crippled creatures, runaways, petty porters, and nondescript migrant labourers who survive like the wayside thorns and thickets along the rutted path on which there is an incessant stampede of those whose lives are not bracketed inside the gaolic strokes of the term 'platform'.

It survives in dreaded anticipation; waiting to grab the fallen crumbs to beat its hunger. Its painful scars lie right there in broad daylight, but are still invisible. To many it doesn't even exist. The adventurous ebullience and pomp and paraphernalia of the bigger world pass over it like clouds ploughing the skies with cotton-soft ease.

The same is the case of the unlived lives on the platforms of Ambala junction. It buzzes with the motley crowd of peasants, railway staff, and passengers waiting, walking, deboarding and boarding. Also mixed in the human concoction are the porters, hawkers, homeless people and beggars. Lost in this jostling crowd are the multitudes of castaways whom the crippling circumstances force to ride the static back of this cemented space along the clattering rails and nettling wheels.

The world of misery exists and exists not at the same time. It heaves like a sighful wave trying to tug at the sleeves of the bigger world. It pours like a mournful drizzle to wash the sandy screen of human apathy. It shines like remorseful rays to light the darkest corners.

It was mid-November. With pining pioneership the new millennium had just started. More than the station sheds—during the daytime—the hazy blue apron of the winter sky was more comfortable to lie under. So these citizens of the kingdom named 'platform'—mired in pain and penury—now basked in open at the far ends of the platforms under the unbiased, indiscriminating and warm beams of the bright father, who seemed chiding the cold breeze naughtily sashaying over the plains after tasting early snowfall in the upper reaches of the Himalayas to the north.

Inshan's hand-pulled cart—on which entailed the fistful of his life (loaded and embaled in fewest of things and circumstances)—was standing at this sunny far end of the platform. The world under the tin sheds appeared unwelcoming, cold, and rebuking.

A train was standing by the platform. He looked thoughtfully into the people swarming its doors. There was an ostentatious penchant to grab a bit of space, a bit of foothold, a chit of more life. Then with a shrill toot the hooter went out and with a jerk the train started to move. Slowly.... People fought their way rapidly. The last compartment was slowly moving away with introspecting sobriety. The cart-puller's thoughtful gaze was distracted by a heavy footfall from the other direction. Having run along the stones and rails, a young man was now cascading still faster on the smooth tarred platform. The law of relative motions in operation, he was running smartly to emerge victorious in competition against the handle bar of the last carriage coldly moving away.

Old Inshan was brought out of his reverie. With agility unfaithful to his age, he rose from the rag he was lying on and ran to cross the young man's path, shouting:

"O brave son...it's not a suitable place for sprinting and climbing!"

The young man swung around and gnashed angrily, "Enough of it old man...next time you do it, I'll break your hand!"

The daily commuters were conversant with this old beggarly fellow's policing regarding the violation of the rule of not boarding a running train. He was a particular eyesore to the adventurous types.

The adventurer just ran ahead. Helplessly, Inshan saw him running to the dangerous end. His dirty, stained, raggish, linen head-cloth draped over his head, standing tip-toe in praying agitation, he watched the heroic feat. The hand gripping the door rail and the legs moving very fast. Time stood still. The young man launched himself but the spring in his feet was not enough. His knees struck against the foot support. On a scared instinct Inshan's eyes closed. He wouldn't open them till the train had chugged away.

Fortunately, the man's grip had worked in proportion to the harsh words to the old porter, and hanging on he had somehow sneaked in helped by the passengers on board. The old onlooker hesitatingly opened his eyes and much to his relief saw that the man had been saved. He was all alone in the world, so considered this vagrant fellow as someone belonging to his own family born of *inshaniyat* and thanked God for keeping his blessing eyes over this inexperienced and immature colt, who had just foolishly jumped into the invisible, inexhaustible, and inexplicable snares of accidents stealthily laid by the God of Death.

Thank God, on this important day in his life no untoward incident had happened! Today he was to be rewarded by the Director of the local railway zone. Yesterday the station master had called him to his cabin and with dignified confidence informed him about it. One day's gap between the announcement and the event only explicitly indicated that it was no pre-arranged official recognition of his services. Still the railway staff at Ambala had been kind and considerate in grasping the opportunity of the Director's visit and honour the poor, homeless man for his service to the humanity.

There was nobody from his lineage he could relate to. Before 1947, his poor Hindu family in a downtown quarter of Lahore survived and struggled as daily wage earners, picking up petty jobs thrown into their beggary bowl by the tensioned circumstances of those turbulent times. Then 1947 saw liberation and the massacres. At one of those long blood-hissing nights, when blood came to be strictly grouped as Hindu and Muslim, they somehow managed to board a bleeding train having more dead than living Hindus. Even those on board had little chance of reaching alive to the other side of the border.

As expected, before it could cross the newly created border, it was stopped by a blood-thirsty mob at a desolate place and unthinkable hacking of humans happened. It was hideous ecstasy. A savage delirium. He was seven years old and was lucky or unlucky to survive. Later at some station, he was dragged out almost dead of fright. They pulled him out all blood stained from the mass of bodies. Blood dripping from the floors, he was lucky to come to Amritsar. He saw all his family members being hastily taken away in a truck overloaded with corpses for mass cremation.

From that day the platform became his home and all its allied crowded phenomena the familial things he could relate to. During his juvenile stage, he grew up doing all types of petty jobs, sufferings all kinds of physical and moral hazards, apart from the ever-persistent exploitation which an orphan is destined to come under. Caught in the eternal encagement of circumstances, he worked as a tea-stall helper, table cleaner in station canteens, dishwasher in railway restaurants, balloon vendor, and peanuts hawker. And when his arms were strong enough to pull a handcart, he became a carter to carry all types of provisions on the small two-wheeled appendage to his beast-of-burden-type existence.

He definitely must have been given some name by his family. It but got smudged under the blood clots and flesh in that train compartment. Hate doesn't kill just bodies, it butchers names as well. His limbs were intact, but he had lost his name somewhere in the gory stampede. How do you keep your name alive? Only others can help you in this by sweetly or sourly speaking it, either in front of you or in your absence in some context. But a name which is never spoken by anybody evaporates like raindrops in a desert. His name had evaporated.

Many a time he would think, who am I, and a blankness struck him like he did not exist at all. He still remembered what his family called him. But just a memory cannot help you in keeping your name alive. You need others to help you keep it alive, and for that you ought to have a social identity. He hadn't any, so very soon he became nameless. Oye, abe, chhotu, motu, patlu, ghamchakkar, etc., etc., roll over you to possess your identity as per people's moods, whims and fancies. And this is even worse than being nameless.

He would have lost his name forever, if not for this wandering mendicant, so prominently bearded and hair braids and all, who was giving a warming sermon to tea-shipping passengers waiting for their trains one frigid night.

"We should try to become *inshan*, a good human being, who follows *inshaniyat*..."

The orphan boy literally stole the word. Kept it safe in his pocket. Repeated it hundreds of times to stamp his identity. And knowing that a name is no name unless spoken by others, he did all he could to be recognised with this name. So he became Inshan, slowly, over a period of years. That was his achievement. He had earned a name. He was not nameless and faceless like scores of other citizens of the platform.

Time's arms swung silently and stealthily, straddling the decades of existence. It was just survival for the sake of it; like surviving itself was the best achievement which could be ever dreamt of. It was 40 years ago when he arrived at the Ambala railway station with his pittance of savings on his frail, prematurely withered 20-year-old personage in 1960. His initiation into what was to become the overarching motto of his life happened just a couple of months after his arrival.

Diwali, the darkest night of *Amavasya*, is followed by the waxing phase of moony nights to reach the milky night's brightest cusp in the rain-washed early winter sky. The moon's unpolluted clarity and cool misty air make the nights smile at their best. During its waning phase after the full dazzle, the moonlight spreads in misty romance over the languorously lying nights. Sometimes during the morning twilight, when there is no mist, it shines like a night sun, casting shadows on earth, beating for some time even the sun's efforts from below the horizon.

It was on one such night when a middle-aged man belonging to some other part of the country was cut to pieces by a train. With disastrous discourtesy the time whirred on it axis. A mishap! And a sinister silence sprawled over the scene. The sight's horrific details struck him with all the fright possible to a human heart.

It was an accident; an unclaimed body; so its removal from the tracks and cremation got mired in the usual hassles which accompany and entail official responsibility. It was broad daylight and the body still lay there. It made the tragedy even more gruesome. A policeman, standing as a sign of the authorities' knowledge of the accident, was trying his level best to get some men and conveyance to take the limbs to the civil hospital for post-mortem.

Coming across the railway policeman's helplessness and gross apathy for the after-death cause of once throbbing life, it was for the first time that Inshan's conscience got those initial pickings, which if welcomed and received cordially blossom into a beautiful moral facade over a period of time.

The wholesale dealer whose packages of provisions were lying in the platform warehouse, having paid him some token money in advance, pulled at his sleeve with the attitude of a master hurrying his slave.

"Oh come on, haven't you ever seen a dead body in your life," the trader gasped huskily.

"Seen sahib...perhaps seen too many to ...!" from the deep dormitory of memories, cries and killings flashed.

Solemnly straight-faced, he gently returned the one rupee coin and offered his services for the final journey of the diseased. The tragedy of these crushed limbs connoted the gruesome massacre in that fateful train. While on the way to the hospital, bloody scenes vividly, massively returned to haunt him. The savage behemoth of memories gripped him so tightly that he went numb.

For a whole week afterwards he pulled his cart lost in a mysterious ennui. Some meaningful outlines were emerging out of the shapeless identity of his poor, destitute being. He had refused money for *that* job. It appeared too sinful and against whatever notion he had of dharma.

After a few months, while he was pulling his cart on the platform, he was beckoned by the same policeman who had asked him to take the unclaimed, unidentified body to the cremation ground. India being a land of teeming homeless masses, someone with a forgotten identity had lost his life on the tracks, at a distance from the station. Again he followed the duty, just getting solace from the fact that his soul felt better for the kind act. He was getting a sensation which even a 10 rupee note, offered more as a tip or charity by a wealthy merchant in lieu of the littlest of cartage, won't give him.

It's convenient to fall in the trap of cold apathy because it is easy and natural just like drawing a breath. Goodness is just one step away. It's another matter that we choose to ignore it. It seems to require a huge effort to take that step. Some people but move out of the rut to take it up. It gives them a certain satisfaction. There is hardly any parameter to measure it, but it certainly exists.

He knew the meaning and essence of his name, so just picked up the abandoned specks of goodness; may be to keep his name alive; to prove that he is worth it. We explore meanings in life. He too had found one. His was a small world and he kept that fragment of goodness, and held it with marvellous stillness.

As the passing years reaped their share of accidents along the steely furrows, his voluntary acceptance of the job, over a period of time, became a duty in the eyes of others. They expected him to do it without even sparing some praise or appreciation for his unselfishness and without harbouring any reservations for their own apathy. Years rolled in this mundane way, interjected with atrophied chunks of accidents which spattered the tracks now and then. He came to be known as the man who carried the dead bodies of train accidents to the civil hospital and even performed the last rites in case there was no claimant for the body.

Now after 40 years, his deeds had accomplished the benchmark of a reward. It was a sort of D-day to him. He drew out his bucket from under the cart and smartly, smugly went out to fetch water from the platform hand-pump. Coming back he freed his old tattered knapsack from its smart knot to the axle of his cart.

The cart was his profession, his house, his world. Standing with its hand-bars raised on the peg-support, it served him as a shelter which enclosed his portion of the world. During winters, he put a tarpaulin sheet over the whole of it and sneaked into the tiny interior. A plank supported on bricks at both ends served as his bed.

Irrespective of all caste, class and all other man-made differentials, every person has a special dress to adorn for the special-most occasion. He too had one. Or rather he had a choice to hit the best combination out of various items: different-sized shirts, sweaters, trousers, and shoes given by the daily passengers who donated on some occasions with different moods with the same motive of getting God's blessings in lieu of the charity. Most of these were oversized for him. The shoes, however, should not be too tight or too large; the rest of the mis-fittings can be somehow adapted. These adaptations are what he thought about tidying up.

He borrowed hair oil, comb and a piece of looking glass from different beggary neighbours, prompting one of the kind commuters, who sometimes spoke to him while coming from or going to office, to say:

"Ho Inshan, are you getting married today?!"

Beaming with shyness he replied, "Yes sahib, it's as important as marriage!"

In all his simplicity, he had assumed that the function was for him specially. Each particle of his poor existence was agitated with nervous excitement and frightful uncertainty. He was feeling a part of the larger world, not just a faceless dot lying on the platform. The people who mattered knew his name. That was the most important thing to him.

He tidied up with a sweeping exuberance. How blissful the feeling! From the dark corner, which sucked all identity and spewed invisibility, he had been put on a shiny stage. He was recognised. They knew him. All the miseries of life didn't matter anymore.

It's very difficult for the world to change suddenly to accommodate such happiness. All these goose-bumps creating sensations were belied very soon as he was made to sit in the last row in the hall. It was some big show for a bigger purpose. He felt being sucked into oblivion again. With joggling force it swept the tiny cottage of his expectations. His felicitation was a mere appendage to the function and that too caused by the generosity of the station master. Still, with a school boy's eagerness and anticipation he saw the proceedings to make the best of the occasion. However, his patience was wearing thin and for a moment he even grew apprehensive that they might just wind it up without even recalling his presence.

Luck but struck for him at last. The station master got up and gave a nice introduction to his deeds of the past 40 years. Goodness in practice takes a long and circuitous route, in paraphrasing however it takes a few words. So the words about his generous deeds lasted a couple of minutes and during that period people cared to look at him like a fellow human being. He found it too burdensome, the gaze of the gentry from the better world, and stared at the faded leather of his shoes in embarrassment.

His hands were trembling as he walked up to the stage. The Director, an enlightened academic man, was impressed by the gilded caption to the long chapter of this unassuming, unknown life. The station master had handed him 1100 rupees to give as a reward to this poor carter in recognition of his services. Deep down in his conscience, however, he felt sad somehow, in some vague manner. Rolling the notes in his fingers, he was lost in thoughts as this beggary man attired in his best dress approached the stage.

The chief guest felt that giving just money (without any souvenir) would be trivialising the silent services of this man. So his senses ran to find something to act as a medallion (the real reward which would last) along with the money which would surely get spent. There was nothing but the bouquet presented to him. He picked it up and handed it to the embarrassed and shy person cowering in front of him, patting him, congratulating him for the show of humanity on the inhuman platforms.

There was the customary round of applause. Inshan just stared absentmindedly at the objects of his reward. With an overpowering emotion, he hugged tight the flowery recognition of his deeds and stammered:

"Thank you for the flowers sir! But I...I cannot accept money because it seems as if today after years I'm taking the price for my services to the dead."

Saying this in all humility, the old carter put out his hand to give the money back to the chief guest. Dumbstruck by the dazzle of this lotus of goodness in the mud of life on the platforms, the Director could not utter a word. Goodness gives its own kind of mild shock which is aesthetically very overpowering. He just patted the frail man on his shoulder. Putting the money on the table and embracing the flowers, Inshan saluted in military fashion and moved out.

For many days to come, he ogled with happiness at the withering flowers, drawing more juice of contentment out of those rumpled petals and crumpled stalks...and still more as the de-juiced, wrinkly petals lost all moisture and turned to pieces.

So he kept on serving in his customary way without any more rewards and without any regrets from life. He carried his iota of self-worth safe in his pockets as he moved around earning his livelihood by transporting goods on his hand-pulled cart.

***

7. Highway Murder

Do you think only you, I mean the human beings, have the right to tell you story? No man, no! Even we trees have the right to tell the tale of our life, especially when the main protagonist is man, the master of nature presently. So listen you all, humans as well as others who comprise nature. The two are different now by the way. Listen!

Well, I am a huge eucalypts tree standing by a road. But since now I stand more as a roadblock, they are killing me. The iron is hissing and kissing the rings of age in my stout trunk. I stand benumbed and in daze. But I have to speak out before I fall. Possibly you listeners will spot the crime and just—at least—get an idea of the pain I feel while I am being slaughtered.

To tell the truth, I feel really sad and bad about it. I never thought the end will come so soon, without any notice. There is no storm threatening to uproot me. It's a very fine day, but all the more suitable to the humans to carry out their act of greed. My killing but is unjustified because I have been fulfilling all my duties assigned by Mother Nature to me.

The way I have gone overboard in carrying out my task, I think I should have been lucky enough to see the majesty of the upcoming wintery full moon. The moon-rays are very naughty I tell you. You may be lost in the brighter self-created neon lights, but nothing can beat the beauty of full moon rays on a winter night. I pine for one more such night! Alas, it seems impossible! I have to take solace by remembering the past only.

See, you may not realise it, but your tools of cutting, your axes, saws, scythes and blades are very painful. I have to impose anaesthesia on myself, for I cannot even cry like you guys. Still I can feel the saw's butchering the bloodless flesh in my guts. But poor me, I don't even have the blood to put forth the evidence of a murder. Even though my flesh is as good as yours, but mine doesn't bleed, so even the sanguine interior as they cut through it, appears simple painless stone to them. But I feel the pain, I swear. Just want to tell. Please don't take my cutting as simple as breaking a stone. And who knows, even a stone might feel the pain!

It's a hazily sun-lit winter noon. It appeared such a balmy day in the morning. I was looking at the people warmly moving onto their destination. But then they suddenly arrived like hounds. We hardly know what cooks up in you guys' minds. I was even surprised why so many of them came and started prodding me, slapping me out of my languorous spell. I don't even know whether to throw my almost harmless, inaudible curse at these fellows. They are helpless themselves. Otherwise why would they suddenly get into sudden killings like this?

The state itself has authorised my murder to broaden this already fat road. But this ***state*** I cannot see, even though it's present everywhere. Possibly, it's bigger and stronger than God Himself. God made me, and is now helpless before the saw of the state. So you can very well guess who is stronger. I feel like bowing before the ***state*** to plead for my life. Hello, ***state*** do you hear me?

Let me be clear on this. It's a murder. You may prefer to call it just cutting wood. But there is a life inside. Never forget this. Don't I grow like you guys do? Don't I do my duty of purifying air and providing shade, and give dead and even live wood, like you people claim your utility?

For many decades, I have been standing as a serving helper to both man and nature. During older times, this metalled road, this carrier of huge traffic and the so called your 'progress', was simply a dirt road. It was my friend taking your forefathers to their common destinations. Nobody was in a damn hurry like you people these days. I stood here as a milestone reached by a tired pair of legs or a rickety bull-cart, who halted under me, savouring the shade I provided. I felt so proud of myself.

This very path has turned a foe now. It's a highway after all, the merciless, fast-paced carrier of growth. It has turned a parasite now. It needs more space. Damn it, they don't need shade and pure air now. These can be easily managed in the metal boxes which hurtle day and night on it. So I'm redundant and old. I have turned a road-blocker of progress with my few square-feet of foot-hold.

Man, again I try to shout and remind you that if a healthy mass like me is no life, then yours is also not so important. By cutting us you are cutting yourselves, for you are nothing but merely an extension of our world, a mere reflection of the nature around you. We gone, even you will be gone. Haa fools, now I can afford to call you as such during these final moments, for you cannot even see the precipice you are heading into.

The chips of my flesh are flying. The strikes are getting harder. Their sweat-drenched faces are wincing with effort. Why do they appear so serious as if it's a war? And I'm not even hitting back. But man, now it is hurting quite a lot. But I have resolved to keep telling my murder story till the axes, scythes and saws send my tiniest of branches to be turned to ashes in some poor household's fire-place.

We trees never recoil with pain as your axes spray chips of our flesh. Just because our flesh is different coloured doesn't mean we don't feel the pain. We do, man, in our own way which you don't understand!

We had equal rights till the mankind was just a part of nature, not the master of it. Now this lethal serrated metal, the extension of your greed, going deeper and deeper into my bloodless guts reminds me of our inevitable fate. Every tree on earth now has a deadly date with the greedy most, treacherous and unforgiving mate.

Haa the cowards! Forever playing so safe! They know that I'm huge. The poor things are afraid of my sudden fall and bring them some injuries. Little do they realise that a tree's pride is in standing tall and upright. And we do it till the last ounce of our strength. I am not going to give in that easily. They have to earn my dead body. It cannot be a cakewalk. Let them have blisters on their hands. It will serve as a proof of my murder.

Little do they realise my commitment to my duty, my oath to Mother Nature. Even in the face of death, I cannot stop playing my part in the natural scheme of things. As they are robbing me of my few square feet of space on earth, my saplings are still giving them life, still doling out oxygen under this winter sun. I am helpless and bound to my sworn duty. I cannot be vindictive and stop fuelling life into their lungs, even if they happen to be my murderers. Even my murder cannot change me, helpless as I am due to my nature.

Now the saw has gone pretty deep. I am getting the signs of that eternal sleep. There is also an unbearable pain in the so called painless mass. Death is death after all. Hope you understand.

Like hangman's noose, thick hemp ropes are tied to direct my fall. From a safe distance, tractors are pulling to bring down this wooden bull. They are worried, but are assured of victory. There are too many of them, with steely human determination to win, to stifle any chance of failure. No, I don't see any chance of a miracle. It's as hopeless as it can be.

Now I feel it. The death blow! The pinnacle of their jeering selves. A cleavage breaks through the portion still holding me to my mother earth. From the softest saplings to the rock hard tissues, my whole self is panicked. But still I have to continue telling the tale of my murder before I finally fall. My saplings are crying like innocent children. The hardest of trunk tissues are shamelessly crying like the battle hard, handsome soldiers on their knees after losing the war. Death is after all death. Who wants to cease to exist?

Who cares? Nobody. This big snapping sound is my death cry. And here I fall with a thud. Yes man, you win. I am dead before I thought I will.

***

8. A Drop of Love in the Poisonous Pond

Only love has the potential of performing alchemy, capable of turning rusty iron of hate into the gleaming gold of humanity.

Many, many full moons ago, there was a beautiful princess in a tiny paradisiacal hill state. As the nature's blooms touched new peaks, her beauty still raced ahead to scale newest charms. The nature spread across the far-flung wild trails sang the songs of her majestic beauty. The cool gusts of pure breeze did its duty to spread the charming tales of her beauty. For miles and miles her fame measured distances in just arm-lengths.

There was a handsome prince in a kingdom which was at war with the princess's state. The effusive tales of her beauty seeped into his thoughts, imagination and dreams. A sweet pining lynched him. Looking at the state of affairs between the two kingdoms, it was futile to nurture such dreams. But he was helpless. Days became boring and nights turned endless. It was just impossible to drive her out of his heart.

The much famed name was haunting him every moment, teasing him, daring him for bravado. Then unable to take it anymore, he untethered his horse and set out in pursuit of his destiny. It was a dark stormy night. Owls were screeching ominously. Wind was warning of risk. And the darkness was daunting. He appeared a futile chaser running after a mirage in a tragic race. He cut all fears and darkness with the steely point of his determination and went full gallop into the corridors of exhilarating uncertainty.

Untamed wind came to subdue his young heart, and spanked his brave, soldierly chest. But he moved without taking any rest. His heart was at rest only in the pursuit. If he stopped for some time, his soul felt unbearable, became restless, forcing him to move with more speed and sturdier determination.

After a weeks-long suffering in the ravines, he reached where the much acclaimed star of her beauty shone. There was a risk of getting recognised, caught and, surely, hanged. He wandered in her kingdom in impersonation. The very air felt so antagonistic, but the pull of her fabled beauty kept him in pursuit. The myth of her beauty came spooling out of every mouth here and there. There were very few who had actually seen the precious jewel of the kingdom. The rest had their boundless imagination and endless stories to satisfy their curiosity.

His eyes were aching to have a sight of her, at any cost, even at the cost of his life. His suffering, pining heart was laden with cold sighs. He had been trained well in all the arts of war and disguise. He was taking out every plan from his well-trained mind and set of skills to meet his goal of seeing her. The enemy prince was just waiting for a chance to get the shower of her bloom to drive away his heart's gloom. In his frantic search, he grabbed a chance at last.

It was a full moon night. The moon was lit at its fairest bright. The princess came out for a boat ride in the marvellously calm lake. He stealthily waited in the shoreline foliage. His chest shook with a thunderous heart-quake. Like the desert sand waiting for the rain drops for years, he lay in wait. The moment seemed so near, and yet impossibly far. Each passing instant appeared like years.

He was just above the princess's safe, secret bathing platform of unblemished marble. The white floor exotically gleamed. The stage welcomed the royal lady with awed welcome. His heart achingly struggled as her boat arrived. Her maidens were giggling and teasing her for her beauty. He held his hand over his broad chest as if to calm down his thumping heart, lest it exploded to make a big sound.

The paragon of beauty was adorned with filigreed silk finery. In silent majesty, she put her adorable feet on the gleaming, cool platform by the waterside. Waves rippled through him with a coquettish chide. Her hallowed figure distinctly glowed over the group of helping ladies. His thoughts stopped. His world froze. And time got stuck up in a trap. It was too overpowering for the senses to take it in a moment. He turned a stone, mesmerised by her beauty. The night was so tranquil, affable and disarming that she decided to take a bath. So her finery no longer covered her exquisitely carved curves. And the earth stopped spinning on its axis.

The naked fairy jammed his nerves. There was statuesque glow of marble on her milky skin. Even the moonlight appeared bathing along the curves of her exquisitely feminine body. A real life sculpture of utmost symmetry and fathomless sensuality! The moon-rays deflected off her curves and panting, pining reached his eyes. Every moment her moon-sculpted body acquired new vistas and highs. Her flowing tresses over her long, slender back lustily shook to her head's gentle gyrations.

Her features were a bit lost in the milky mystique of the moonlight. But he heard the words spoken with mythic softness. He was dying with the urge to see the face of the fabled carrier of the unparalleled beauty. So he came closer to fulfil his young heart's only desire. How can you stop a sunflower from turning to the sun? The nature suffuses our selves, our beings, with certain helplessness. And such pining vulnerability paves the way for what we make of our lives. They decide the path we take. They set up the course of our destiny.

No flight lasts forever. Gravity pulls us down onto the plain of reality. He was noticed by the female arm-guards. Their well-toned, almost masculine, arms tossed into action and grabbed the sword hilts. Surrounded by trained female warriors, he still had a decent chance of escape through a fight. But how could he put a blot on this night by getting into a bloody scuffle with her guards? No, he was in no mood to go to war, even if it meant risking his life. The female armed guards advanced and surrounded him. The prince was thus caught. The scandalous air of the happening filled up the moonlit panorama.

The next sun rose with its curious, perplexed rays, eager to see the consequences of blind love. The tale of his reckless misadventure was doing the rounds. People were offended, more so because he was the enemy's son. The King's throne literally shook with the young prince's impudence and mindless transgression. He was seething with anger.

Revenge, revenge shouted the petrified air. It was the enemy's unforgivable crime. The King sentenced the enemy prince to death at his youth's prime. However, even when blinded by the scornful blasts of rage and revenge, kingdoms have their own laws, the inviolable laws which hold their bastion even in the face of almost unpardonable sins. Well, that is the thinnest line dividing the domain of mankind from that of heathens.

The prince's royal blood deserved the fulfilment of a last wish before his death. When they brought him out for the public execution, the masses were jubilant. How dare he enter into the private place of their fairy like princess? He came out with the regal confidence of a prince. His face still carried the finest smile possible on a handsome face.

When the last wish was asked, as the law demanded, he just asked the permission to see her face in full light of the blazing sun, no cover, no veil, just her much-fabled face. He simply requested an eye-full brace of her magical features.

God, why thou create such bewitching creatures? During his final moments before death, he was led to the courtyard below her ornate, marbled balcony. He stood there like a victorious soldier. His head held high, his chained hands placed on both sides of his slim waist, his broad shoulders drawn firmly and chest puffed up with the pride of a journey completed.

The star of countless eyes was then led onto the balcony. She beat the sun in the dazzle of her finery. It was the finest creation of God he had ever seen. A smile curved down the corners of his lips and he took a deep breath as if to soak the moment till eternity. Her sad eyes looked down at him without any hate and malice. It was almost impossible to be otherwise with that beauty. The prince too was no less on the scale of looks. On his manly features, the smile lurked with such ease as if it won't be dislodged even by the gravest threat of death.

The princess knew that her face had been the bait, which would soon seal this life's fate. She looked deeply into his eyes and tears welled up in those almond cups of beauty and love. He looked at her with such unmoving intensity as to take a deep, deep imprint of her beauty on his soul, where no dagger would reach.

She was taken away. And he was led to the public square for beheading. His every step but told the tale of a victory.

A sea of sorrows surged painfully through the princess's delicate self. She fell at her father's feet with an utmost painful entreat. If he, the prince of an enemy state, was ready to die for the cause of just a look at her face, she was capable of going a step further with her feminine bravery to save a life, an admirer, a brave man, a man having a heart full of love. It boosted her guts. She was ready to go to any length to save him.

"Father, it is not his fault, but the result of my well-meant kiss! He is not a stranger. Your daughter secretly tied the knot with him. If you kill him, sorrows and sufferings will cross ocean's brim. A father would widow his daughter. For ages known will be this slaughter! And if you still send him to the gallows, another death surely follows!" she was crying profusely and fell at her father's feet.

The King loved his daughter more than his own life. He didn't remember her tears through her lifetime, for he had always undone any cause which may bring tears to her beautiful eyes. How could he let this darling flower wither away? Thus, smiled on many fates a new ray!

A drop of love transformed the pools of poisonous, hateful waters. It turned into a fountain of brotherhood, non-violence and cooperation. They were ceremoniously married. The decades-old animosity was buried. What a humane outcome of her wise, flowery whiff of courage! For the newlyweds a marital bliss, and for the two states a friendly kiss!

Long live love! The only substance which can consume the endless fire of hate!

***

9. The Undying Flame of Love

Many, many years ago, a sage was meditating on a Himalayan peak. Majestic dales and solitary vales sprawled around were all aglow with the divine streak.

Though the birds chirped songs, and rain poured down in throngs, he was unmovable, lost in a deep trance.

In winters, icy cold storms blew and the snow around and over him was all aglow with its chilling primitiveness. His soul but was safe somewhere in the cosy warmth of transcendental realisation.

In autumn, wind-fallen leaves sailed down with slumberous tumble, and ripe fruits fell proudly, adventurously for a juicy, pleasant crumble. He still was somewhere else when the nature opened these marvellous jewels from her treasure trove.

In spring, wild flowers fully unfurled their fragrance and smile, and honey-bees engaged in dawn to dusk toil. He but was unmoved and transported into a state where the ecstasies of natural bounties don't mean anything anymore.

Summer's warm days sprayed desultory, eerie uneasiness around, and cool nights proudly embraced this son with his soul heaven-bound. Still it didn't matter. He was undisturbed and was silently moving on his meditative path.

Once it was a full moon autumn night. A fairy was flying amid milky delight. A perfect calmness pervaded the solitary vales. Everything was asleep, bathed in the softest fluffy shades of white. The fairy flew low over the peaks glowing under the moonlight. The seer was lost in his trance in front of his cave, the beauty of nature sprawled around meaningless to him.

She saw him and hovered around the sanctimonious air of his sagehood. A small, harmless mischief rustled in her young, innocent heart. She circled in the air above him. Her laughter touched the milky sea around and created soft ripples. Her unbelievably soft dress rustled in the gentle breeze born of her circles. It but did not have any effect on him. He was engrossed too deep in the cosmic balance beyond the sensory contradictions and dualities. The more she looked, the more was the urge in her to bring him back to the beauty of this world, to fetch him from the deep ocean where his soul had dived.

His exquisitely masculine physique and persona created tempted sparks on her magic stick. She tried all juicily leering feminine tricks. But her desire-lorn swirls in the air failed to move him even a bit. Helplessly she descended onto the earth. There were almost tears of helplessness in her beautiful eyes. She sat in front of him with those rose-red lips pursed in a heart-breaking frown.

Her marvellous eyes were lost in his handsome, bearded, well sculpted face. It was mesmerising. There was not a single worldly trace on his face. She herself was caught in a trance and lost the sense of time and the laws of the fairyland. The night sped away as if in a jiffy.

The day rose. The sun arrived with full earthly delight. There was but terror in her eyes. The hope to return to her realm died. She had broken the law of her land by not returning on the same night after the brief terrestrial sojourn. The realisation crashed against her soft self like a thunderbolt. Her utmost sensuous bare shoulders heaved under the tremors of this unpardonable fault. A cry involuntarily tore through her slender throat. And then it was a still bigger violation.

His serenely flowing meditative phrase met this sinful, full-stopping dot. His communion with the divinity was broken. His long-closed eyes opened. The world of his penance lay scattered. His fiercely burning eyes stared at the flower in sobs and sighs. Her large, flooded eyes pleaded for mercy. But the fire in his unforgiving eyes was unrelenting and cursing.

The fabric of his serenity was torn. The sage thundered, "You proud, vain woman of egoistic beauty, become an ugly bush of thorns!"

Mowed down by the spell of his cursing energy, an ugly bush stood in place of that angelic beauty. All shaken and ravaged, he left the place. A thorny branch, meanwhile, got entangled in his loin cloth, as if for meek, pleading forgiveness and brace. He but scornfully jerked it apart and headed to some other place for a new start.

Time then took to its heels on swift horses. The seasons changed. The spring's colourful patterns were rearranged. The summer's warm kisses melted the snows. The autumn's harvest uncomplainingly fell to the air's chiding blows. The winter's snowy blanket covered the peaks. And rains lashed down in stormy freaks.

This pleasant wavering of nature, however, couldn't shake the sage from the meditative maze high there in the hills. Faraway down the hills, the accursed bush was shrouded in thorny haze. It struggled to sprout fruits and flowers. Even cursing has a testing time against soft, innocent glow of purity. How can something having a fairy core remain ugly and thorny for too long? Her pure soul entombed in that thorny shrine prayed for penance. And see, a flower of her fruits sprouts forth!

A flower blossomed among the thorns. So beautiful! It lit up with life among the thorns and pale brown branches. It appeared juxtaposed by a miracle, like it had dropped from the heaven and got stuck there. It was the day when the enlightened sage arrived from the north. Contented with his cosmic realisation, he came down the beautiful dale. As he passed the bush, his purified soul sensed the thorny shrub's plaintive wail. His feet disobeyed him and he couldn't move. The lone flower among the thorns fell at his feet in holy-most obeisance and greet. He picked it up and was lost in its fragrance.

The thorn was ugly. The flower so beautiful and fragrant! What contradiction! Flowery heaven and thorny hell together! The latter born of his cursing condemnation; the flower born of the beauty behind the thorny bars. It was a jolting earthly realisation. Hadn't he broken the beautifully set laws?

Torrents of repentance cut through him. He bid penance at the altar for a long time. His repenting self set around a reformative shrine. His soul drenched in painful chime. He braced the thorns with the love and affection purest of the pure. It gave him bleeding fingers so many times. He caressed and cared for it like it was the beautiful most flowery shrub. He was practicing his penance now, of love, of surrender, of repentance. What else can be bigger than these?

When his soul had been salvaged of the sin, nobody could bet against her for a win. There she blossomed in front of him. Beauty, charm and grace filled to the brim. Her smile was forgetting and forgiving. It was the beacon of her penance, of love, of beauty. Inside the stony walls of his heart, a new luminosity was now thriving. The sage embraced her. She, who had been separated from her loved ones, got the earthling she had fallen for. Happiness, bliss and calm opened a new door to the start of a fresh cycle of life, love and humanity.

All but the sage had been extinguished by the cataclysm. The lone and forlorn survivor, he had been striking at the doors of heaven with his endless questions. Now there was no more pursuit. The endless had manifested itself in a small sip of love. Now they lived as a man and a woman. New hopes, aspirations and progeny began to thrive.

Thus were sown the seeds of another spell and cycle of life, of creation. Their unchecked love in those flowery vales left countless exotic trails. Gurgling brooks gave company to her primordially sensuous laughter. His instinct's procreating sprouts mingled with the mirthful waters of her receptiveness.

***

10. The Parrot and the Old Sparrow

After a long, hard and wearisome journey, the parrot realised it was no longer possible for him to fly anymore. The sunset was imminent and along with the great fire ball, his willpower was ready to surrender and call it a day. His wings tired, his temper losing its balance, and his beautiful colours mired in the hard journey's perspiration--although it was winter--the parrot landed on a branch.

It broke his heart, this inability to continue on his march to meet the lowest-set milestone for the day. But then it had been a very tough, cold and stormy day. There was no sunlight during the day. And when at last the sun prevailed over the frosty chaos, it was the time to call off its duty, pack its bag of brightness and light the other part of the world.

The winter was at its peak. And anxious, drooping, panting was his beak. With every precious moment left of the day, the saffron slanting rays were melting into the misty bay. More emboldened, the cold was creeping up. Its pinch was becoming bold to take everything in its hold.

With sad eyes the parrot looked at the setting sun. His run had been too long and taxing. He had long forgotten the flight's fun. Where was that fleeting, winged pun? With each breath and laboured purr, restlessness crept further into his perturbed fur. Each moment passed, pinching him with the realisation of loss and failure. With each mile, the journey had become a drag. The vigour and energy, which had lifted him with brag, were now dumped in a deep pit, from where it was not possible for him to retrieve even a bit.

Then even the last ounce of strength was hit. He was fighting to save himself from a fall. After all, he had so many miles to go. The height of his flight was becoming continuously low. Finally, he bowed before the eventuality and anchored his feathery weight on a branch's restful bait. Halting, but, didn't bring the relief it should after a long march because he still had far, far to go.

"Merciless, frost-fanged will be the night!" he thought to his misery's delight.

As the warmth vapoured off his body, shudder crept over with incremental ease. Anxiously, he ruffled his feathers as if to loosen the cold night's siege.

"Where to spend the cold night?" he pondered from dejection's highest height.

Everything appeared alien, uninviting and antagonistic in this freezing twilight. The night moved closer with a scary chuckle across the gray shades of the dreary dusk. The night was so near! It again put him on his toes. He realised the importance and utility of the remaining traces of the day.

He looked around. The forest was lost in an eerie silence. The day's last vestiges bade goodbye like the feeble truth emanating from a sad couplet. For miles and miles everything appeared surrendered to the gloomy pal of a freezing, imminent night. All the woods around looked solid, unwelcoming and creviceless; without that hole which can become a bird's hall. His despair and agony touched another peak.

His sad reverie was broken. He heard a muffled, breaking-free, old, juvenile chuckle. It was an old sparrow. The greyish patches in his fur long put under time's harrow. The oldie was flapping its feathers in a water puddle. So old and bathing in such freezing winter's hold! The young parrot's senses went into a chilly huddle, while staring at the scene in the puddle.

Even to a tired body, dejected mind and subdued soul, advice comes very easily.

"Hey such a cold night is waiting! Take care, it doesn't become death's baiting! Old fellow, you must take care and should not extend your dare to the limit of catching cold, fall sick and lie on death bed!" the warning came with ease from his beaten, sulking self.

The old bather, the fun freak, stopped in the middle of an ecstatic shriek. But within an instant his seasoned enthusiasm regained its footing. Again the old punster squeaked, chirped and tweeted to match the huge heaves of happiness sashaying across his old turf.

"My old coat has enough room for the water to turn to warm vapours and shun and beat the death's creepers. Each moment has to be lived like a full day before I fall asleep forever. Before that I have to live fully and fear nothing, worry about nothing, and get everything which can be drawn from each and every moment. I have to milk the time's udder totally dry bro!" he tweeted, whistled and made a frenzied display of dancing in the muddled waters.

The old sparrow had raised a storm: a riot of happiness; a cascade of mirth. In between, he paused and pantingly opened his beak to fill his old lungs for more life, more vigour and more strength. Everything falls short in old age. The young, beaten, subdued and defeated parrot looked on from the branch. It appeared silly and illogical to him.

"What could have happened to make this oldie so happy?" he wondered.

With his saggy, drenched feathering, the sparrow heaved his old bones to fly up to him for a hearing. The moment he landed on the branch, he brought exciting, adventurous jolt of mirthfulness. The branch shook with the force of his liveliness. The young parrot tightened his claws and ruffled his feathers to maintain his perch. He was hardly done with it when a vigorous pat landed on his tired left wing. The old sparrow's right wing landed with a casual, supportive and friendly force. Again the force of the old bones jolted the tired young bones.

"Tired!" the oldie asked.

"Yaa," the parrot could manage a weak squeak.

"Well, most often we get more tired in the mind than the body," the oldie puffed up his chest, ruffled his feathers, and twitched his tail to rearrange his gear.

There was a little shower on the parrot. He shook with a sense of cold and moved away a bit. The distance between them was too short for two strangers.

"New to the place, humn," the seasoned native of the land asked the visitor.

The branch was still swaying with the inertia of the vital last drops of life in the old sparrow's body. The newcomer insecurely, apprehensively, worryingly gripped the wood. A cold night and darkness was all playing in his mind.

"Where are you flying to?" the oldie asked softly, suppressing his enthusiasm, feeling the parrot's discomfort.

"I have to go far. Shouldn't have stopped at all. But then my wings gave in," the parrot sighed, traces of defeat and loss all strewn over his green.

The sparrow gave an assuring, comforting smile. "During the day, do your best. Night is just and just for the rest. No flight can last forever. Rest is not stopping. It's just the beginning of another league in the journey," there was mystic calmness in his old, dim eyes.

The parrot looked at him and sighed. He wanted to say so much about his trials, tribulations, unmet goals, crushed dreams and scattered ambitions. Too much was striking inside to pour out. He preferred to keep quiet.

"Why sit here and ponder over the path which you can't even see in this impending dark? Dear, I have no family and live in my palatial hole in the trunk of a banyan. Come with me, my place is at your service!" the sparrow spoke with the grace of an old patron.

There was almost no choice for the parrot. In the hot pursuit of another mile, he had missed many a nice shelters on the way during the evening. Little did he realise that one has to stop. Stopping isn't a defeat. It's biding time for the victory. And when his body and the day's last rays both gave in, stopping was enforced. He had to stop and now take the option which presented itself. He thus followed the old sparrow to his wood-hole. The latter whistled all the way, chirped songs and tweeted notes of strange happiness.

"What makes him so happy?" the parrot following the sparrow again wondered.

They sneaked into the cosy, warm confines of the sparrow's wood-hole. It ran deep and appeared perfect for the best sleep. There was a nice bed of softest sinews. The sparrow's raw, bursting enthusiasm had turned to a palpable silence, contentment and restfulness which pervaded the wooden abode.

Outside, the weather turned as bad as possible in a single night. A horribly chilly, stormy night. No light for miles in sight. A furious rainstorm lashed the tree as if to uproot the earthy shackles and set it free to fall. But the tree was strong. After all, it was the choice of such a seasoned player, the master who knew the strength and fragilities of the woods. The banyan withstood the deathly throng.

“I live here all alone, but in constant company of my peace, rest and happiness,” the old host spoke with half-closed eyes, resting his slightly crooked back against the wood.

“What makes him look so happy, no longer in pursuit of anything?” the guest again wondered.

“Though the memories and reminiscences sometimes sneak in through my door to moan over my beautiful, active, youthful past. Darted when I fast. Wooed damsel sparrows with mischievous finesse. Raised families, driven by my instinct’s pull,” there was a loud thunderclap outside and the narrator stopped.

Lightening struck somewhere. It shook the earth. A sinister flash of lightening sneaked into the shelter. The parrot shook with fear. The sparrow laughed and assured him of safety. He had seen many such storms.

“The storms aren’t there to kill. They support life, even though it may not appear on the surface. I have seen it. Most of our fears are phantoms,” he chuckled.

The parrot listened. He again made himself comfortable.

“Well, coming back to my past that sometimes sneaks in to disturb like this lightening did to you now. Age then caught with me. Most of the beauties lie at a distance, teasing you to run after. My eyes but no longer see them. Feeble eyes you know! When I completely shut them off, my eyes, they even sense the death’s blood-thirsty hound. So I open them and just be myself. Me with my weak eyes. I just see the small, dimmed world sprawled in close proximity to me," the old host paused and pecked his saggy feathering with his blunted beak.

"So his happiness is a compromise with his disability and old age," the guest thought.

"You know what," the host broke the parrot's chain of thoughts regarding the compromise resulting in an enforced happiness. "To justify a well-lived life, when the force of youth is on your side to propel you towards your goals, the conclusion, the slowdown also has to be well-managed, well-paced, voluntary, not an accident. Ending is as important as beginning. With an accidental, aggrieved ending the essence of the beginning and build-up gets lost," the sparrow's slow-paced words again dispelled the parrot's just derived theory of enforced happiness born of old age and weakness.

The parrot's body was aching and he would have fallen dead asleep, if not for the question which was puzzling him to the extent of forgetting the pains of his fatigued self.

"So I live happily as the tail-end of a great life lived. The force of beginning, starting, acceleration! And the path of letting it go, losing the pace slowly, gracefully, receptively. The deceleration. Slowing down with effortless muse. To stop finally. It can give as much excitement as the force of starting. And then the final rest. During the slowing down phase, the time becomes slow, the world is a small puddle around your feet. You live like in a dream. A slow-paced one, minutes stretched like hours, days like weeks, weeks like months, and months like years. In slowing down gracefully, effortlessly, one can live a dozen lives lived in the beginning mode," the old sparrow coughed a bit, and then with a smile, telling his guest that all was well, took a pause.

Some swift sleepy grip would have drawn the parrot into a deep slumber, but then he heard the words again. He driven and lynched by the starter's force; the other one leading the rickety carriage to its stopping shelter. A journey completed by two characters. A life lived by two protagonists, separately, but summary being just one life. A beginning and an end. The latter part was so comforting that it appeared to seep into the turbulent phase of his own first leg of the beginner's journey.

"Enjoyed I the choices which the fate sieved for me. Just thankfully took my share. Now I pick up and play among the coarse, discarded chaff which remains unwanted above as the fine particles, much in demand, trickle below. But it's great fun, I tell you. In youth, we just think that life means rolling in the sieve's fine brew. However, life can be equally enjoyable among the discarded heap, little malformed grains, sand-grains, specks and twigs. Now I roll like a child in the rubble of the past, which was once waylaid by the youth's blast. It is now the precious wealth of my old age. Mellows down the rage in this haze. There aren't any takers for it now. So I enjoy it alone, without that competitive drone," said the old host, away from the fire, cosily lying at the margin, where the faintest traces of warmth touched his old fur before moving into the cold darkness.

The majestic slow down, as important and enjoyable as the headlong thrust of the beginning. The source, the beginning, and the slowdown. And the end. A cycle.

"And try even to get bold against this winter's hold," the oldie chuckled, patting his faded fur with the end of his wing.

"Has he achieved all he wanted in life to make him so happy?" the parrot wondered.

"During youth, I flew majestically high to beat the cold with my blood's warmth. Now wisdom swarms. I don't go out in the storms. I just go along the gentle breeze's pace. So I find ways to brightly light my days with these feeble rays. In this cosy wood-hole of mine, drunk I'm with my age's vintage wine. I know that I may not go out of this hole to ride softly on time's back at some new dawn. When death will pick up the pawn, leaving this old fur and feathering engraved in this wooden hole. But it doesn't make me sick. That time hasn't yet come. And I have the leisure of stretching moments till then to the capacity of my old bones. Also, that sleep doesn't appear different from the ones I enjoy now," a gripping calmness emanated from the each word he spoke.

Outside, the storm was tossing with a self-ravaging fury, consuming itself, jolting everything around, breaking, snapping wood. The banyan was but sturdier beyond any storm's destructive lust. It stood firm as if the calmness from the old sparrow's restful soul was seeping into the wood, giving it strength.

The parrot had been in the hot pursuit of the orchards beyond the forests, deserts and ocean, where the fruits of unheard sweetness lay more abundantly than the grass below, where the sweet cooing female parrots, of unparalleled colours and beauty, seduced youth to the pleasure's farthest end. His happiness lay too far. How could he be happy till he got all that he desired?

"The pitcher of desires no longer exists. I dropped it long time back, realising its weight. If you have it, the desire to get it full can be a real pain, I tell you. Even if you kill yourself to fill it, and suppose you succeed, still there is no escape from the torment. Then the fear of losing it strikes. So where is the rest? I have been having beakfuls of fun. No storage, nothing. It has all been a majestic flow and marvellous fluidity. Like the unforced march of a trickle of water down the slope, moving with the gradient, with acceptance and surrender," the old host closed his eyes, feeling the soothing touch of that flow with life's natural pace.

"But I'm happy. It won't be possible if I hadn't been happier earlier. To die happy, to happily slow down, one should have been happier earlier during the blasting stage," the old sparrow tweeted and whistled as if recalling the happier times.

"This old fart must have hit gold during his youth, and now he is just rolling in happiness as a pensioner, munching the leftovers," the parrot thought.

"The sinews holding life to my body have become weak and almost bloodless. These will not feel the pain of the final cleavage. It will be just like an autumn leaf being painlessly windblown into the oblivion. In this tepid existence of mine, between hot and cold, amid warmth and coolness, a misty torpor pervades my old bones. Beyond the extremes of pain and pleasure, I spend my time in some pleasant, vague proportions of reality. Happiness and sadness seem to have lost their specifications. Neither both exist, nor they are dead altogether," with a deep look of serenity, the old sparrow looked at the guest.

The parrot appeared restless even in this cosiest of a safe hideout. How could he be restful? A bigger storm of unhappiness was raging inside.

"How come you look so subdued and sad?" the sparrow asked. "Have the conditions been so bad to rob all the real charm and leave the colour on the feathers and soul so dull and poor?"

The pain inside broke all check-dams of restraint and the parrot spoke out.

“Though I’m young but the spirit seems to have sung the last song of life. Too much has been the pain and strife. My courage appears to have run dry now, although the colour on my feathering holds somehow,” the parrot spoke dispiritedly and sighed.

Outside, the storm touched a newer peak. The wind screeched. Rain lashed. Lightening struck. Some tree nearby fell with a huge snapping, cracking sound. The parrot shivered with fear. The sparrow calmed him down. Taming his emotions a bit, the parrot spoke again.

“When just a hatchling, father was gone. Grew I up hearing mother’s moan. The paternal sun thus never shone. However, the biggest consolation was the mother’s caressing, preening, feeding beak. Ate I fruits at love’s supreme-most peak. As the sole nestling, I was fattened on her love’s labour daylong. And then went to sleep hearing her lullaby and song. Aha! Sweetest dreams came with a throng! My whole existence was tethered to her maternal pole. Me, the brightest attractive-most star sole!” there were tears in the parrot’s eyes.

The young visitor was lost in his mother’s memories. The old host looked on sympathetically.

“Under her great grooming, colours on me came bright. Lavishly my green and red flashed as I fluttered and flapped for my first flight. Unbelievable was the pride and compassion as her souring soul’s maternal shades touched the brightest delight. In her eyes I saw a new light. How marvellous was the sight!” the parrot smiled and then stopped as if some painful recalling stabbed the smile.

“Alas, her incorruptible love of yore was arrowed by the fatality’s shot. Again the cupid’s arrow came hot. I became a past, ignorable and with rot. She was now in another spring of love. Incipient love for the future in her womb, I was the past buried in a tomb. I thus became an orphan although both my parents lived. After many cries and anguished, aimless flights bereaved, life's burden with my soft feathers I heaved. Young and handsome, I flew with the time's oblivion and balm. Intoxicating is the youth's charm," the parrot paused with some shine in his eyes.

There was a smile. The sparrow nodded knowingly.

"Inevitably I fell in love. Heartfully I cooed with my beautiful lady. Those love-drenched days when the heart was ever ready to sing an ecstatic ditty! Such abundance and happiness was in my kitty. So sweet, silent, mirthful and undaunting were those acceptances of the nuptial responsibilities. Those watchful, eager searches for the hollows in the tree trunks for our nest! Tirelessly we looked around for the best," the aroma of sweet memories raised the pal of gloom from the parrot's face.

The sparrow beamed as if dabbing his old beak in the sea of happiness.

"Guided by the love's brace, we found our place. In that comfortable, safe hole, nothing else but we had all the muse and role. Our identities melted into each other's. How proud was I when I became a father!" the memory suffused the parrot with a fresh gust of energy.

The parrot stood, flapped his wings and preened the fur with his luscious red beak. The sparrow too got onto its old claws and stretched his wings to unstiffen his old body.

The parrot's voice had a strained note now. "I will not become like my parents, I thought. I will not be ensnared like they were caught."

Some traces of that determination still seemed to raise his spirits for a moment.

"So I clung to my possessions with youthful pride. Alas, the inevitability arrived with chide. In full bloom of youth and colours, all of my brood flew away. My lady-bird came to be infatuated under someone's cooing sway. It was another fine day when she bade adieu and flew away," sorrows ran through the parrot's fatigued, sleepless body.

The old sparrow sighed, stretched his wings and patted the visitor on his shoulder.

"I embodied all forlornness. The loss was glaring in my face. Monstrously unremedied! So I decided to leave that place. And my sulking wings did brace to take up the longest possible flight from the place, where such pains and unfaithfulness abound. So flew I as if pursued by the fearsome-most hound. For many days I have been flying, my soul aching and wings crying. I won't stop till I reach the place where happiness is not checkmated by such tragedies," the parrot looked outside through the opening.

"Why should we enter into a relationship and love somebody so completely, if it is bound to go into the gutters? Aren't all such temporary dives into the life's stream futile and vain? Aren't we just mere cogs in the hands of those inevitable, unstoppable machines of fate which make us cheat on each other, abandon the once loved ones and more?" the parrot had burning questions coming out of his aggrieved self.

The old sparrow, full of wisdom, the undisputed king of his life's small kingdom, looked with solace and simplification of age. Perched safely where youth's dilemmas and puzzles no longer haunt with their pinch and rage, the sparrow said:

"It's like a flower ruing and ruminating over other blossoms because its beauty will not last forever and will go to the glooms. Dear, it's not we who are the ends, rather the beautiful phenomena like love, marriage, procreation which decide the trends. We are just means to these beautiful ends and destinations. So become an uncomplaining tool, tilling earth without any expectations. It isn't that love exists because we *do* love someone. Love is the primordial sea without any limits of space, time and individualities. It's we who sweeten a few moments of life with it till the full stops arrive with a stopping hit.

"Do we procreate to cling to procreation throughout life? No, we are made to procreate to become the unselfish means for the propagation, for handing over our batons, to perpetuate these beautiful phenomena of love and relationships. We do not leave behind an offspring, but a possible instrument which may come in handy for the sustenance and survival of those very precious moments which got us the taste of love, happiness and friendship at their best. If we recognise it, our spirit gets a solacing rest. If not, we get caught in an acrimonious net.

"We cry and put up a bet that I completely loved her and became the cause of young lives. It was I who caused that buzzing in those hives. But such limitations would have been meaningful had our survival been unlimited, or say the course of our life was uninhibited and unrestricted. But our journeys are to be ended. So just cherish those moments which you tended. If you cling to the stream of these phenomena as if they are your inheritance forever, they then become a drag around your neck, making you a prisoner behind the bars."

The sparrow stopped and shook his fur as if trying to find some last trace of such bondage.

"Liberate fella, liberate yourself! Just be a journeyman who understands that young flowers on a plant or adolescent leaves on a branch do not lessen themselves or the spring in not ruing over their wispy autumnal fall. They inculcate phenomena. They help perpetuate nature. They sustain the amazing natural gifts of love, beauty and bloom. They also served in a similar way, made some new ray, very feeble though, to defeat a bit of gloom under the shadows," the oldie's dull, watery eyes sparkled with hope and satisfaction, as lightening flashed and reflected in them.

The parrot was at long last feeling the vibes of happiness and rest which comes with the acceptance of simply doing the duty and completing the task with full heart.

"So the only way to remain happy is just to ***be*** happy, no matter what the circumstances are?" the parrot had his doubts.

The old host chuckled, tweeted and cleared his throat. The visitor was near the point, although still with his doubts, which was natural.

"Yaa just ***be*** happy, no water what!" the sparrow lowered his voice as if in cadence with a divine mantra. "It's basically we who repel happiness away from us. We don't allow it to come to us, embrace us, take hold of us. We set it as a goal too far down the lane in future. Some house, some grains, some accumulation of pleasure, some relationships, etc., etc. We set up goals as the preconditions for our happiness. And the goals keep on piling up, over the years, and set up a wall between us and happiness. And happiness keeps on getting more and more distant from us. I will set up a home and then be happy. Happiness delayed. And then I work over the years. There is no end. I set a goal to raise a family and then be happy. Again it sets up a wall between happiness and us. Like frustrated human log-movers, whom I see in the forest, we just push on. Happiness stays thus a distant goal. Never to be achieved. We make it conditional on endless goals, which are never met, because it's the destiny of a goal to merge into another bigger one. They never die, only we die. Huge immortals they are. The goals and destinations! In pushing for them, we die; separated from happiness which could have been the greatest gift of life, had we not pushed it away from us."

The long fabric of the stormy night was slowly melting over the banyan. Outside, the stormy chilliness was fleeting before a promising twilight. Chances were there for a day bright. Clouds parted for the sky's delight. The parrot's spirits appeared to cut through the shadows after turmoil and inner fight.

Holding onto the visitor's traces of hope, the old host tweeted, "The remedy lies in taking away happiness from the far end of our endless goals and keep it safe in our house, like I do store some grains for the harsh winters, near me, in the safest part of my house. It has to be cut away from the trail of endless goals and ambitions and kept with the self, in the present. It has to be set free from any conditions of meeting some goal. It's a state as good as being healthy. Just being and living for a day. Separate ***being*** from ***becoming***. You can be happy if you set your happiness free from the chains of your lifelong dreams."

The parrot smiled. It was the dawn of truth.

The wise oldie continued, "You should be pushing towards yours goals as a ***happy*** person, rather than somebody who wants to ***be happy*** in future after completing the goals. The goals never come to a halt, only we do, at the moment of our death. So we die unhappily, separated from the natural state of happiness which could have pumped our life with unthinkable contentment and satisfaction, only if we had set it free from the chains of goal-setting and placed it unchained from those unreachable spots in the future."

The parrot stood erect like a disciple in front of his master.

The sparrow raised his voice as if carrying his old furred body over to the peak of realisation. "Let happiness be a precondition for our doings, not a poor outcome of our efforts. Do everything as a happy person; instead of doing the deeds to become a happy person. Happiness is a state of ***being so***, not the specific result of some hot pursuit. There is only one way it can be availed. Either we embrace it in the condition we are in, or it just eludes us. Keep it with you while you fly. It will boost your determination to go far and high."

The sparrow was beaming with such rest and repose, as can be provided by being happy unconditionally.

The peaceful oldie looked out with hope. "The day today will be warm and sunny. The dawn promises sweetest honey. Youngman, I'm in hurry to go out of my hole, and play my chirpy role on the great stage set around. My feeble soufflés and dim light in the eyes are still enough for the spirits abound. I still see my own sun in the down-hilly twilight."

The parrot looked on happily, deeply drinking the sips of solace and comfort pervading the wood-hole.

"You go high because the forenoons are there for you with their multiple hues. Go, so that you don't rue over the day aimlessly lost. Do justice to the old spirit of your host. Take some lessons from my soft feebleness. It will boost your courage. Take clues from the manner in which I make a day out of my night! And top of all, decide to ***be happy*** before you take flight!"

The old sparrow came to the parrot and patted him with his faded wing. The parrot lowered his head in gratitude for a great lesson taught. Thanking the host, the visitor flew away into those swathes of promise, where new life, new love, new aspirations and new relationships held sway. But all that was secondary, in future and to be worked upon. More importantly, he was happy in the present. He had decided to keep happiness as a routine, like eating fruits and flying.

***

11. A Gram in the Heart and a Ton in the Mind

Two monks, one young and the other old, were crossing a stream. A beautiful woman was also standing on the bank. There were lines of worry on her striking face, her mind calculating the risk. The stream appeared daunting to her elegant, feminine self. In the spring air, the bird songs appeared to carry sensual notes.

The old monk looked at her. He understood that she needed help to cross the stream. His moral training of being kind to others fetched the idea of helping her to his mind. But the mere thought of touching a woman shook him up. It was a bigger no on the scale of immorality. He got goose-bumps. His rules of celibacy forbade him from touching a woman. So chanting mantras to clear his mind of the thoughts about the woman, he moved onto cross the stream.

Reaching the other end, he was horrified to see the spectacle behind him. The young monk was crossing the stream. The woman was sitting on his shoulders. It was scandalous to the elder monk. He was gripped by scores of emotions. He felt jealous of the younger monk, for taking the initiative basically; of becoming someone he always wanting to but denied himself from being. He then forced his jealousy into anger over the violation of the code of monastic conduct. He was seething with helpless rage. The thought of touching a beautiful woman was gnawing at his heart. He was again denying some basic instinct as he had throughout his life.

Reaching the opposite bank, the younger monk helped the woman down. She thanked and smiled. He bowed and followed his religiosity to the extent of keeping a straight face and moved away with respect, peace and dignity. The monks started towards their hermitage.

They had been walking for hours. It was evening when they neared their place of penance. The check-dam of the old man's thoughts broke. Finally he burst out.

"You touched a woman. You have broken the code of conduct. I will complain against you once we reach," he was still wondering whether he was jealous of the young monk or was it really anger over the violation of the rules book.

The young monk smiled. He put a comforting hand on the old man's shoulder.

"I left her on the river bank itself after helping her. You are still carrying her in your mind," he said politely.

The older monk was ashamed. He tried to put her out of his mind as they walked. The younger monk meanwhile walked with a rested mind, appreciating the marvels of nature in the forest.

The message is clear. The things which ought to be simply done, should just be done. Otherwise, their shadows linger in the mind. They grow heavier with the passage of time. This invisible weight is heavier than the stones we see around. Simple, harmless acts of appreciation, of enjoyment, of helping someone cross a stream are better done and closed with a full stop. It's better for a healthy mind. Otherwise, they linger like conspiring shadows over our conscience.

A missed chance of being good will definitely cast a shadow on our mind. An effort to help the self in being good, on the other hand, will hardly leave any unbecoming imprint on our conscience for pinching reflections later.

Only goodness has a legacy and a future. Hypocrisy and meanness are just bad examples and leave repentance most of the time. To do good is instinctive for a human being, it's however another matter that we stifle the urge most of the time. To be bad, on the other hand, is not intrinsic to our nature. It is wrongly reflective, a miscalculation, a tragic bypass of the instinct of goodness.

Nurture the seeds of the instincts of goodness like the younger monk did. It gives peace of mind, clear conscience and makes the journey enjoyable. Avoid it and you carry the burden in your mind like the older monk.

***

12. A Soul's Pyre

Hate, fury and violence burn to eat their own self. Only love, peace and harmony survive and sustain. How long you have seen a storm screeching? The stronger it is, the faster it eats its own self.

There was a gang of robbers in a forest. Its leader was a bloodthirsty soul. He took pleasure in robbing people of their wealth and possessions. It gave him strange, paranormal pleasure. He relished that look of fear in the victims' eyes for losing the valuables. But he needed more pleasure from the victims' plight. More than the dread of losing valuables, he was addicted to the terror in their eyes as his people wounded and tortured them before the final kill. This horror of injury, blood and death in the victims' eyes gave him more pleasure than the costliest diamonds. His delight reached its peak when he saw the ultimate fright in their eyes--the fear of death--as he went for the kill.

One day his band came across an old ascetic. The brigands hadn't robbed and killed anyone for the past one week. They were thus thirsty for money and blood. A mendicant though won't give them any valuable, but the terror in his eyes while facing death was no less for the gang leader's evil soul.

They tied the ascetic and a huge bandit raised his sword to behead him. Death was imminent. The outlaws expected an outpour of panic from the bearded old man. Their ears were ready to receive the very same plight of crying words, pleading to be spared.

The head-bandit was looking at the old man's face. His bloodthirsty soul was waiting water-mouthed at the spectacle of fear and cries in the face of death. But the old man was as serene as before, totally unaffected. To break his calmness, the leader even brought death an inch closer by ordering to count till ten. The beheader was to strike at the count of ten. The head bandit thought now it was impossible to escape fear as death approached in just ten steps. He had made it visible, just ten steps away.

One of the bandits started the count. With each number, a brighter smile surfaced on the old man's lips. Before the final count, the bandit leader stopped his striker. The old man kept on smiling.

"You are smiling! You have no fear of death!" the head-robber asked.

"I have experienced death and its pain. It's not as scary as we make it. To stay alive can be more painful," the ascetic replied.

"But the experience of death makes it even more fearsome," the bandit frowned.

His ego had been puffed up over the years; swelling on peoples' fear for their possessions, injuries and finally the life itself. It had been his driving force: a bloody calculation of his progress in life; a measurement of his devilish desire; the scale of his monstrosity, which he took as excellence and superiority over fellow human beings.

Now the foundations of his treasure were breaking down. There was a challenge to his bloody conviction.

"I was a warrior one time. I was renowned for the power of my sword. I had enemies and unable to defeat me and inflict wounds on my body, they killed my family. I cried in pain over their death. Then I slaughtered them to the farthest known links of even their distant most relatives," smile had gone from his sagely face.

The bandits listened in rapt attention.

"I bathed in their blood, laughed to the capacity of my lungs over their painful cries. I was trying to bury my pain under the pile of their bodies. Though I increased the number of my revenge killings, the pain inside won't go. I was thinking that I am removing my pain, I was but making it mountainous. Then I came across the wife of someone who had himself beheaded my wife and children. Killing her would have given me the maximum pleasure. I raised my sword to kill her. She was pregnant. Just a week or so from delivery," he closed his eyes.

The bandits sat down, laying their weapons by their side. It was an audience now.

"She was imploring me to kill her after she delivered the baby. She said she would consider it the kindest act done to her if I spared her life till the baby was born. She was in a way asking me to spare the baby. I told her that it won't serve any purpose because in any case I will kill the newborn also after killing her. But not in her womb or before her eyes, she asked this much favour. She was holding my legs. I was trying to shake her off but something stopped me. She was a mother. I remembered my own mother, the way she must have been killed. That left me shaking. I was ready to kill an enemy's wife for revenge. But my hands were trembling to kill a mother," tears were rolling down his bearded cheeks.

The bandits were listening as if to a sermonising seer.

"I decided to postpone my revenge for a week, thinking it will add to the pleasure in killing both the mother and the newborn. She gave birth to a girl after a week. The momentum of killings was still on my head. It still possessed me. I killed the mother. When I stabbed her I was shaken by the look in her eyes. She still carried the look of acknowledging my kindness in postponing my revenge. She had it all through the week. I had thought she was trying to save herself with that look, trying to arouse pity in me to spare her and the child's life. But I was wrong. She had fulfilled her promise that if I spared her life for a week, she will consider it the kindest act done to her by anybody. That look on her face while dying showed it clearly. It robbed me of my hate. It killed the devil in me. And it condemned me to die each moment till I really die," the old man looked into the sky.

There was pin-drop silence. One of the bandits even felt like offering some water to the old man. But he checked himself.

"The baby girl was my punishment for the revenge killings. I tried to kill her but my hands gave in. The game of death had possessed me. It had gripped me with such force that I was not living. I was already dead. I was roaming around as a dark agent of death. I was not living, I was already dead. I died long before my body will die. I went mad with repulsion. I hated my bloodied hands. Leaving the girl under the care of a friend and paying him for her upkeep till her marriage, I ran away. I was running after my death. But even death seemed to have discarded me. It laughed sinisterly from a distance. I tried to kill myself. But I was so weak that even self-injury won't come. So I roamed around, neither accepted by death, nor by life, just a ghost lingering between life and death. Years of roaming around have left me detached both from life and death. As I take a step forward, I don't know if it is meant for life or death. This melting of difference between life and death has at least removed the scars of blood from my soul. I can sleep for a few hours peacefully. And I can smile. Death thus has lost any meaning to me. So has life. Nobody can restore life in me. That's impossible with so much blood on my soul. But if you give me death, I will consider it as a favour," the old man seemed to implore the bandits to come and strike.

What was there for the bandit-head to feast upon? This old man didn't possess any valuable. More importantly, he did not even have the fear of death. What will he take away from this killing? The food, this game of death, appeared stale, meaningless. He asked his group to throw their weapons. He had tears in eyes. He knew it was easier to continue the life like before and some day die at the hands of some more ferocious robbers or soldiers. That would be the fine end to it. And exciting as well. But to live differently to die another way was almost impossible. In fact that would be the real punishment.

This old man had meted out the punishment to himself by dying every moment, dying while life thrived abundantly in the forest around him, leaving him alone, not touching him in any way. So he decided to change. Not for a better life. Not for lesser punishment either. But for a prolonged death, recalling all his sins. Drawing sips of death instead of life for years before death claimed a body whose soul had escaped long time back.

***

13. The Old Moon and the Imperilled Landscape

It was very cold and the time was frozen around half an hour before the morning twilight on January 13, the day celebrated as *Lohri*; a day before *Makar Sakranti* on the full moon next day. The pallid rays of a pale moon had quickly grown feeble during the last hour before the morning twilight. The night had been chilly, clear-skied, frosty and fogless: an exceptional January night, not in being chilly because cold and January are synonymous, but in being clear-skied certainly. The moon, just a day from its rounded fullness, had been exceptionally bright.

Nightlong, almost near the peak of its circular beauty, it had fulfilled its luminous duty. Its milky beams over-rode the pointed shafts of light from the distant stars. After all it was his world; the stars had their own at mammoth astronomical distances. The moon was thus the brightest, bulbous star, eager to brush out every strain and tainting, shadowy tar. Its beams spread like snows over the sleeping horizons across the sleepy distances and languorous miles.

The beautiful countryside was lying in sleepy abundance under the frosty, milky blanket with slumberous pride. Everything was open to the celestial torch with nothing to hide. Cold-basking fields were huddled under their croppy sheets. Above was grandmotherly gloating the marvellous moonshine. The wheatlings stood bow-headed in reverence with dewy crowns fine. The marigold flowers were frozen in kissed silence by the milky showers. The flowers appeared happy to surrender their colours to the lover's mysterious smiles and disrobing powers. White pea flowers boasted their augmented whiteness. Aha, such dolefully beneficent had been the moony brightness. Even the trees did not appear merely dark spectres lurking shadowily over the horizon. They appeared boats of foliage floating in a misty sea.

In the background of such a brightly lit stage even the sky seemed eager to come onto the earth. Across the milky transparency, its bluish-dusky veil lurked and through it only the brightest stars smiled and showed that there was a world beyond as well. Scattered in the docile swathes of this moon-baked countryside, the villages seemed as mammoth ships silently floating in the white wavy sea of milky light.

At this moment, the moon was well past its prime, as if in shining too bright, to use the full charms of a fog-free night, it had committed a harmless crime. Its setting quarters lay in the north-west, from where it was eager to slip down for some rest. Its strength and vigour had drastically plummeted down, paleness eating into the guts of its plump milky brightness. An old, setting moon, away from the youth's boon.

Dislodged of its shiny crown, it ogled with a meek, even irritated, anguished, helpless frown. Its sheen was rapidly fading out. Its yellowish pale rays almost eager for a wailing shout. Glumly it was fading over that reddish-brown sandy undulation carrying fields, furrows and crops on its gently unfolding dome. The shiny fruits born of sweat-drenched hours by the farmers in its sandy loam. Accusingly the moon threw pale, protesting shadows towards the south-east. There urbanism, consumerism and crass commercialism blatantly, proudly held their seat commanding metropolitan, capitalist feast.

The area had been earmarked for some development project. It now being defined by a tiny space bound in a map issued under the state government's gazette notification. A mischief by the developmental hand, ever eager to bulldoze over the nature and turn it into uncomplaining, lifeless sand where lustrous stones will be built over the nature's burial. Heartless, wanton and depraved! But the nature has no oratory to baulk the words. It but repays in kind.

This pale, mournful moon was preparing to set soon into the misty gloom of the twilight. A new bright sun of consumerism and commerce will be ascending to its dawning height. And the soft natural delicacies will scamper with fright.

Those reed stalks which swayed to the cold shove of a gentle breeze without any greed appeared to say good-bye to the moon. The latter plummeted down further with a bloated face and a sigh. Its pallid face grimacing with a painful nostalgia. Its fading, setting rays tainted with a peculiar dullness, the death, the demise, the oblivion. Its oblong teary face looking down at the landscape: sleepy fields, beneficent swathes of wastes and fallow lands.

Mighty lessons were taught here by the nature to itself and all. The farmer going to the fields with his gear. Those long, painful and oftentimes fruitless days, and at the end the setting sun's eager rays peering at the sweaty trove on the farmer's back carrying the shirt's hoe. Where the long, brooding nights arrived like the deeds accomplished. Where the failures galore, but the hard work was never a bore. The failures defined the success, as the losses stood just as a testimony to the karmic gains. Where the hopes, aspirations and desires varied with the changing hues of the weather. The farmers pawning everything for the feathers in destiny's crown. Gold forming immaterially—or minimally at the rate of a dust speck for tons of sweat—in the toiled soil reddish brown.

All this will be gone. The moon was also dying with a moan. This charming mystery of the landscape: why the hardest labour fetches minimal returns; why a bit less harder toil results in a soul-satisfying speckful of returns that seems the wealthiest load. All these beautiful, aesthetic, curvy, circuiting strings, the mysteries of the landscape, of destiny, of the see-saw battle between happiness and suffering, between pleasure and pain, between penury and sustainable as well as gluttonous gain, between life and death, between a smile and a tear, all will be lost.

Everything will be gone for a direct, straight, materially penetrating needle of surety: the commercial, unflinching and fixed use of the landscape in a concrete form, where profits will boomerang in proportion to the short-cuts; where compromised humanity, ideology and conscience will not face any ifs and buts; where there won't be any sweet scent of labour, which will be replaced by mechanical, greasy, muddy panting of merciless competition and mad grab; where concrete blocks and apartments will replace these wondrous solitudes and petalous platitudes basking in unrestrained, free, natural air; where sheaves, stalks, straw and reeds will not sway to the breeze, but blank, rigid, ironed towers will stand mutely, inflexibly to the nature's cooing calls from increasing distances.

Now the sorrowfully yellowing death rattle of the setting time was arriving with a finishing chime. There on the opposite horizon, the day opened a window to sneak a peek at the imperilled room of the night. Wispily, there was the twilight with its mixed day-night delight. In its mysterious lap, the old moon met a slightly premature death, slumped as it feebly, freely into the silvery sea of mist hung over the tree-line. Slithered it into the sea of death and plunged into invisibility.

The twilight mischievously winked with its unfaithful, teasing look, asking favours both from the night and the day. The old moon was gone with its last ray. And the soon-to-be-doomed panorama, unmindful of the fatality in wait, came out of its dewy slumber. A crane's clarion call cree...ked over its yawning bosom. The sun prepared to cast its first ray. The fields got up for another hard farming day.

***

14. Ice Cubes on Desert Sands

Summers. North India has started to burn. Heat has broken the record of many past decades. Temperatures above 40 in the last week of March! Something seems to have gone wrong with nature. Heat emerges with bumper buoyancy. Hot dynamics grip everything with such force that all will yell prayers for the Monsoons.

In the desert state of Rajasthan things must be even worse. The sand as the birth soil isn't too attractive. It may have its nostalgia, but on a day-to-day basis it appears a curse. Ask the ones who are born there. So many people come out of Rajasthan to avoid the burning cauldron during the summers.

Two lanky boys are moving across the streets of this Haryanvi village. Haryana is a semi-arid state. But for somebody belonging to the desert state, semi means almost full: full with life; full with bread; full with water; full with green trees.

They are tall and thin. They have migrated from the desert state. Necessity has pulled them out of the sand like water flows from higher level to the lower one. They have to beg. But begging has its own share of pitfalls including reprimands and harsh words.

"Why don't you study? Why don't you work?"

So they have put the saffron sail-cloth on their poor boat to navigate safely, holding onto the winds of faith. Their clothes are soiled. But the saffron sashes around their necks indeed cover a lot of holes in their personas. They expect to be taken as wandering ascetics. They have even mastered the artful words of bringing blessings to the house they stand in front of.

The woman chides them the moment they knock against the rusty iron gate. They but decide not to be deterred by the initial rebuke. Stealthily they steal glances at the two small cars parked in the front yard. These are old cars. But to them a car is a car. Hummer or Maruti 800 doesn't make any difference.

So they continue with their blessing words of good fate, long life, endless prosperity, and more. It's morning and yesterday it hailed and rained a bit to take temperatures a bit down. To them it seems like a land of perpetual rain and prosperity, although it rains just marginally more than their homeland. They have thorny bushes there; here there are some semi-arid varieties like *neem* and acacia. And that changes the world for the best. It's a shift from the worst to the best.

They feel that the woman cannot cross certain limits to turn outright abusive and threatening. This is the chink. They have to prod their way in.

"You have hard words but a heart of gold. You can never think ill of others even if you sound a bit impolite," the elder one nails it.

"What do you want? No money I tell you! I can only give you some wheat flour," her voice mellows down somewhat.

They let their foot further in. It's an opening.

"There is no better deed than feeding the hungry. It's a direct holy feat. God sees it instantly," they take their chance.

She seems to be awaiting God's attention on some front, so agrees. They barge in. It's a spacious house with peeling plaster and mundane furnishing like you see anywhere in a village in Haryana. To them, it's an abode of prosperity. They sit down on the unplastered brick-laid floor in the courtyard.

It's too early for the family to have their lunch, brunch or whatever. So she makes chapattis for them. The vegetable curry is already done. They can see the chapattis are coming straight from the *tava*, not the stale leftovers from the previous night which people usually give them and throw to the stray dogs also. Every time she comes to put another chapatti, they are ready with more words of blessings from the God.

The younger one asks for ice. They must be having refrigerator, he has guessed it right. It is available in every household here. Ice is a big luxury to him. He comes from burning sands. Pitchers burn like hot oven there. They drape sack-clothes around pitchers and pour drops of precious water to prevent it from boiling. He already has many ice cubes in his water utensil. He opens the lid and checks out to see how far these have melted. He is concerned. The ice is melting. He wants replenishment.

"Please give me ice," he is literally pleading.

She laughs at him. "It's not that hot this morning. There is cool breeze," she says.

But he looks at her with eyes which are crying for ice. She has to get it.

As she pours ice cubes from the tray into his cheap, dented aluminium utensil, she can see the twinkle in his eyes.

Ice that is just ice to her, is something more to him. He has seen fire in life, the fire which seeps into everyday life in the desert. Ice has a bigger meaning to him than anyone else around here.

She notices it now. His clothes are also wet. Not dripping exactly, but he must have been completely drenched thirty, forty minutes back.

"What happened? Did you fall in water?" she asks.

The elder one is laughing. "Water turns him crazy. Hardly any water back home. We take bath just once a week there. When he saw the pond outside the village, he straightaway jumped into it like a mad frog," he is laughing.

Water that is just water to her, is luxury to this boy. She tries to fathom the reason for his ecstasy over ice cubicles and pond waters where buffalos waddle, but fails to understand. Little does she realise that people run out to count drops of rain on the sand at his native place. So water is a treat to him.

Like most of us fail to understand that the things which seem dustbin cheap to us might be the symbols of opulence to so many others. That a broken doll on the garbage heap, a shiny wrapper, and a single-wheeled broken toy are still items of magnificence to many unfortunates. If we do, then we won't begrudge most of the problems in our life.

***

15. Gone with Colours and a Smile

On Holi the colours go riotous. It comes with spring, rejuvenation, resurrection and blossoming. The rigidities melt and stiffened souls flow to embrace a bit of fun, a bit of sunshine. Everybody takes a sip from the weather's cool cocktail. And the effects go cutting across ages. Childhood dawns.

Colours fly, water is raining around, although there is no rain. Even mud finds a way, especially when playfulness mixes with the speedy horses of angry mischief. The drunkards dance as women beat them. The drinkers have a heyday. Bhang flows unchecked. There are cries: playful, challenging, querulous, sneering, sniping, chiding, mocking, and above all flirting. As the floodgates of festivity get opened, inhibitions and taboos take a backseat and people enter the zone of a rare freedom, a chance let-looseness: flirting, teasing bonhomie.

We celebrate the festivals for life, love, hope, light and keeping the dreams alive. And when there is a death in the near neighbourhood, within a fortnight or so of the festival of colours, the spirit gets damp. The colours get a black cast in the mould, some extra mixing, a discoloration.

The old lady was on her deathbed for the last three months. An averagely good woman, but more importantly very unfortunate, was the summary of her life when people discussed her plight and even prayed to God for a hasty, smooth and painless end. For that would be a relief to the good old lady, a painless death.

Such suffering puts up a speed-bump even on the life-road of those around. All of us fear the same fate; so like a horrible nightmare, wish a prompt end to the tale of agony that reminds us of the inevitable chapter in everyone's life. But then Holi was approaching. If she had died within weeks before Holi, the colours would have been lost. But as it happens, such last sufferings get prolonged—extended to break the last sinews of attachment still clinging to the body, to free the soul. Surviving on water just by tea spoons, the old woman kept hanging there between life and death.

******

She was deaf due to old age and missed most of the words shouted almost into her ears. But then sometimes unwanted comments and jibes sneaked into her ears like a distant golf-shot incidentally falling straight into the hole. And then it would create a ruckus.

It was on Holi that her life went colourless. Not once but twice, one exceeding the other in the measurement of pain and loss. A few decades back, it appears like ages now, she then a young wife disposing household chorus like a nimble-footed sprinter, one-year-old boy suckling her full breasts, singing lullaby and mollycoddling, was preparing to participate in the festival of colours.

In the black and white of a tough peasant life, Holi stood out as a colourful intervention, when all their life's rough and gruff melted in the coloured waters, *gulaal*, street mud, beatings, drunken sprees, and quarrels that arose like water bubbles and went down unnoticed.

Her husband was known among the rural hamlets as the master crafter of wheat-chaff domes. Massive, almost three storey high domes of wheat-chaff bore a testimony to his craft. These were storage structures, storing hundreds of quintals of the dry fodder meant for the off season usage. The circular base, made of the hard stalks of dried *arhar*, was dug into the ground. Over that *bajra* stalks and paddy hay was built into circular layers in conjunction with the wheat chaff filling inside inch by inch, hard pressed by stomping feet. The ropes made of reed and hemp took it upwards to end into a well proportioned and perfectly symmetrical dome, ready to save the storage mound against the worst of weathers. Of course it required special expertise, matching that of a weaverbird's effort in notching out the marvel of a nest in terms of safety and symmetry.

Two days before the festival of colours, a rainstorm had lashed the farming hamlet. Lightning struck and blew away the crown of the chaff mound. If further rain fell, water would seep from the top to spoil the entire dry fodder. So on this day of Holi, before surrendering to the fun and funstery of it, her husband, after being repeatedly requested by the neighbour to repair the open-skied chaff store, got onto the top and started with his expert hands. It was a sight to watch him working so diligently almost three storey high in the sky. All was going well. But then accident takes the fraction of a second's goof-up, just like normal routine needs miles of straight moments. He slipped, fell headlong , broke his neck and died.

The death and tragedy overwrote the festival with its swiping black colour. The festivity was gone. Colours were banished from her life and she got a permanent white as her identity. And life moved on.

In the black and whites of a widow's life, she still had some colours hidden deep in her dreams for her son whom she brought up single-handedly, sweating out on the plot of arable land. Irrigated with the moisture of her sweat and blood, manured by the maternity of her motherly self, the flower blossomed. He turned out to be a handsome young man and was readily taken by the army.

Post training, his first posting was in Kashmir, the state that was on boil in 1989. Post a horrid winter, while the ice was thawing, and spring was beckoning all humans to calm down and listen to its open-armed charms, the turmoil touched a new peak as casualties touched a new high on both sides in the spring of 1990. There was another young soldier from the same village in the company. Their patrol was ambushed by the militants. Amidst fierce gun battle, the widow's son fell to bullets. It was found that he had died while attempting to save the life of his fellow villager.

Blood spread with a sprawling sanguineness on the melting snow. It was a Holi of agony and pain. Elsewhere in the plains, including their village, people were busy in obviating the miseries of a hard life in the coloured frenzy. Barely recognisable, panting with riotous play, surrendered to the spirit of the festival to deface their mundane existence, they stood stunned, as the news reached them in the evening. Again the black shades had been splashed suddenly by destiny.

This time Holi had robbed her of the colours of her dreams. Her plaintive wails killed the last trace of festivity hiding in some part of the village. Holi had restamped its authority to drive away all colours from her life.

There was another common thread which separated the tragedies by two decades. The soldier, whose life the widow's son had saved, was the grandson of the chaff mound owner, repairing which the dead soldier's father had fallen down. This fact rose over the merciless paradox of Holi repeatedly robbing someone's colours, first from the real life and then from the dreams also.

She cursed Holi as much as she cursed the family which unfortunately, accidently, came to be linked to the tale of her irreparable loss. After that they couldn't so much as raise their eyes if they happened to face her. It was a meek acceptance of their incidental link to the tragedies in her life. Not that the rest of her year was better, but come Holi and her soul would burn in the boiling cauldron of limitless agony.

******

Since the last week before Holi, anybody could have said she may die any moment. However, the feeble flicker kept on burning, as if it didn't want to become the reason for postponing the colourful fair by one year. And then there was the Holi dawn. She was taking last laboured breaths. The festival started with its customary worship at the shrine of the village God. Then *gulal*-smeared children ran amuck through the streets, men-folk got to drinking in order to benumb the senses against beatings, ladies prepared hunters of twisted cords of headgears, which otherwise keep them chained into docility and obedience in the patriarchal society. But today the roles were reversed. For 364 days of submissions and even thrashings, they donned the role of beaters on this special day.

It was then the same thing: children shouting and clapping, men mimicking bravery, while the women pounded then like they were letting out all the pent-up fury born of their subservient position in the male-dominated society.

The festivity was on its downslope—with ladies all drenched and smeared in every possibly way, and the men with dead tired bodies still holding ground to keep their sense of victory even today.

Around four in the afternoon the news spread. It might be the end. People gathered around her cot. She was dragging her breath with a guttural sound. Her mouth was open and dull grey eyes, sunk deep in her skull, had a look of overawe and fear like you are face-to-face with the fearsome unknown. She already looked like a corpse.

A little boy from *that* family, which destiny had put up as a sorrowful factor in her tragic life, all smeared in colours, was also standing near the cot. From nowhere her eyes rested on him. With one last effort in her life, she raised her hand in his direction. They pushed him forward. The scared little boy bent over her. God knows from where did she manage even that much of life. She moved her finger to take off a bit of *gulal* from his cheeks and put in on her forehead. Her eyes closed, as if she was wishing herself happy Holi, a smile surfaced on her shrunk lips. The smile remained, and the eyes closed forever.

She was gone with a bit of colour and a faint smile. She had crossed a milestone to start again.

A night with a corpse is too long and unbearable in a Hindu house. Funeral was to be arranged before the sundown. If they missed the deadline then the ordeal of nightlong sitting around the dead body, placed on the ground, awaited them. Of course anybody alive, and wanting some rest after heavy drinking and Holi lynching, would prefer rest in bed instead of guarding a corpse.

With sobered senses, beaten bodies and unrecognisably smeared in colours, the erstwhile revellers, like sleepwalkers, got busy with the funeral procession, most of them drunk dead, trying their best to force sobriety and sense, to hold ground, to walk straight, and talk without a slip of tongue. The dead have their right to respect. They knew this. The setting sun seemed to make up for mourning through its pale rays. It was a queer funeral procession. Their glide down from the high plane of festivity had been suddenly checked, and the happening like a strict and unsparing teachress put them in a line to behave themselves.

In intoxication, a man isn't completely in control of the reins over his emotions, so tears which would never have seen the tired sunrays flew freely in many eyes, the eyes that hardly had seen the old woman on the deathbed of late. Many were freely philosophical about the questions of life and death. The procession walked silently. The drunk mass minding its steps pretty well. The biggest onus was on those shouldering the *arthi*. They had to walk without the slightest falter in steps. It was such a task at hand. Some steps still staggered.

When the pyre burnt much to their collective relief, many a battered limb felt the soothing warmth. Their conscience then repulsed all such feelings of ease and comfort at the pyre-side.

***

16. Love More, Hate Less

I come out of the tunnel and see the light. I smile, have a restful inhale of the fresh air, open my arms and embrace this world, my world. It welcomes me back with a brotherly bear hug. I smile again and close my eyes to look inward and take a sip of peace from the sea of tranquillity inside. Again I open my eyes. Miracle! The world has changed. It's far better now. I have changed my eyes to look at it differently.

Earlier, it was dark and daunting. It was as much frightening and intimidating as it was painful. The tunnel was as much dug by the external circumstances as the negative tools of my own mind. I had entered a cave, a little recess in the mountainside of life, a routine trouble in the scheme of things. Then I became my own enemy and started digging earth in the direction I shouldn't have.

I was digging a tunnel, an aimless futile struggle; my depressed, bruised mind digging earth faster and faster. It was taking me deeper into the womb of darkness. Directions became meaningless. No light, no sun, only dense layers of darkness, piled layers upon layers.

It was like digging my own grave. A bruised brain and injured mind are the potent tools of a self-gravedigger.

Sweating, soiled clothes, aching limbs, now I come to the other side of the mountain of life. Out of the self-dug cave that almost became a grave. Life has changed its meaning. The poles have reversed. I take credit for the small act of having kept on the digging job. It's a new beginning. I know myself better. I even wonder did I even know myself earlier. I stand as a stranger to my old self.

It's a new sun. The air is so fresh. The earlier life seems futile, all this self-gravedigging job.

However, as I close my eyes, a feeble smile on my lips, and inhale the essence of a new, redefined life, the journey seems worth it. As some wise man said, the moment you reach the treasure trove of your destiny, everything which happened in the past becomes relevant. Nothing goes waste. Even the garbage of the past has played a big part in the shiny present and still shinier prospects of the future.

Life is almost on a pause now; so slow in motion that I see the marvels of nature around. They are for me as much as they are for anybody around: the spring sun kissing the winter-beaten leaves; the songs of birds; gentle breeze ruffling bits of peace lying around; and the swirls of a footloose bird in the sea of cool air.

I inhale the fathomless fragrance of peace, harmony and integrity from the farthest part of the cosmos. Cosmic harmony. Endless orderliness in orbits. Ever-going periodicity. Supportive synchronisation. The fury of explosions and astronomical speeds tamed to harmless, slow acts of space-time continuum. Me and my environment feel like an iota of this cosmic concord.

I allow myself a gentle smile. Ripples of peace cascade through my soul. I close my eyes again and look inwards, deeper than the superficial world of my body and my worldly circumstances. I can travel far deeper than I ever thought. There are undisturbed paths leading to my true self. It's a replica of the cosmic orderliness. I am on the path to meet my true self, the self that is destined to be happy and at peace with itself.

It awaits there, the self, with unlimited dose of happiness, comfort, compassion and peace. We only deny ourselves the dose of this cosmic healing pill by looking out onto this world, the superficial world of frustration, jealousy, hate, futile rat race, mundane cravings, illusions, assumptions, fears, apprehensions and cravings. It doesn't allow us to smile, to close our eyes and start the journey inward. No wonder we have hardly travelled in the real sense even if we are lucky to spend hundred years of chronological age in a lifetime.

The journey to the real inner self, on the other hand, is not bound by the puny limits of time and funny horizons of space. It's open and there are unlimited dimensions. In minutes, one covers cosmic distances. And when you smile and look at this world outside, you see a replica, a reflection of the inherent beauty. You are better now and happier. You look at this world with a healthier mind and sturdier brain. More importantly, you have a better heart. You are capable of loving more and hating less, the hallmark and definition of a human being.

***

17. Pegs and Ropes of the Mind

The night was falling. A camel caravan was passing through a desert. The caravan-head decided to spend the night at a *serai*. There were hundred camels and the store wagon had pegs and ropes for each one of them to keep them safely tied though the night. Ninety-nine camels had been safely tethered in front of the inn. But they had lost one pair of rope and peg.

The caravan-head was much worried. If the remaining camel was left untied, it will surely run away and claim its freedom. He asked the inn-keeper for a rope and a peg. The old man had none. But he had a solution in his experienced mind. He asked the traveller to playact the whole process of setting the peg and tying the rope in the dark to the camel. The middle aged weather-beaten, tough traveller laughed at the joke. Still he decided to take it as a comedy even at the cost of losing a camel.

They made a false show of the process, made sounds of hammering a peg into the ground, then one of them fiddled around the camel's neck, making it feel that it is being tied with a rope. They went to sleep and the night passed the baton to a pleasant dawn.

Much to everyone's relief, and surprise, the camel was found sitting comfortably next morning. It was almost a miracle. The camel had allowed himself to be tied to a non-existing peg with the invisible rope.

The caravan prepared to leave. They untied the ninety-nine camels. These camels got up to move onto the journey. Thinking that the hundredth camel will also get up of its own to join the rest, since it was already free, they didn't approach it. The camels moved. The hundredth camel didn't. They kicked it to get up, but it won't move.

Much worried, the caravan leader went to the old man and told him about the camel.

"What have you done to it? I know you performed a magic but please now set it free. We have to move. We are getting late. It will be a very hot day," he was almost folding his hands before the old *serai*-keeper.

The old man smiled. "You had tied him in the dark. Now you have to untie him in the light. Do you think pegs and ropes exist only in reality? They exist in minds as well. And the latter are even stronger," the old man chuckled.

The caravan-head understood. Thanking the old man, he asked his men to playact the whole process of taking out the peg and untying the rope. They did it and the camel, taking it to be free to move, got up and joined the others waiting to march ahead.

Pegs and ropes exist in minds also. What else are our false assumptions, fears, anxieties and worries? They tame and condition the mind to a basic level, a very small level given the unlimited potential of the human brain. They literally make one human almost a carbon copy of others in settling for smallness, in being labelled like any other, like they do in factories, just labelling for small, convenient sameness.

It is very convenient for the religio-political ruling class to tame the minds with pegs and ropes of fear, ignorance, assumptions and apprehensions. Brahamanical Hinduism does the same. It is an elaborate system of putting the peg and tying the rope in the form of rituals, taboos, do's and don'ts. The priestly class was ever apprehensive of the capacity of free minds.

A huge effort was put over the centuries to instil fear in minds, to cut them to smallness, to be less daring, more obedient, and less creative. It was a systematic effort to create meek followers and stifle any trait of confidence and leadership. The Brahamanical orthodoxy hammered down pegs and tied ropes around meekly accepting necks.

Religiosity was kept limited to the skin of mankind. A check-dam created to tame the free flow of the rivers of human spirit. No inward looking and self-realisation to reach the light of an enlightened, aware soul. Elaborate system of pegs and ropes. So you just get conditioned to your inherited miseries, your caste status, your untouchability, your bad karma and the mirage of getting better luck in future births through meek following of the skin-deep religiosity. So that you just keep sitting, accepting your fate, like the camel with a false peg and rope. So that you don't look deep within and beyond the narrow confines of your outer world. So that your spirit doesn't roam free, breaking the barriers of false fears and exploiting rituals.

We had a chance of practicing mindfulness, of breaking the shackles, of melting the fears, of realising the potential, of being the leaders. It was Buddhism. Buddha taught nothing but mindfulness so that you become aware of your potential irrespective of your low caste. When you go beyond mere rituals and meditate, most of the false ropes and pegs burn away. You roam free as per the vast horizons of your free-roaming, liberated mind.

Unfortunately, Buddhism was bundled out from the land of its origin. The shrewd Brahamanical connivance packed it off to faraway lands. It thrives in East Asian countries. You can very well compare the chained and liberated minds. Buddhism cuts the chains through training the mind. Brahamanical Hinduism chains the mind through fatal conditioning with the help of fear and meek acceptance.

Look at Japan. Such a small country. But look at their technological excellence. It is nothing but the fruits of centuries of setting the mind free through training the brain.

Meditation helps you reach the top of awareness, to know more, to dissipate ignorance, to be more of a human being, to become different and daring.

Blind rituals are just the first step leading to the endless flight of stairs to evolution and freedom. Unfortunately, Brahamanical Hinduism just kept the people grounded at the first level, to keep them the prisoners of their minds, their selves chained to false pegs and ropes of fears and taboos.

***

18. The Rapist

There are softly moaning sounds in the dark, dingy room. The screen light of a smartphone is the hallowed sun in the dark. But instead of light, it seems in connivance with the dark. Sunny Leone is doing what almost every Indian man dreams about.

The porn clip is sucking the damp air into the funnel of lust and greed. His hands are moving faster and faster. He is visualising himself as an active player in the game. His very soul is on the boil. He finds himself hungrier, more aggressive and better endowed than the male in the porn movie.

He wants her. Or for that matter anyone looking as beautiful as her. He tries to hold but soon surrenders to the climax. Even the feeble light from the screen shifts its shade. He lets it out on the screen, trying to reach her body. It's a strange demented pleasure.

Long before we see the flower, the process starts at the roots. Fruits as well as thorns are the result of a long process which begins with the seeds. The deeds or misdeeds are not sudden sprouts; they also carry their seeds, their incubation period, their structural building and growth before the final appearance.

The idea of woman and sex has mutated so strangely over the years in his mind that he wonders how can anyone just love a woman, especially when there are better uses like lust and sadistic violence. He has been masturbating for a decade now. He started the experiment while in the fifth grade. Now at the age of 20 he has come a long way. His father once caught him and gave him a severe thrashing. He had committed a crime, he realised. He hated his father, so did it with more rampancy, even willing to be caught again to show him that he didn't care.

Sex is the nemesis of Indian society and carries such a taboo, the quintessential *gandi baat*. It exists everywhere, basically in the minds. The more they try to deny it, the bottled genie keeps on growing. He liked this defiance of his. He loved the sensation of doing it right under their noses.

While playing with girls he pinched them. They cried, not understanding, taking it just a hurtful prank among the children. He but felt a strange excitement. He hated this sweet-faced little girl. She was so friendly with a well-behaved boy. But after the last pinch she started to avoid him. He was thus looking out to pinch her once more. He tried. The well-behaved boy saw it and intervened. There was a fight. The good one proved stronger than his appearance and threw him down. He carried a big bluish dark bump on his forehead. The children laughed at him. He seethed with anger.

The studies didn't mean anything at all. He belonged to a lower middle class family. His parents were entangled in the struggle for bread and butter. The school was co-ed till fifth when he had just started masturbating, visualising the girl who had got him a bump. The trigger had been the elder boys' experiment. The group of elder brats had rented a CD player one night and played it in the scandalously moaning secrecy of a room. As they moaned with masturbation, he, peeping from a window, carried out his initiation. After that there was no looking back.

After the fifth standard, it was the boys' only class. With months and then years, invisible walls crept in between him and the opposite sex. Driven by the way elders spoke, or the manner everybody pretended, the way his father thrashed him that day, sex, women and girl started to acquire the exciting shapes of huge taboos. And inevitably it became the favourite haunt of his mind.

It was eating his mind, taking big chunks of fantasies with each passing day. The society appeared to ordain that sex was to be avoided at all cost. It appeared the worst thing a person could even think about. If somebody was explicitly or implicitly found to have something to do with sex, the society would condemn him as a person without any character. It was the hallmark of a good person to have nothing to do with sex. It was such an evil act, to be shunned and avoided at all costs. He even wondered how people gave birth if it was so bad. And continuously thought about whether a married couple had sex or not. Why would they, if it was so bad? The idea kept on bouncing from all corners of his mind. He suppressed it outside but inside it was an ever-haunting mirage.

One more crime against women in India. It happens so many times that it doesn't sound like news anymore. Harassment, molestation, eve-teasing, domestic violence, rape and murder, the evil deeds which have become part and parcel of the modern-day life. These don't occur just randomly, rather take long and winding roots over an individual's soul.

These are but the news items he runs after. He scans the newspapers for rape and murder cases. He hears people around expressing disgust, but somehow he doesn't agree to the vehemence of their anger. He keeps silent. It gives him a strange excitement to visualise the incident given in the news item. Invariably he ends up getting excited.

They have their poisonous seeds. Their building processes. Long before they sprout with thorny branches, the soil is generated and the seed is sown. It is a common social soil, a cumulative shit that piles over generations. It takes a long time, this process of soil formation. Tradition and patriarchy rake it up over the ages.

He remembers how his father mistreated his mother. In fact, he grew up wondering whether they had sex at all. Sex then appeared as the instrument of his father's dominance over his mother, an apparatus of exploitation. *Of course, man is superior to woman at any moment.* It's the most verified fact to him. He has grown up feeling so proud to be a man, the *taker* from the woman, the *giver*.

He has thought so much about sex that now it has acquired a monstrous shape in the secret corridors of his mind. You weed out something, it grows multiple times in the secret recesses. He has been involved in orgies with paid women. But he returns hungrier than before. The act itself no longer counts as sex. It's cut down to some filthy bargain, some moments in the grimy room, cold staring looks, corpse like impassive body, some soiled notes changing hands and the lower garment going up with as much ease as it had come down. To the sexual monster in his mind, it falls grossly short of expectations. It feels like buying a pack of cigarette.

The sight of normal girls puts his soul on boil. He considers himself to be sewage dirty and them as clean and respectable beyond measure. They appear like getting repelled from him like they would from dog shit on the pavement. He cannot even so much as muster up courage to speak even a single word to a girl. The chasm between them and him is increasing. He resents when he sees a *good* girl going around with a so called *good* boy. He feels cheated. He has no role to play in this socially clean set up.

His frustration is building up, putting huge pressure on the check-dam. It is about to burst any time with criminal consequences. The girl has overshadowed the stormy sea in his mind. She laughs and enjoys so much in the company of this boy. They go on bike rides, movies and restaurants. He is following them. Each spell of laughter and the moments of holding hand put a knife of agony through his heart.

He has convinced himself that they are having sex also. And still they are clean and he so mucky, just because he visits prostitutes and no good girl would even look in his direction. The more she smiles in her boyfriend's company, the more he seethes with rage. Society appears hypocritical. They pander it through such relationships and shun it in the case of people like him. He is revengeful. The other day, he sees them coming out of a cheap hotel, having been inside for a couple of hours and during which time he wandered outside like a lunatic.

She is plum red, shaken and diffident as they emerge from the hotel. The boy seems scared and insecure now in the broad hubbub of life after sneaking into the cavernous vaults away from the civilised society to steal a few golden moments. As she moves, her eyes hooked onto the ground, walking carefully to somehow be away from the scene of the taboo, his blood is boiling in anger. He spits in disgust and condemns her as a slut. A cauldron of fervent emotions shakes him up. He is beyond himself and follows her. The boy has taken a different direction, their conscience dictating them to part ways after the union. It is weighing heavily on their sense of right and wrong. They literally take themselves to be the condemned culprits.

He is following her and is completely beyond himself. He is bursting with erection and anger. How can she just walk away after wallowing in the gutter and again merge into the cleanest corridors of the society. He just cannot come to terms with this. It appears like there is someone else inside him as he hears himself shouting *randi* after her.

He is blood red with excitement and beyond himself while splashing the derogatory word. He is walking behind her while narrating his interpretation of what had happened. She quickens her pace but it's not possible to outpace him. She is horrified. He is spilling over the scandal in broad daylight. It appears like she will lose all her standing in the society. Like one clutches at a straw to save life, she plucks at anything to save her *ijjat*. She just finds herself turning back and slapping him. He is stunned. There is a crowd. A painless ennui. He is just vaguely aware of the kicks, slaps and blood in his mouth.

Now he isn't scared of any consequences, the worst the better. He is the wronged person, and redemption his right. The society, generally, and she, particularly, have to pay for it. All that pent up hunger of many years is lolloping its fiery tongue to chuck out the moth of her honour. His face gets flushed with excitement, lust, revenge and some gory illegality.

His tiny house is located in some poor locality of Bombay. Just across the street, the scene shifts to a lower middle class neighbourhood. Her better house is just across the street from his. Now he can very well relate to those snubs she gave him even as little ones, in that forgiving and unknowing childhood zone where the kids crossed class and social boundaries to play together. He vividly recalls that fall of shame when her boyfriend, then just her playmate, had held him with a hesitating grip around the neck, first scared himself, but then finding that it was having some effect, pushed on with it, himself not sure where it will land him. Recalling those moments he spits with disgust.

She appears to be carrying on with life almost normally. It pricks him even more. There is a corner on their roof where he can stand, unseen by the neighbours on his side and most of the houses on the other side. If he stands there, and with luck nobody being there on the roof of the two or three neighbouring houses on her side, he can grab some moments to vent out his fury from a distance if she happens to be there at the opportune time. He is lingering on the roof, and makes lewd gestures when she happens to be on the roof across the street. Even this seems to leave no effect on her at all. And this offends him further. She appears like she doesn't even know that he exists.

He has turned purple. Seething with excitement, his soul has turned sadistic. She is laying clothing on the wash-line. There is no one else on the roofs across the street. His hands are shaking as he unzips himself. He makes a grunt as if to clear his throat to draw her attention. She seems unbothered about him. When she turns her head towards him to work on a tangled shirt, he starts masturbating. He is sure that she is looking at his flashing from the corner of her eyes. Disappointingly there isn't the slightest change in her mannerism. She stays normal. But he is sure that she has seen him doing that. He is feeling proud of his swollen endowment, hoping out of hope that she will now prefer him over that silly *chickna*.

The storm is over. She is gone. He stands spent. Now he is scared of the consequences. What if she tells her parents about it? For the next few days, fear nibs at his lecherous being with a dull intensity. And then the apprehensions clear out. Nothing has changed. He is happier and bolder.

Through common acquaintances, he has a brief idea about what is happening at her end. They are planning to go to Goa, he comes to know. He puts in extra investigation, fuelled by hurtling desire and smashing hate, to find out when and how of the trip. She has told her family that it's a college trip for three days. He shakes his head and chuckles with ill mischief within himself, rubbing his hands in excitement. Now he has taken her for granted, being sure that he can go to any extent and there won't be any reprisals.

It's four days to go for the trip. He is busy in planning a complete makeover so that even his parents won't recognise him.

Early in the morning of the day of the trip, he sneaks out to his friend's house and there the entire turnover in his appearance is brought into effect. He gets his head shaven, puts on false beard and dons sunglasses. He goes beyond this make up to wear clothes he had never worn in life, hippy type, and changes his mannerism completely.

As a new day's hustle and bustle starts he is ready there, lurking around the counter for the buses to Goa, keeping a sharp eye over everybody entering the bus stand. And there they are, coming with excited springs in their walk. He boards the same bus as they do, they in the front part, and he as a skilled follower at the back.

Now he follows them as a bug in the tail of their young, flagellant love. He takes a room in a cheap run down hotel across the street from theirs and peeks at the exit from his balcony smoking cigarettes. They don't come out for the rest of the day. Hungry dog and the bitch is in heat, he mutters.

The next day is more fruitful. He is following their autorickshaw on a bike he has taken on rent. He maintains a safe distance. The further they move from the bustle of the city, the more he gloats over the prospects, like he is waiting with a snare for the fish and the poor thing is on the way.

The sea opens up with greyish blue murkiness, a shadowy, heaving horizon very much in tally with the machinations of his strayed self. They are walking along the shore to reach the farthest end where the coastline is mobbed by greenery. He is walking at a distance through the palms inland. He moves expertly like a hunter with slithery prowl, his heart berserk with criminal anticipation. He feels bold enough to any extent. They are too far from home. Nothing happened even when he flashed right there in front of her house.

They have come a bit too far from the last human seen around. The sea splashes in desolation. Against the background of infinite spread of the sea, his eyes peer like a wolf at the couple walking in majestic oblivion, holding hands, moving to that corner where they will be just *they* with their budding love. Sea gulls screech. Waves crash against the coast. There are only two things that matter: he with his hate, and they with their love.

They are kissing very gently. He is very caring and considerate and lifts her in his hands. She is giving him peck after peck on his cheek. They titter and laugh in full freedom. Only the sea is the witness, they think. No they are wrong, there is someone else too.

He is shaking with bursting excitement. He never felt this much jealous in life. The all free-flowing love of a girl; doled out herself with full heart. It seems unbelievable. The girl holding out her own heart, her whole being, voluntarily, happily to the boy. No need to take it by force. No need to pay for it. How could he be so unlucky and her boyfriend so lucky? He is gasping for breath to keep pace with his racing heart.

He is taking her into the safety of coconut trees. There is healthy undergrowth on the ground. Isolation undertoned by the sea waves welcomes the lovers. Her lover stops in a clearing. Gripped by passion, they surrender to the basic instinct and entwine their young bodies. They are rolling with ecstasy. He looks on from behind a tree. He cannot make out whether he is shaking with hate, jealousy or lust. Possibly all three have rattled his being.

Such an open-armed acceptance of the male passion by the female! He stands as a deprived soul. She appears utterly promiscuous and shameless to him, totally unlike how a girl is supposed to be in the society they belong to. He condemns her as a fallen woman. He spits in disgust. She is putting her reputation to pieces.

The foreplay is going into the seething depths of passion. His soul is burning. Just before they start making love he strikes. He hits at the back of his foe's head. The guy rolls over in agony. The girl shrieks. Her voice is eaten by the sea waves. They are too far from the nearest human ear to catch the distress signal. He jumps over the injured boy and smothers him down. It has been a painful strike and the boy's head is spinning. Now he is venting out the full fury of his fists on his face. There is blood. The boy whimpers with pain and is unable to stand up. He is almost unconscious.

In the scuffle, the aides to his impostorship come off. She recognises him. They are face to face. She is holding her clothes against her breasts and the middle part. He carries the ugliest of a smile on his lips. She tries to run but he easily overtakes her and grasps her like a wolf tames down a rabbit. She tries to fight back, digs her nails into his skin, shouts obscenities but soon realises the futility of it. She is crying now and has fallen at his feet, pleading for mercy.

"Get up, be as much shameless with me as you were with him," his voice is frozen in coldness.

She is folding her hands and crying. He slaps her and she falls. He repeats his order. Can you kiss a thorn with as much love and smile as you do a flower? She is shivering terribly but still tries to kiss him on the cheek. Her courage gives in. A violent sob misbalances her. Again she falls at his feet. He kicks her and she groans with pain.

Again she tries, this time on the lips. It fails and ends up like she has spitted on his face. The poor girl just cannot manage it. He is furious and whacks her down. He then gets all over her.

He is walking back carrying the scratches of her resistance on his skin. A strange ennui has taken him in a mysterious grip. He doesn't know what to plan further to escape. He understands the futility of it. He knows he cannot escape the law forever. Still by instinct he is planning some escape route.

Another rapist is born. He walks like any other criminal. Still another rape victim lies there to get justice, carrying the stigma of ravaged modesty, waiting for justice to take course which would ultimately put her on further path of shame.

Only the rapist doesn't carry the burden of culpability on his sick head. The social system that breeds such thorny seeds shares the cumulative crime. A poisonous seed doesn't land from another planet. It has its supportive forces. It has its environment.

The rules of conduct and tradition certify your sociality and civility if you pander the taboo from a safe distance. Avoid women. Stay away. Only pour out your frustration through passable, ignorable acts of minor mistreatments. These are passable offenses.

Away from the skin-deep dilution of the taboos, the beast lies in the mind, tied with the ropes of patriarchal conventions. The ropes are strong, it takes some time to break and claim criminal freedom. Before that there is a long drawn out phase of passing remarks, molestation, eve-teasing, staring, and criminal visualisation in the mind. The beast is struggling against the ropes. The ropes aren't getting stronger. The beast is claiming power at a furious pace. The beast of skewed ideas in deprived brains has unlimited potential to grow strong and break the ropes. It is no longer satisfied with passing lewd remarks and brushing against the taboo in crowded buses. It wants more. It's an untamed criminal now. It has got a helpless body to carry out its evil design.

A rape happens. And, of course, murder in the wake many times.

It's not that a rapist's scale of depravity can be gauzed by the act of rape only. A person capable of raping can be worse in any other possible manner for a demented mind. He can also harm humanity in any way imaginable or unimaginable.

Rape is a symbol of the evil itself. The grip of the evil is genderless. It can grip a male with the equal felicity it can do a female. Females can also be equally mean. Badness after all is no domain of man only. It doesn't discriminate in infesting a male or a female brain.

***

19. The Point Where Duty Turns into Hate

The master was telling a story. His peaceful face and deep eyes bound the audience--traders, peasants, masons, carpenters, ironsmiths and many more--into one social unit irrespective of their different roles in the society. Many seemed freely lost so far during the sermon, but now drew their mind to listen attentively.

In Japan someone killed a Samurai's master. Now, it was the tradition to avenge one's master's death by killing the murderer. The Samurai went after the culprit, duty-bound as he was, and won't leave any stone unturned in fulfilling it. Bringing this person to death was a matter of honour to him and nothing was more precious to a Samurai than his honour.

The sinner was a very wily man and gave him a tough time. It was not before many years of relentless pursuit that the Samurai laid his hands upon the criminal in a deep forest.

The Samurai raised his sword to kill the person and salvage his honour by fulfilling his duty. But just before the strike, the man spat on the Samurai's face. Possibly he expected a quicker death in one stroke. He had tried to further aggravate the anger in the Samurai. The unexpected happened. The Samurai held his sword back and asked the man to take his sinned face off his eyes.

The murderer was surprised. Much relieved to be still alive, he but couldn't check his curiosity. "Why did you spare my life?" he asked.

The Samurai was visibly trying to overcome his anger.

"For so many years, I was following you to kill. But there was no anger in that pursuit. There was no hate involved. I was just following the tradition and duty of avenging my master's death without bringing my ego in between. But when you spat on my face, you changed all that. You got me angry. You brought my ego into the play. Now if I kill you, it will appear like I killed you because of being angry after being spat upon. It won't be an objective, egoless pursuit of my duty. I cannot kill you as an angry person. Please go away for the time being. If I can detach this personal anger from the cause of my duty, your death, I will go after you again."

Sometimes, a doing, carrying the same effect as an act committed under a spell of anger and hate, can be beyond the germs of ego, hate and rage. It then becomes a duty. The challenge lies in finding where duty stops to turn into revenge or hateful reaction. Check your ego. Tame it within the limits of duty. This world will become a far better place and life more enjoyable.

***

20. A Mouse on the Ground, A Lion in the Mind

He has done it again. The feeling of victory is carried by the air around his puffed-up chest. These are the proud steps of a famed warrior. A victorious fighter walking triumphantly can literally create an earthquake with his stomping, forceful steps.

The King was effusive in praise when he emerged as the most skilful swordsman of the kingdom once again. The Lord's words are ringing in his ears as he steps down from his chariot. Holding the most coveted sword of the state, he walks down the flower-bordered path to the entrance of his impressive mini-palace. He has been awarded and rewarded so many times that he has lost a trail of the achievements of his swordsmanship.

The competition has been long, tedious, tough and even bloody. He bears many cuts as a testimony to the arduous path to the trophy. He is tired and wants some immediate rest. There is group of female servants who run to help him ease up. He just dismisses them as if he doesn't even feel they are around. He wants to soak each and every moment of the victory. He appears willing to retain his scars for some time. It keeps the smell of victory nearer for some more days.

It's getting dark. A restful night is around the corner. He is belching, full with numerous delicacies the King had ordered in the royal kitchen to celebrate his victory. He ate and drank to his victorious self. The champion swordsman is full of food, praise, pride, glory and victory. He doesn't put off his robe for the night. He decides to go to sleep like he is now, just to carry the feeling the next day as well.

The sword, but, needs to be placed on the well-ornated sword-holder on the wall. It's a sanctimonious ritual. He loves and reveres his sword. As he moves to place it where it should be, he sees a mouse on the cushioned chair by the wall. The tiny trespasser is twitching its muzzle, almost like poking fun at him. He gets angry. How dare a mouse keep its presence longer than required—which shouldn't be more than the fraction of a second—in front of him? He expects the little thing to scurry away at the mere sound of his step. His anticipation is scuttled.

His ego gets a dent. By natural instinct, his hand grabs the jewelled hilt of his sword. But then he shakes his head in irritation for even thinking of using his sword against such a tiny irritant.

"Just the sound of air through my nostrils should be sufficient to scare this idiot!" he thinks.

He has let out a few noisy breaths. The mouse but is relaxed on the silky cushion like it is a special guest. The champion swordsman's irritation is turning to anger. His hand is itching to just finish it off in one masterstroke. But won't that it be an insult to his sword? To use it against such a small creature!

He moves on to place his sword at its place expecting that his crossing the room will scare away the tiny piece of annoyance. As he turns back, he is surprised to see the mouse still there, unmoved and relaxed like the room belongs to it.

"This is too much! This little one is inviting sure death!" he claps and expects the mouse to literally faint with fear.

As we all know, it's all but normal to expect a mouse to be the most cowardly creature. It is linked to so many tales of chicken-heartedness. However, the mouse is still unmoved.

"This bloody tick of a shit seems to be deaf and dumb!" he mutters.

The defiance seems to be a challenge to him. He picks up the wooden practice sword and waves it around hoping the airy swirls will be sufficient to scare the mouse and make it run for its life. His expert swings in the air in front of the mouse fail to budge the tiny opponent. Now he is flabbergasted.

"What the hell! Does it want to commit suicide or what? How can I put a dark spot on my heroism by even accepting the challenge from something that will be buried under my shit?" he is offended.

The things which take a detour from the normal, of course, unsettle us. He moves towards the cushioned chair, hoping the cowardly creature will scuttle away, twitching its tail. They are face to face. Still the mouse isn't moving.

Now it's getting into his nerves. He feels like putting it off in one strike. *But then to stoop so low to start accepting challenges even from a small mouse.* His ego is whispering. After all, he has slain mighty warriors in bloody combats. He seems intent to give the mouse more chances to run for safety, accept its defeat and let things remain normal in the world.

He puts the lower end of the wooden sword on the cushion just inches away from the little rival. The mouse is still unmoved. Now it's really eating into his nerves. He is in no mood to jokingly pass off such things as trivial one-offs. The bursts of clapping, shouting and sloganeering are still echoing in his ears.

"And now this bloody mouse! Go little one go, don't mess with my patience. I don't want to put a blot on my bravery by being a mouse slayer."

He feels like cutting it in two smooth pieces even with the wooden sword in an expert stroke. *But killing a mouse with your artistically bravest of swordsmanship*. The voice of ego from inside is even stronger.

"This little nuisance is worthy of being killed with a stick. Poor mouse," he raises his practice sword to hit back like a stick.

But to strike a sword, even if it is a wooden one, like a stick is an insult to the holy art of swordsmanship. His hands just give in. He cannot do it. He cannot use his sword like a stick. A mouse is too lowly a creature to be killed by him. His mind is full of so many ideas that he even gets panicked for a moment regarding his dilemma.

"This suicidal chit of a bird-drop needs a suitable punishment. I cannot bring myself so low to turn from a demon-slayer into a mouse-slayer. The fate of a mouse is to be slaughtered by a cat. Yea, that seems justified and natural! And this little rascal will pee at the sight of a cat. The little devil!" he is angry like he has been given a tough fight by some combatant.

He is thinking of an appropriate punishment to the mouse without compromising his sense of heroism. It's fair between a cat and a mouse. He agrees on this and already has the instrument of punishment in his mind. The fat, well-pampered cat of the wealthy man in the neighbourhood! He feels a sadistic sense prevail over him as he visualises the cat chasing the shitty little one, putting its teeth into its soft fur, and mowing down the squealing bastard. His hands are itching to grab this moment from the space-time continuum of happenings.

A servant is sent to fetch the cat from the neighbouring house. Now, the cat is listening to the exaggerated version of what happened in the warrior's palace.

"Just imagine the guts. The devil is not scared of anything. Not even the bravest soldier of the land. Not that he cannot kill it. Of course he can. But he doesn't want to put a blot on his name by being a mouse-slayer on the day he has been crowned the state champion. But this little piece of arrogance by the tiny creature has forced him to mete out the harshest punishment to a mouse. And that is to be hunted down by a cat."

The cat is listening. It doesn't sound normal. There is something in it. It doesn't seem like any other cat and mouse encounter.

"Of course, it means it must be some special mouse. Otherwise, why would my master take all this trouble to look out for a cat? He could have taken rest after the hard-fought victory," the servant is nailing it down.

The well-fed and amply pampered cat is becoming serious. Many things are playing in its mind. Its paws aren't itching to slice through the soft fur. Its mind is clogged with calculations. It seems a daunting task. It doesn't appear like any other cat-mouse encounter like she has done hundreds of times in life. The poor mouse scuttling away at the mere sight of the cat, the cat preying upon, a minor one-sided scuffle and the inevitable happening. So easy! But this one seems to be different.

The merchant is very happy over the prospect of being of some service to the King's prized fighter. Holding his dear cat he walks with swag to the scene of the looming encounter. With each step the poor cat is becoming more and more conscious of the fight. The news has spread like fire and people are toeing after. The procession moves.

"The mouse is definitely some special devil otherwise why would these humans make such a show of it," the cat's mind is getting bombarded with countless random thoughts.

Her judgment is getting clouded. All the natural sequence of hunting down a mouse is getting stretched to miles with so many distinct steps. And she has to face a mouse that stood up to the mightiest warrior of the land. Thoughts are randomly scurrying across its head. The chaos of thoughts are now changing to numerous apprehensions, which in turn are eating her natural inborn confidence and mastery in doing a small task like killing a mouse. Today it's not about hunger. It's about a challenge. The cat is fully fed. Still it has to kill with the impunity like it is the hungriest beast on the planet.

"What stance I should take before preying upon, and from what distance it would be the safest to pounce upon? Should I put up a fierce avatar with my hair standing up, tail taut, and mewing and growling like a tiger? No. Yes. But wouldn't a cool approach will ensure a better shot at the aim? Yes. No, because the idiot may take it as lack of character in me. Should I, shouldn't I??" each word from the people around is putting out questions after questions in its mind.

At the end of it, the cat feels like they are taking her to the altar to sacrifice her.

"Who knows, it may even be a devil dog impersonating as a mouse!" she has completely forgotten about its experience in killing mice.

By the time they reach the warrior's house, there is a terrible pandemonium around. The cat's head is buzzing with thousand questions, thoughts, fears, apprehensions and what not. It can barely see what is happening around. Now she is in a total daze, not able to think at all. It's not about killing a mouse; it's about defeating ***THE MOUSE***.

Before she realises, she finds herself placed at a distance from the mouse. So many eyes are prying over her. Her natural instinct, her inbuilt dexterity, her inherent skill, her easy-going call to eat a mouse has abandoned her. The cat is conscious of the effort it will take to make a swift dash. It tries to think, but its mind has gone empty. Abandoned by all conviction, it sits there indecisively. It's puzzled beyond measure.

It's a blind, futile rush. With a very awkward movement it leaps. The mouse coolly shifts to its right by a few inches. The cat doesn't know what is happening. It goes rolling like a lump of earth thrown aimlessly. It hits it head on the wall, loses balance and a brass utensil falls on it from the windowsill. There is noise. Its senses are in a riot of panic. Yea, it's not some rat. It's the devil himself and I am attacked. The cat runs away for its life. The mouse looks curiously at the peoples standing at a distance.

Well, that's what happens when a mouse become ***THE MOUSE***.

The news spreads far and wide to reach the King's palace. It's no ordinary mouse. It doesn't scamper away at the sight of swords and cats. The King's still more pampered cat listens with its innards shivering with fear. What if they send me? What if even I fail? I will lose all this royal luxury. Lost in the painful reverie, the poor thing doesn't even realise that the onerous duty of dispensing justice has already been handed over to her.

Now there is a bigger hoopla. Lot more people are talking about the incident. There is more clamour and clatter. And consequently thicker are the clouds of nervousness in the royal cat's mind.

"It's not scared of a sword, nor of cat, and now the presumably the finest cat in the state is summoned to get it done. It cannot be a mouse even if it is impersonating like a mouse."

Simple mouse is becoming a still larger ***THE MOUSE*** with each step they take towards the place of the incident. The royal cat seems surrendered to a doomed fate. They appear like enemies who are pushing her to doom and fall from the royal grace. Her worst days are coming. There has been a shift in her destiny. The winds of misfortune are pounding the fabric of her well-pampered self. Chronic panic has set in. She thinks of everything expect the art and craft of the natural skill of killing a mouse.

The royal cat is in a far bigger dilemma by the time they put her in front of the defiant mouse, who seems hell bent upon retaining the seat like it is the crown of the universe. The cat is shaking with nervous excitement. It goofs up even more miserably. The mouse just jumps to its left and doesn't move. The cat seems to have wasted all weapons in its armoury.

Even before the fight she has been thinking of the aftermaths. How the King will laugh at her and kick her impudently. She is thinking of her life away from the palace in disgrace. More than killing the mouse, its mind is plagued with thoughts of where to run away from the humiliation. So having missed the aim, the cat simply runs away from the scene of its dishonour.

The news blasts through. There is an unheard of mouse which is not afraid of cats and swords. Almost everybody appears unwilling to put his cat through the ordeal and the impending shame. Nobody seems eager to be called the owner of the cat which can't kill even a mouse.

An ascetic stays in his hut outside the state capital. The task of accomplishing the deed reaches his doorstep. He listens to them patiently. There are long and wordy narrations of the incident. It is made to appear larger than life. People look overawed of what has happened. The ascetic's demeanour is calm. He listens to the tales with a smile on his lips. His kind eyes shine with a divine understanding. Knowingly he looks into the eyes of his cat. The cat too appears unperturbed.

"Go and do what you always do with the same attitude and mindset. A mouse is a mouse. Remember. Always. Everywhere. And expect a mouse to be just the same mouse you have eaten so many times in the past," he pats his cat affectionately.

The molehill has become the biggest mountain. It is being talked like nothing else. It beats the pulsating humdrum of a thoroughfare. Everything seems to have been pushed into the background. Everybody is talking about it. But the cat is beyond all this hoopla. Its mind is the same like on any other occasion.

They place the cat in front of the mouse. It twitches its tale with the familiar conviction. There is surety in its movement. It holds its head at a convenient predatory angle. It beats the mouse in the dozing game and buries its teeth into it. The mouse squeaks. The people cheer around. A great thing has been accomplished.

"A mouse is a mouse only. Why burden your mind with so many things which a poor mouse itself can never relate to in the wildest of its dreams," the ascetic is telling the people who have come to return the cat.

The cat has eaten the mouse and mews contentedly. There isn't anything complicated about it.

It was a simple, straight matter torn and skewed into numerous phantom shapes and appearances. And when that happens, even a simple mouse becomes ***THE MOUSE***.

It's better to treat a mouse like a mouse only; spare the lion treatment just for a lion. A mouse under the misfitted conduct of apprehensive minds becomes still more significant than a lion.

***

21. The Hangman

Prominent, generous features on his plump, lined, old face didn't make him that clichéd hangman, who is often featured as black, coarse-featured and thick-muscled. Sparse silver bristles on his round head shone in the silvery haze put over the shiny palette by the approaching winter during this last week of October. Intricate wrinkles on his face showed the rough and gruff of the life he had led.

Yes, for a professional hangman this old veteran had a rather peaceful face. With half-closed eyes, he rolled his stubby fingers over the elaborate lines on his face and gave all the indication that he could very well have done better with some other profession.

Wearing an undersized shirt—a put-away of his son—the buttons tightly shut over the bulging belly, he looked a gentle monster, who would do more good than bad. For the lower garment he had a shin-length blue checked coarse cloth draped around his hairless dark legs. On his feet were the ubiquitous Bata *chappals*.

Belonging to a family of professional hangmen, he had seen the capital punishment's demise from its earlier position of a fierce redemptive sun chucking out darkness to a distant, faded star of justice. Free India had gradually seen him disburdened of his hangman's job.

In fact, it was five years back that he had performed his duty the last time at the age of 75 years at Tihar jail in Delhi. In any case, a hangman's blood ran through his veins; and though his hands shook with age this time, still at the moment of pulling down the handle, he didn't flinch even for the fraction of a second. He did it without showing any emotions and sentiments. After all, he was following the Godly injunction of punishing the sinner, as he, and before him his ancestors, had always believed.

He believed in justice; considered himself to be just the plucker of the ripe fruit of justice at the end of the chain; thought that the fruit having ripened flawlessly through the machinery of judiciary, it was now required of him to give the final pull to bring down the process to its justified conclusion.

It was the much hated and discussed serial killer; the one who roamed Delhi streets and its surrounding satellite towns with deadly impunity. The victims came from all streams—children, young, old, beggars, wealthy, haggard and smart. The murderer killed with otherworldly craziness. When this psychopath was nabbed—a haggard, middle-aged man—there was a vast sigh of relief and feeling of security.

He was tried in a fast track court and to increase the circumstantial evidence against him, the spate of mysterious murders stopped during that period. The society's scourge was sentenced to death. There were jubilations over this collective redemption of the society's woes against the sinner.

Our old hangman, Mastu Pahalwan, became a minor celebrity for carrying out this collective will. His old, peaceful face came to symbolise the maliceless, unbiased face of justice. So the proud old man returned, with his tiny rewards of paltry hangman's remuneration and a few newspaper snippets having his picture, to his home in a village in western Uttar Pradesh.

The hangman now lived on a small few hundred rupees pension. His children survived by doing all sorts of menial works because gone were the prospects for official executioners. Although during the modern times, the crime graph has increased both in numbers and heinousness, yet the demand for justice has remained just vocal, not so much in effect on the ground, in a democratic set-up.

So the official hangman of the Allahabad jail now passed his old days in turkey farming in his backyard to augment the sparse income of his sons. He raised robust, large birds both for meat and eggs. A few full grown turkeys matched his hangman's fees (at the rate of INR 600/turkey). He felt no qualms while seeing a male turkey being fed to reach a weight of around 7 kilograms (and a female half of that) and then selling these in the meat market. It was, after all, a sequence of lawful events.

"A few turkeys do for me what the noose around a criminal's neck does! A criminal is just worth a few turkeys!" he often mused with his simplest calculation and still simpler logic.

But then more than the monetary remuneration, it was the call of duty—the duty to lawfully execute the notorious criminals and murderers with the instrument of gallows—that mattered the most to him. This inheritance defined him, like it defined his ancestors.

None of his four sons had shown eagerness to don the family mantle. They, in fact, laughed it off as a worthless job in which you yourself become a murderer (though ordained by the law) for a paltry sum of money. Nonetheless, the old man would fight with them against this insult to the family's hereditary occupation.

There was a time when his forefathers had worked almost restlessly in the oppressive jails under the Mughals, then the Nawabs and other princely houses and later the Britishers. They then worked on the wheels of instruments of torture for slow death; made the final execution in myriads of horrifying ways. Then the Britishers with Western wit said sending the culprit to gallows was fit to be called the civilised way of taking away criminally antisocial lives.

Mastu's father had worked as the notorious device of torture during his prime years—with no time and intention left with him to do anything else. When not in the Nawab's jails—other princes also sought his services when some notorious criminal or dissenter or rebel had to be broken—he tortured his wife.

However, after Indian independence, he was mostly left twirling the rope in his hand, as the state-sponsored instruments of finishing the criminal lives turned milder, gentler and prolonged. The disgusted old man gnashed his teeth over the new impotence in which the criminals grinned, while the cases stretched endlessly in court corridors. So like a vulture he waited for the prey to fall his way. Whenever some odd death sentence came his way, he did it with the mammoth sense of meting out justice with a quick stroke of handle. Not that he drew sadistic pleasure out of it. It was just that this is what life meant to him. All of us have an idea about life. His was only this much.

"To kill a criminal has been the religion of our family. It's a pious deed to finish the wretched existence of a sinner on earth," he would sermonise young Mastu honing his dark, muscular body in the *akhara*.

Mastu's father appeared as dark, menacing and strong bodied as the occupation required. A red cloth tied around his elf-locks; his oil-smeared bulging bare torso would make him appear like virtual Yamraj to the condemned convict. So he trained his son to be the one who would become water-mouthed at the opportunity of hanging a criminal.

"I'd prefer beheading. But it's considered unsuitable and uncouth these days!" he even grumbled sometimes.

He had a big store of good quality ropes. He wouldn't believe in authorised provisions in this regard, for these were the victuals of his religion. However, despite best of his efforts, he could not bring about that sashaying current of lolloping sea inside his son when the latter donned the mantle. However, the son took the job without much hassle. But whenever some appointment arose, the senior hangman could not see that greed for dispensing justice in his son's eyes. Mastu in fact, quite contrary to his father, did his job passively, without any cherishing emotion. Like a mechanical device doing its duty without pleasure or pain. Sometimes, the slightest of a pinprick would tug at his apron, but he just brushed it away without much consequence to his routine.

"If such educated people deem it fit to finish off a criminal, there must not be any question about it!" his simple hangman's logic thus kept him firmly on the path of his duty.

******

During his last years, Mastu's father turned out to be a psychological wreck—a victim of hallucinations and delusions. In his dreams he saw sky-high demons, the criminals, chasing him down treacherous paths, yelling, "Now we want our justice against you!"

He felt that some ferocious moustached monster was sitting on his chest and trying with all his might to suffocate him to death. With riotously lamenting cries, he would get out of his cot and try to run away. After many such mad escapades through the dark, they were forced to tie him to the cot lest he took final mad steps to death during some night. So the old man tortured his body against the trappings around his body. All his feelings, thoughts and reasons gone down the rubbish drain, he looked the most grotesquely tortured being at the hands of destiny.

One of the culprits condemned to death had expressed a wish to listen to a folk song as his last desire before being hanged. The kind jailor had obliged the man about to leave the world by arranging a performance by a famous folk-lorist in the jail premises. The about to die person sat there like a VIP of the show. Now that song buzzed in his head for hours on end.

At other times, he felt crawly sensations under his skin as if some mysterious fingers were tickling for a cat and mouse game with him. In the name of treatment he was being given electric shocks and hydrotherapy, but his nerve cells which had gone haywire never aligned themselves along the vector of normalcy.

Whatever might have been the opinion of the society while he was wielding the common remedial handle of justice, now but they put the full onus on him for his horrible condition. When he tortured the criminals, they appreciated him for being such a strong arm of justice. Now when his own self was torturing his own body, they let out the simple logic of karma.

"It's the result of his karmas. God knows how many innocents must have been killed and tortured by his unsparing hands!" they now opined.

So the once strong executioner and torturer died as an unnerved wreck. It did, in fact, shook Mastu's belief in the profession.

"Is it all that safe and free from being a sinner in performing the duty of a hangman?" he now found himself questioning.

However, the inertia of the rolling stone of myths, legacies, tradition and conventions pushes one in the same direction for a considerable period of time; even after the pushing force is gone a long time ago. So like an impassive stone—even though the debate regarding hanging, in full colour and multifarious viewpoints, kept the society busy—he kept on following the call of duty when on certain intervals he was called to complete the judge's broken pen's promise to dispense justice.

Mastu sincerely believed that God Himself sat on the chair of the judge. It was thus his duty to follow the instructions. However, all that foundation of unquestioning belief in the profession came to be rudely shaken after that satisfying hanging of the evil incarnation who had been held guilty of killing many people at the whims of his criminal fancies.

Even before the city could complete its sigh of relief after the hanging, one more gory murder took place in the dark of night. The pattern of murder was exactly like the previous ones. It was extensively highlighted in the media. The serial killer was on the prowl again. Special police teams were formed to track him down. More than the lengthening chain of victims, the media highlighted the gross lacunae in the system which had resulted in the loss of an innocent life.

All these headlines accusing the system of sending an innocent to gallows struck old Mastu direct in his wrinkled face. Just as he effected the system's verdict on justice dispensation, he felt that all this was written against him. He had had his little share of heroism from the media, so now when the scribes mulled over the issue of an innocent man being sent to the gallows, he felt himself to be accused by the whole educated world. He could barely read. So others read out to him the hot issue.

Certainly it was a crime against the dead man. Then who is to be held culpable in this matter? The judge? The police? The whole system? Or he himself?

"Maybe people were right when they branded my father as a sinner fit for such suffering!" he mulled over in his simple head.

"In my ignorance, I've killed a man. In the eyes of the law, it's not a killing, but a mistake. But it's not my mistake. It's the judge's mistake. Or the police in that they caught a wrong person? Even those who bayed for his blood so profusely? The media...the country itself!" he was feeling the pangs of unprecedented guilt.

He had come to fetch a Tom turkey from the group to sell at the meat shop, but could not muster up enough courage to grab the young and healthy bird's bright plumage; for now everything gripped him in its parameters of sin.

He had been proud of his lineage in his own silent way. In his unique unbragging manner, he prided himself for holding the baton of justice on the real ground, the baton once held by his illustrious fathers whose deeds ensured a safe society and instilled fear in the evil-minded people.

"We have been the loyal servants of both good and bad masters. But only God knows whether the sin lies on us—for we actually perform the deed—or on the ones who give orders either out of ignorance or being led by their cruel fancies?"

There were some poor layers in the group who brooded over the eggs for weeks to hatch out the poults. 'They want to become mothers and I whisk away their eggs,' ran in his conscience. In order not to qualify as a sinner he freed these. Piteously he looked around at the sacks of bran, shell grit and poor grain.

"Ultimately my every deed stinks of a sin!" he sighed.

Led by a thunderbolt of pity for himself and the birds, he opened the creaky gate onto the backlane leading to the pasture.

“I can melt down the sin, the sin of their slaughter, by taking these to pastures and let them have a fill. Then I’ll give them fish today. But for what purpose?” his frail old mind in his saggy fat bulge was giving a free lease to troubling thoughts.

“If God wants the criminals to be punished and executed, why doesn’t He put His own hands on them? A clever fellow God is! Plays always safe. Always keeps his apron clear. Makes up puppets in this game of justice, sin, crime, good and bad. But maybe these are the hands of God Himself!” he stared into the rough old skin of his thick, veiny hands.

“Oh, how I wish now that these were not my hands! But cannot help it now. Either my hands or the God’s, these have done their deeds. Then who is the real culprit in this affair? The judge? No, no me! It was I who pulled the handle. He was after all some poor, homeless mad man who sometimes talked cleverly, who couldn’t defend himself. A murder indeed! And the murderer...or the murderers? Who will punish them? We won’t punish ourselves by our own selves. Then who is left out to punish all we murderers? India! No, it cannot send so many fellows to the gallows. There will be mercy petitions for saving many of us. Then who will? That leaves God only. But then if God has to do it Himself in select cases, why doesn’t He do it all by Himself? Why does He drag we poor people into the game? But then maybe there are too many sinners in the world. Poor God can’t tackle so many cases. That’s why He takes up the select cases like us who can’t be punished under the law on earth. Oh my God, I hope His punishment will not be that harsh! Gallows I’ll bear easily. After all, it’s a matter of seconds. Is my crime big enough to get me into the tub of boiling oil? Ah, how I wish we could talk to the people who have gone to His court! Babuji hanged hundreds of people. Against how many of them I stand as a sinner, as a murderer? Whatever might be the number but that would certainly leave me as the biggest sinner among all the people I have hanged. The way I have suffered on earth, and will continue to suffer till my death, would it be sufficient to mitigate the sins of all the innocent hangings? Only God knows what would be left in my account book of good and bad when I will be finally pushed into His court. How many I've hanged...and how many murdered? This one for sure has been murdered. I hope I have only one murder to my share! If a few Turkeys are worth a man's life then I owe many more murders. Oh my God, either I'm all of a sinner, a murderer, or no sinner, no murderer at all! God, I can't decide whether I'm a sinner or not!"

His old head was buzzing with tormenting sensations. For a moment, terribly scared, he took it to be the magisterial voice of God reading out His verdict. However it wasn't so. Much against his will, his old head cleared a bit and he was left alone by God to sort out the puzzle himself.

"Oh God, please tell me whether I'm a murderer or not! For if You don't tell me while I'm alive, how'll I come to know. If you tell me after my death," he struck his chest, "then how will I come down to tell myself about this, for by that time they will burn me? God, it is a sin to keep mum like this. I just want to know the truth. However harsh it is! Speak loud...speak louder...please...if you don't tell me I won't own my guilt. I tell you, I'll flatly refuse to own even an ounce of it. And then you too will commit a mistake in knowing the truth. Do you also commit mistakes in dispensing justice? If you do, who will punish you? You won't speak because that will open the lid of the secret of your mistakes. A nice ploy you hatch...remain unseen and unheard so that nobody accuses you for your..."

He was ranting loudly. Neighbours gathered around the yard fence.

"Do you think I've gone mad like my father? Let me tell you sinners that it isn't so!" he shouted at them.

"A mad man never admits him as such!" someone was pretty straight.

He was nervous and fidgety during the next few days. After that volley of oracular bursts at the Godly vault, he went into a silently brooding, almost impassive, state. Smile and energy were all gone from his face. Sometimes during nights he saw long loops, coils of ropes hissing like snakes and suddenly woke up from the nightmare with a cry, his whole body sweating profusely. Thus he walked the tightrope, his mind on razor-sharp edge of sanity and insanity.

During these five years the case had made much headway. The real serial killer had been caught, identified and condemned with almost infallible veracity. Charges against him were based on the firmest of grounds; police investigating team piled up—leaving no loopholes anywhere—evidence after evidence against him; sending down nails after nails to seal his case to the farthest limits of truth. The case thus had moved slowly. So it was not before the 80th year of the old hangman that the sentence was pronounced to be carried out in actuality.

This time too he was supposed to finish the job with perfect smoothness—devoid of any malice or pleasure. This profession had after all become his identity. Such life-long identities are very hard to break. He was too poor and old for creating such a cleavage. So helplessly he followed the instructions. Going through the gloomy corridor leading to the hanging yard, his old mind—physically he was still strong though—was full of hazy ideas.

He just muttered a prayer to the God, "Forgive me God for my deeds because I don't know whether I commit a sin or do a good job."

Standing a bit stooping over the handle of death, he saw the culprit being led to the platform. Their eyes met. He tried to grope into them to sneak into his inner being to find out whether he was still the real culprit or not.

"God please assure me that this time we aren't committing a mistake!" his hands shook as he took the grip.

However, God doesn't seem to give such assurances to us in our everyday mundane lives. His hands were shaking on the handle-grip. Palms got almost flooded with sweat.

"Take care old man! You aren't that old and incapable of taking a judgement for yourself as you think. God is too far and too busy to settle such earthly matters," he was thinking, trying to muster up courage to pull at the drop of the cloth.

Now with a full penetrating force of his feeble, old eyes he tried to peek into the hooded face of the prisoner and instantly recalled that mocking, cold look of those slanting, brownish eyes before they covered his head with the black cloth. He hadn't seen any remorse in the eyes; nor was there any fear.

"Either he is a saint or the said killer," the old hangman waited with thumping heart for the jailor's signal.

"If he turns out to be saint then I'll be surpassing all the combined sins of all my ancestors," his power seemed to fail him.

"Is he more likely to be a saint or the murderer?" he questioned himself.

He searched for saintliness all over that figure clad in washed, clean prisoner's dress. He but couldn't find any.

"Maybe I'm too big a sinner to spot saintliness. So I must look for the other. The presence or absence of the other will prove the presence or absence of the former," his old feeble mind was working rapidly now.

"Saint or a killer?"

"Saint or a murderer?"

"Do I commit a sin or a good deed?"

"Am I a sinner?"

"Am I a good man?"

The questions over the silver strands on his head went on increasing. Its hook struck around his old, poor being. The prisoner's hands were being tied behind his back. The noose was being fitted around his neck. The jailor looked at his watch to give the final signal. Like most of the moments which find us indecisive and uncertain, the crucial moment arrived similarly. With his hangman's instinct he pulled the handle. However, it didn't come smoothly like earlier times. The old man virtually drew out every ounce of his not so feeble strength to pull the death-gear to its full length. It almost rattled his bones like he had lifted a whole mountain.

Nonetheless with that herculean effort something snapped inside him. It was, maybe, hangman's equanimity and balance. His movements became disordered and abnormal. Once bed-ridden, though it was a ripe age, people didn't forget to remind him that it was on account of his profession.

"But all of us have to die...get old...get bed-ridden...grow feeble...unable to move...Almost similar fates! Then maybe all of us are sinners! Or...or nobody is a sinner!" he was entering a state of delirium.

His condition worsened. More than his old body, it was the mind that lynched him hard and sucked him into the whirlpools of death. One afternoon he died an unknown death.

***

22. The Remnants of a Dream

Time's hands were not speeding fast to force people to realise about getting late on this Sunday morning. Time further slows down for the school going children on a holiday. They need not rush to get ready for the school. Madhavan was peacefully asleep in his tiny bedstead in the small room of their semi-concrete little house, situated in a small fishing hamlet off the coast, about two kilometres from Velanganni near Nagapattinam in Tamil Nadu.

His sister Jayachitra appeared even more angelic in her sleep. She carried a smile while sleeping, as if an ever-persistent sweet dream safely blanketed her. It was about 8:30 a.m. Their father, a moderately well-off fisherman from the tiny settlement, had left for fishing in his fibre catamaran. Their mother, not expecting the children to wake up for another hour and half, had left for Velanganni about half an hour ago.

Madhavan's house, a little semi-concrete hutment with whitewashed walls and red sloping roof could well have been called a small fisherman's pride. A safe cosy world; an axis of long-cherished dreams; a small world inside the bigger world of the quiet fishing village, the latter still boxed up in the larger world of the houses on the shorefront. At a short distance, light blue waves of the sea gently surged and receded. The sea all welcoming and friendly, except on occasions when there were storms.

Life as usual, mundane life dragging with surety, keeping routine, maintaining hope, retaining society yoked in practised roles and responsibilities. Beach sand, mud, masonry, planks, boats, jetties, and beach huts: a fishing world. The sea and the fish rule the air.

Menfolk going into the sea. Women taking fish to the market. A slightly boasting air sailing over the wealthy fishermen's small villas with their red-tiled roofs, fluted columns, *verandah*, and tiled floor. Golden sand ready to simmer under the sun, like any other day, waiting for the sun to add to its elevation.

In the background, the bluish calm of the sea looking meditatively into the Bay of Bengal. A morning as vivacious like any other, so dreamy that a passing angel might have been struck by the majestic calm and languorous beauty of this unit of the world. Specks of grey white clouds in bluish expanses of the sky. Greenish black silhouette of the fishing trawlers moving on the watery bosom. Even the celestial flier may not have an inkling of what lay ahead within a time-span of just fifteen minutes.

It was the fateful morning of December 26, 2004 when a Tsunami wreaked death and destruction across coastal areas in the whole region. When hurtling waves swallowed many a dream. The times when the nature forgot its objectivity to turn furious. Boxing Day Tragedy: a frightful gift of death, doom, and destruction by the sea as it opened its Christmas Box. A black Sunday when white silvery sandy beaches were spattered with calamitous mud wherein rolled the boats, fishing trawlers, and bungalows. The day when cars, buses, and trucks were washed away like toys in a miniaturised play-act of flooding by the children on the beach on normal days. When even mighty bridges and sturdy railway lines collapsed like pack of cards under the monster wave.

So the fate of this little hamlet appeared sealed for the wrong, just at the moment the first tidal wave came silently wreaking havoc like a poisonous snake.

Madhavan's sleep was broken by an angry shake of the tiny house. A boat's bow came in splintering away the feeble resistance of the door, the very same door that their mother closed behind her every night, leaving her two children in the warmly protecting air of the little room. Before he could make out what had happened, water was greedily coming up the little height of his bed. Was it a bad dream? No, it was something worse.

Their house was at the outer fringe of the high-tide mark of the first wave. So giving them first hurried warning, the water swashed back even more dangerously than it had arrived. Elsewhere lower down the coast, the waves swept defenceless people desperately trying to reach higher ground. The things which had been done in years were undone in a momentary swash. In Nagapattinam, Nagore and Velanganni vehicles, boats, humans, animals and houses were converted into a tangled mass of wood, metal, and bodies.

As the next wave came upon their palm-fringed little hamlet, proudly holding its settlement-lore for the sake of these simple fishermen, all structures were razed to the ground. The boat came dangerously smashing in and hit the wall. The evil progeny of the submarine slumping flooded the room in all its muddy flurry.

"The sea has gone mad!" Madhavan's panic-stricken voice cut across the roaring rage and reached his younger sister's ears.

On many occasions in the crowded bazaars, his mother had left them alone in the past, instructing him to take care of his little sister. Even in the face of this terrible moment, the instruction overcame his danger-struck senses. Jumping into the boat's bow, he dragged Jayachitra safely into his brotherly arms.

Just a few seconds later, the house was blown away and the boat was lifted to the level of the top palm branches, whose height once filled him with curiosity, awe and surprise. He was grasping his sister as strongly as he could manage. Luck throws a tiny handful of survival chance in such chaos. Who gets it is beyond the comprehension of any law of determination.

A motley crowd was running futilely away from the sea, unmindful of a costly car turned upside down right in the middle of their path. Nets, masts, fishing trawlers, canoes and mechanised boats lay in a tangled mass. Water muffled the breaking and snapping sounds of the world built with so much of focussed passion. Only the sea roared, subduing all other lesser noises.

A young man was running away from the beach with a young girl's body in his supposedly protecting hands. However, the monster was grinning instead of grieving over the massive loss of lives and property around. Plants, wood and damaged boats lay over dead fish. In just a few minutes, it was a changed world; the world which was almost the same with its mundane routines over the years.

We have been running miles ahead of our dreams. As concrete buildings cluttered the seafront, the fisherfolk moved within the perilous vicinity of even storms, not to mention a Tsunami. The angry sea rebuked: destroyed communities, vandalised beaches, mutilated bodies, and twisted boats. It simply pushed the table, scattering everything like broken crockery. The beachfront engulfed by the disaster, there was only one anatomy recognisable. Disaster's.

The massive keel and hull of a ship that moved proudly, smoothly, for fish, money and life, now stuck up, torn and bruised, among coastline rocks. Water is generous to fish and ships. A liveable world to the former, to flap, to swim; a soft road for the latter, to move, to almost run on an even keel. The sea had perhaps momentarily abandoned the customary role. The fish lay dead, hurled inland and left to die muddy death in the world outside. The ship lying on the rocks, tilted to its right on its keel.

A crushed world. Fear hung in the air over the debris. Rumours did perilous rounds. Every now and then people, like tiny insects, began running helter-skelter, away and further away from the sea. The sea that spawned death and destruction. The gigantic seismic waves unleashed by the super-massive undersea earthquake loomed large in the panicked air. Buildings, huts, fishermen and tourists became just tiny testimonials to the wanton destructive power of the massive geological plates pushing against each other with demonic pressure.

Fractured images in a broken mirror. Fragments and pieces of broken dreams. Lorries, pushcarts, and the pilgrims to the seashore on the full moon day were mercilessly moulded into a muddy slush. The twenty-thirty feet sea wall smacked two kilometres inland, destroying secluded mangrove paradises, people working in salt pans, breakfasters, as well as fishermen out in the sea for catching fish and prawns.

Decimated coastal fishing hamlets and battered fishing canoes, torn-apart beach front and an incontrollable mother crying over the shirtless dead body of her daughter of Jayachitra's age, bore mournful testimony to the madness of the killer wave. People were happy in their varied ways, now they cried for the same loss, a monotonous line of loss of relatives, family and houses.

Hundreds of bodies were lying in the sand. Holding his sister's hand, he passed by the body of Kittoo, her eyes half-closed and her mother, robbed of the diamond of her maternity, crying so loud that Madhavan dragged his sister away from the scene, horribly terrified. The dead little girl had been friendly enough to offer him a lollipop as their mothers introduced them at a local thoroughfare a few months back. He still recalled that particular taste as he moved away. However bitter the life around, a child but has an innocent little world of sweetness. He carried that little world in that taste in his mouth.

There in the dangerous sea, he saw the coastguard ships braving the unusually ruffled sea. For a moment he was wonderstruck as to why the sea was behaving so madly. The sea appeared playful even. A joyous memory: the boat's rough planking, painted freely, artlessly in red and white; his feet struggling in the bow, stomach taut over the gunwale, his hands holding her sister's as he laughingly dragged her to the edge. A smile on his lips cracking the bloody crust on his lower lip. Pain. Again he was pulled back into the scary reality.

He thought his parents will return. They will all be together in their sweet home. A child's hope as vast as the sky. And till then it was his duty to take care and protect his little sister like on so many occasions in the past.

The titanic Tsunami caused by the fifth largest earthquake in hundred years occurred on the twenty-sixth—a date that has become synonymous with the destructive face of nature. On 26 December, 2003, it was Bam in Iran that bore the brunt of the raw, unnerving, shaking forces of nature; On 26 January, 2001, there was epical devastation by the Bhuj and Latur earthquake. And now it happened again on the same date—quite unexpectedly since Tsunami is such a rare phenomenon in the South Asian region. It just caught the people on the wrong foot.

All hope seemed to have vanished from the people's Tsunami-tortured faces. Whenever a VIP visited the relief camps, the people folded hands with such desperation and helplessness like they had never done before any of their Gods. There was so much to say for so many losses, for so little of the help that might come their way now. Some even vent out their desperation to the hilt during these rare fleeting moments as the hurried VIP chickened out of the mess lest there might be some mud smeared on his clean shirt.

Holding his hands over his smashed head a man was crying inconsolably. It was the mournful acme of sorrow. Just tears and cries didn't appear sufficient to give expression to the grief born of the terrible loss of his little son, daughter and wife. His very purpose in life had been washed away. The four-five years old boy, who had given him so many reasons to start out for work and return home after finishing a bone-breaking schedule, was now lying to be buried hurriedly in line with his eternally asleep sister. The mother's covered body appeared sleeping comfortably under warm clothes like somewhere in North Indian winters at the time.

On every face 'missing' and 'homeless' was written. Explosive tidal waves which had taken many countries in their destructive spectrum now haunted the tormented psyches of these displaced, hungry, and destitute masses. Hospital morgues were choked with unclaimed bodies so there were mass burials. Multihued coastal community that once glittered with the sea's softly gyrating waves now bore horrific testimony to the all-battering sea-surge.

Massive relief operations, on the other hand, were turning out to be a small and feeble whiff of desperation. Still people managed a hopeful talk in the stinking relief camps, narrating the miraculous tale of an infant's survival, written inexplicably on a floating mattress. Kudos to life—one single flicker of life lighting up the endless depths of thousands of lost lives. Well, that's life!

This earthquake off the coast of Sumatra was so powerful that geologists claimed it made the earth wobble on its axis. The evil aftermaths of this emission of energy, caused due to the undersea slippage of the fault-lines, were felt in every nook corner of the earth. Like tiny insects, people were scurrying to safety, impassively carrying the leftovers.

A battered woman was moving expressionlessly carrying a colour television set on her head. Her little home, fishpond and vegetable garden all lost and other family members still missing. How was the television set saved? It could have been another story of miraculous survival. We cannot expect it to be dry at least. It must have been in water and not in working condition. But after losing your present, you salvage survival crumbs from the past and look into the future with certain shared memories. It was the tiny idiot box that had seen so many moments of their togetherness. She carried the spoilt box of memories on her head, still catching onto the thin strands of hope, to meet her family, to gather the sinews again, to make a nest once more.

Madhavan saw Nikhita. The left side of her face smashed. In place of the childish smile, a purplish scar and reddish right eye gave her a fearsome expression. Seemingly unmindful of her serious, unattended open injury, she was munching a crumb which had luckily fallen in her pleading hands from somewhere. In the face of such calamity, you have to grasp to the streaks of life filtering through the screen from the unknown world. Also you have to be lucky among thousands of hands which try to hold that iota of life.

They had played together on many occasions. It was but no occasion to play. Jayachitra smiled at their neighbour carrying a different face now. The girl was too young to feel the pain of loss; she could just sense the dull pain in her head. Nikhita, however, was grown enough to have an idea of the loss, and knew it was not the time to reciprocate a smile. They remained sitting silently. Unable to bear some hushed unseen agony, the once agile chirpy girl got up and moved limpingly. He watched her almost lifeless body move away with undecided steps. Where is she going? He thought of following her, but then dropped the idea because she appeared not to even know them.

Whenever something worth eating fell in his hands, he first gave it to sister, happily looked at her as she ate, and with enthusiasm thought of the praise he will get from Pa and Ma when they will come to know of this. He seemed to forget all the hardships as his present melted to make a happy picture of the future. When they will be together, they will go to the school, their mother will cook, and father will go fishing. His hopeful eyes putting the scattered pieces together.

In what can be termed as the largest ever relief operations during peace time, all three wings of defence forces were notching out every ounce of their professional efforts. However, the extent of the tragedy was such that even the most humane of their efforts appeared lost in the mishandling chaos around. Life had derailed, and so were the common-most expectations.

The dead bodies had lost reverence and respect, and the scenes like carrying a dead body tied to a wooden stick jolted the last bit of optimism still lurking around. It appeared strikingly unreligious as the dead are given utmost reverence in normal times. Under such disharmonic times, however, all civilised norms get thrown into the dustbin of survival, and humanity sucks out draughts from the same to somehow survive and see another day.

Volunteers were dragging dead bodies on all fours to save them from still worse fate of rotting in the open. Relief and rescue personnel worked mechanically; clearing away the rubble and the bodies with the same expression. There was no other way.

It was frightening, more so for his sister. You have to be brave, he recalled his father once telling him. Embracing his sister, turning her face the other way, he braved the sight, breathing heavily and heat beating fast.

Having lost each and everything related to her, an old lady was wailing piteously. Her wide-open, toothless mouth and lost dull eyes drowned in the salty surge of the sea of tears. Her face was questioningly raised to the God's eyes somewhere in the sky.

Madhavan had seen her earlier. He recalled vividly. No doubt it was she. She had grinned and acknowledged his father's greetings, while he looked happily wearing a bright red shirt, walking with his father on some Sunday, going to the market holding his hand. Now her hands hung limply in air; palms wide open having lost each and every belonging linked to the lines on them through the inexplicable and invisible chord of love, relationships, and life's abounding pleasantries.

Badly battered living bodies were walking upon hundreds of others still buried in the sand. Their vibrant fishing hamlets wiped out of existence. The fishermen robbed of their catamarans and nets looked at the sea as if it was some perennial foe; broken was that sanctimonious bridge which links a fisherman to the sea like a farmer is linked to his plot of land.

The army had dispatched various columns to somehow undo the horrendous extent of this catastrophe. The whole of humanity seemed to have been stranded in a tortuous quagmire. It was a struggle to survive, to move in the mud to gather the broken pieces, to find the surviving family members, then walk a bit more to take on what remained of life.

The Coast Guard, Navy and Air Force were carrying out aerial reconnaissance mission to salvage some pride from the human side in the face of this gruesome attack of nature. Temples, churches, mosques, schools and offices were being converted to makeshift shelters for this badly battered section of the modern humanity.

Bodies in hundreds—naked, half-naked, black, brown, some already showing initial signs of purplish decay; others still fresh like they were asleep; children, men, women, old, young, middle aged—were waiting for the final rites. Nobody was bothered about their caste, class, creed or religion. It was just a gruesome mass of corpses. Manmade differences melt in the face of assault by the larger forces.

Relief workers were frantically digging a big mass grave to provide a quick burial place, where these victims could be laid to rest within the shortest period of time. No ladder was available to carry the bodies to the bottom of the pit, so even the last respect that could have been given to the once-thriving life had to be abandoned. The uncomplaining corpses were thus thrown into the pit. The hands alive and moving being forced to carry out this apparently inhuman burial, almost feeling ashamed and carrying bruises on their conscience. No God-fearing eye could spare even a single look at the jumbled up limbs once the work had been done, so closing their eyes the workers threw earth over these unknown and even casually acquainted faces.

The nearby beach—a little shiny patch of softness to absorb fatigue and tension—had vanished in a deadly jiffy. The beautiful sand-work was unprotestingly swept off as the waves came rising in a flash and then completing the first calamitous cycle, the water subsided as hurriedly as it had surged. Here Madhavan had spent many hours with family and friends on holidays waiting for his father's boat to return from fishing.

The seaside hotel, from whose balcony he had panoramic view of the paternal extent of the sea while his father supplied fish to the kitchen, had been ransacked by the mobbish waves. He looked at the rubble. Some happy memory waved at him to bring a smile on his face. He looked more intently into the rubble to rebuild those nice times. Even his childish fancy failed him. That world seemed to have been ripped apart. No, it wouldn't be the same again. He was suddenly scared. 'But I shouldn't get scared because I am elder brother and have to take care of Jayachitra,' he worked up a little resolution.

On Christmas, the visitors had put offerings and money in boxes in the church. The priest was now distributing the same to the needy lined up, of all faiths and beliefs, having lost their colour, mired in the same dye of tragedy, mere battered human beings. The priest distributed the things with a peculiar sense of detachedness as if it didn't matter anything to him anymore.

Madhavan held his sister in front of him in the queue. Putting some coins and some candies on their open palms, the priest put his hand on their hands, first on the girl and then her brother. It was the first human touch of sympathy since days. It appeared so long that he hardly remembered the last time he felt the same. He felt like crying out and ask the elderly priest about his parents. But then the queue moved on mechanically and he just stepped ahead. He knew it was futile. How will the priest help him in finding his parents, he calculated the impossibility of the task. But then who will?

All he knew was that he has to take care of his sister and continue looking around to catch a fragment of his lost world. But the world had been shattered in a way that all broken pieces appeared the same. These seemed to belong to all and none at the same time.

The gigantic rupture in the earth's womb whiplashing deadly ripples on the open bosom of the sea, which gained horrific momentum over hundreds of kilometres, had broken the languorous calm of that Sunday morning. Hoping to see his father's boat he went to the fishing jetty. It but was decimated, only tiny vestiges remained. Some sullen fishermen were helplessly looking at the angrily lapping watery tongues, more dangerous than fire, hissing against the broken stone and woodwork.

Much to the playful cry of his tiny heart, a big mechanised fishing vessel had been washed ashore. It was lying on its side like a big whale stranded on sand, like a broken toy on the table. It appeared damn funny to them. They laughed, gesticulating like two little monkeys, pointing towards the funny tragedy. Children can laugh, even if there is hardly any reason to.

Children cry as easily as they laugh. He cried. He ran weeping, holding Jayachitra's hand as tightly as he could, lest the chaos snatch her away. She was the only possession he was left with. A trench-like long and deep mass grave was being dug. Coming to its edge, he saw the horrific sight of a girl being carried to the bottom. He cried loudly and ran with his sister, scared that they had gone mad and were burying girls and might snatch his sister to do the same to her.

"Father and mother will get angry at me if I don't take care of her," he was calculating with his innocent mind.

He was now moving towards Velakanni beach hoping to find their mother. On the way, he came across the water-work done by the seismic onslaught of the waves. Leftovers were being dragged out of the devastated fishing hutments. Rubble-strewn landscape glittered with Tsunami's calligraphy—mud smeared utensils, battered clothes, smashed trunks, tattered cupboards, broken chairs, unhinged tables, open chests, and dislodged cots.

Many a time, they went crashing into battered fishing canoes. The survivors, wailing hysterically, were being led to relief camps and hospitals. Municipal lorries were carrying dozens of bodies to dump them into huge pits and municipal graveyards. Killing the last emotion for the dead, their relatives just handed over the bodies to the relief workers for burial. Most of the bodies had been smashed beyond recognition. There was no need for post-mortem now, so the hospitals were getting rid of corpses as soon as possible.

The huts and semi-concrete houses of Seruthur, a fishermen colony about a kilometre from Velakanni, had been rubbled beyond recognition. Subramaniam uncle, a fast friend of his father, was not at his customary place today to greet him. He just stared at the place where he supposed the house to exist.

A little shrine of the sea goddess, worshiped by the fisherfolk with special protective prayers offering toddy, turmeric water and *neem* leaves, stood half ravaged. Trail of death and destruction around it still grinned wantonly.

He had seen his mother praying. 'God listens to your prayers if you pray with a clean heart,' he remembered her telling him one day. He went up to the broken shrine to pray with a *clean heart*. He wasn't sure whether he will be able to do it with a *clean heart* or not. 'In any case the God couldn't save its own house,' he felt like making fun of God and turn a little joke of it. But then he was scared the God might delay meeting with their parents. Recalling all mannerisms of his mother, he sat down to pray. The agonised air continued to tickle him, the sounds around, and he gave up the effort to muster up a *clean heart*.

Collapsed walls and roofs meekly brandished the signs of destruction at the VIP and official vehicles buzzing around. A fishing trawler had been rammed into a minor bridge. Sacrificed coastal life had been offered at the seismic altar. Boats, electric poles, nets, planks, boards, roof tins, clothes and ropes were scattered over the grotesque mud. Hopelessly people wandered through the mud and water puddles. Everybody seemed to be hopping around like children, sullen-faced children rather.

Jayakodi, the fisherman uncle who talked to him so lovingly and confidently that the child in him considered the big fisherman as the bravest man in the world, bore the sight of a big mountain collapsing. The big bulky man's spectacularly heart-rending mournful abandonment to the incessant stream of sobs made him more curious than scared. The more the big man tried to control himself, the more uncontrollable became the stream of sorrow shaking his body with piteous convulsions. Bending on his knees, he was holding his boy's lifeless hand against his left eye as if to prevent the stream of sorrow. His wife was wailing by his side, her face convulsing on the boy's chest.

Madhavan thought the boy was lucky in having his parents by his side. But then the boy will not get up to smile at his parents. He knew death meant the point of no return. They were, he and his sister, but alive and would smile on meeting their parents. Then his heart beat faster. What if, if Ma and Pa don't smile when we meet them? He was gripped by fear. The scene of him and Jayachitra wailing by their parents unsmiling bodies flashed in his head. He had seen too many dead bodies, so the picture came vivid. He started crying. Seeing him cry, his sister cried even louder. He heard her crying, recalled his responsibility, embraced her, and caressed her to smile again.

Everybody appeared robbed of something most precious in life. Against this background of black-music of death, the sea thundered demonically, forcing the badly pillaged human beings to rush inland and cram the make-shift relief camps. The people were just simply fleeing away from themselves; away from their God-ordained right (or duty) of performing the final rights of the dead bodies coming their way whom they recognised as their direct relatives and dear friends. Their badly smashed selves dithered from taking up this responsibility.

Chinnapillai from a neighbouring colony was bravely putting a flower garland around the twisted neck of his girl wearing a pink frock. His wife's body lay at some distance. Around them dead fish littered the muddied landscape. He had seen thus jolly person. Their small family had been a guest at his house, last year, and had lunch at their place. Yes, he remembered her dress. Pink. Was it the same? He peered into the frock to find out if it was the same. No, he wasn't sure. He was staring at the dead girl, or at her frock rather, when he shifted his look and found the unfortunate father looking at him. He thought he will recognise him, but then realised the man was just seeing through him. He was alive, but perhaps he didn't see any longer.

Quite anxious to lay her frail hands upon something useful for the life staring into her feeble old eyes, an old woman, clad in a tattered sari, was furtively roaming around in the Tsunami battlefield. Plastic cans, broken dented utensils, plastic chairs, and a sack of clothes were the things that lay around her waiting to enter some badly contrived shelter. Her once cosy shelter having been blown and scattered away like brittle matchsticks, it was a humungous task, at this stage of life, to make a beginning, to regain a foothold again. The Tsunami had left behind many a dangerous sea resident on the land. Angrily the old woman threw a big stone at a scorpion, as if taking it as the veritable representation of the deadly sea. A boy wailed nearby, fruitlessly pleading that he had been bitten by a snake. In normal times it would have been news, driving people to rush to his help, but not now.

At a short distance, people were running to beg rations from the relief workers. Most of them did not know how the sudden shifting of the sea floor and the consequent vertical displacement of water created disequilibrium in it giving birth to this evil child of death and destruction. Now survival meant with how much strength you could stretch out your begging hands as voluntary organisations came with food and clothes. There were hundreds of hands jostling for the littlest of piece. Hands stretched out flatly, tautly on their all five; lines on the palms—the webbing of luck and fate—glaringly evident like death-sentencing signature of the Tsunami.

He, having made his sister stand at a safe distance, tried to fight his way into the faceless behemoth of the beggary, pity-faced, soulless, multiple-handed creature, jostling, shifting and restless to survive, to grab the morsels of life. He was pinched down in the innards of this ever-hungry creature. Gasping for breath, scared for life, he howled and found himself pushed out.

An old woman, beggar before and beggar now, got him up and handed him a handful of plain boiled rice. Smiling through tears, holding the treasure in his cupped palms, he ran to his sister. He held it to her mouth. The little one was hungrier than he expected and ate all of it, like a little puppy gobbling greedily from a bowl. There was rice around her mouth. He wiped these last grains from her face, put these on his palm and ate, closing eyes. He was happy that she was no longer hungry and will not cry for some time now.

The black Sunday had gobbled everything. Temples, churches, mosques, and an odd *gurudwara* had been razed to the ground. The survivors had put red rags as signs of reverence at the former shrines. Here hundreds were trying to sew up their tattered faith and pray for the survival, well-being and finding their near and dear ones. Faith and its symbols had been cut down. It will take some time for it to heal, to grow. Well, all this takes time of course.

One cannot know from where this devastated young couple got dry wood to cremate their four-year-old twins, son and daughter. Two little pyres were burning as the unfortunate young mother buried her face in the sorrowfully heaving bosom of her husband. Though it wasn't cold, he felt a little shiver as the tide of some strange sensation welled up the pores of his skin. He saw the fire. Felt like getting some warmth. He needed some warmth of love. He stood by the pyres, solemnly as if he was a fellow mourner. All he felt was the warmth. Flesh burning. Fire crackling. Then he got scared and ran away to his sister whom he had instructed to stand at a distance.

Some priests were carrying out a religious procession towards the sea for its pacification. One was saying that it was the disaster born of an angry sea God. "No, it's angry Varuna, the water God!" the other countered. Someone was trying to romp in his point that it was a sea goddess who had caused all this.

The twisted time was taking turns to get itself free of the knot it was entangled in. Then some missive triggered a panic wave. An early-morning warning from the Ministry of Home Affairs to the Chief Secretaries of the affected states went around the devastated mobs in rumoured versions. Fearing another sea storm, people abandoned whatever little things they were left with and took to their heels. Horns were blazing. Vehicles and humans competed to beat the swift forces of death chasing them.

The Tsunami *tandava* had been too fearsome to be faced twice in a lifetime. Noise made by the relief planes and helicopters was mistaken as another sea-surge. Many were injured in the stampede. The brother and sister also ran, imitating others. His sister's small legs gave in and she fell. He got her up, tried to carry her in his arms and then run. His mind was up to the task, but his small body wasn't. They both fell and crawled away from the stomping feet to hide by a broken wall.

That fateful day, Fatima's four-year-old son was playing on the beach imminently facing the sea's watery wall. He tried to scamper back as the Tsunami struck. She had her infant son in her lap. She also ran towards him to protect him from the perilous wall. Nonetheless, this crippling natural disaster was beyond any of her prayer to the Almighty and snatched away the boy. Tragedies defy all logic, miracles do even more. Clinging to a floating plank, she still clutched the infant and was pushed far out into the mud, and when the sea retreated with even more force, she found the board struck in the branches of a tree.

A day later some gutsy fisherman got the mother and child onto the ground. A young mother, she was now feeding coconut milk to her infant daughter. Her dried motherly bosom now spent of its contents, while the heart heaved inside promising recuperation as soon as possible. She was a mother. She had to give life even if she was almost starving.

Madhavan had sometimes seen his mother talking to this woman. He ran towards her for support and succour. She did not appear to recognise him. Her glassy eyes just stared into the murky horizon where the sea hissed. Mechanically her hand was raised and she caressed his little head, but then the thought of her own son overcame her like another Tsunami and she started wailing so loudly that he was scared and forced to retreat.

The symptoms of post-traumatic stress infested the foul air inside the relief camp. He had forced his way in, like it was their home. He tried to find some known face. Hundreds of orphaned children were trying to come to terms with this gross reality in feebly-lit makeshift tents. Some were lying with eyes closed but sleep was nowhere near. Some were eating from paper bowls; others were just staring at still others who did the same in return.

Doctors and nurses were trying to forestall the battle against the impending epidemic. He saw some familiar faces. He had definitely seen them. It was on that fine morning, the weather being exceptionally calm, his father had taken him in the boat. Christian fisherman Miller, Minsha and Bapsha had greeted so lovingly that his head felt their blessing touch as their fishing boat passed along. He raised his hand towards them. They just looked. Memories had melted in the heat of the tragedy. Possibly they did not even recall him whose son he was. He just allowed his hand to drop down and caressed the little head of his sister.

Collapse of clean water supply had brought the camp to the verge of cholera, typhoid and other diarrhoeal diseases of poor sanitation. Sickness loomed large in the air.

Still unburied bodies, petrifying, now placed in a nearby camp, turned dogs on the path of scavenging their once masters. A policeman, Sanjeevan, stood guard to chase away the canine onslaught. A month back his father had a row with another fisherman and this policeman had come to their house, had been extremely polite and helped to resolve the matter without aggravating the issue further.

He remembered this kind, moustached face very well. He might help even now. He ran and tugged at his baton. The policeman did not remember him, but as a humanistic gesture took him to the stinking corpses so that he could recognise some acquaintance. He carefully left his sister outside and pinching his nose against the shirt end to keep the stink away, inspected the corpses with utmost seriousness belying his little years on earth. He did not even know whether he was relieved or sad over not finding his parents there. The air, the stench, the corpses jolted his senses. When he came out, he was much older in years in his mind.

Military field hospitals and temporary shelters were being set up to provide basic amenities, drinking water, clothes and utensils. However, the extent of the damage along the 2000 kilometres southern coastline was so huge that the relief effort proved to be a molehill before the mountainous need.

He had taken up parental responsibility for his sister. Having been almost trampled to the pain of his bones, he grabbed some clothing and toiletries from the military relief site and rolling his sleeves up, sat to the task of bathing her under the tap, like his mother used to do to both of them, carefully recalling each and every nuance of the art.

Kamlawati whom he recalled as the condescending elderly lady, who shared some anecdote with his mother in the vegetable market, appeared to recognise him. She sat to the task of bathing both of them. Like tiny puppies finding their mother in a stampede, they felt safest in the world. They had at least a fistful of the lost world. But then life had been jolted so terribly that everybody had lost footing. Before they could even come out of their initial childlike shyness for the casual acquaintance, the chaos grabbed the benefactor, and they lost her face in the unhitched humanity around. They were alone again in the crowd. For a while he considered to search for the old lady instead of his parents, but then looking at the disorder around dropped the idea.

A woman at a specially erected *pandal* was lamenting over her inability to save her elder son. She appeared brutally traumatised by her ordeal to save only one of her sons. The one-and-half-year old squeezed against her bosom, she was haunted by those flashes of memory as the perilously swirling and debris-strewn torrent snatched the other one away.

Theirs was a little heaven on the palm-fringed shore before the 30-feet water wall brought overwhelming devastation. Their little hutment was twisted and snapped off its foundations as the Tsunami came crashing. The boy was clinging to her right hand while she grasped the infant with the left. Paddling for life, she knew their fate as combined three had been sealed, so in a stony ennui she allowed the waves to snatch away the boy, somewhere inside her knowing that she could have held onto him for some more time, but that surely would have been the peril of all three.

As a mother she had to salvage something out of the doom. She cursed herself for allowing him to be offered at the altar of twisted wreck all around. All silent and sullen now, she stared into the distance and safely cradled the baby in her arms, an expression of incalculable guilt written on every pore of her being. Mud-smeared school books, diaries, papers and photographs from some unknown house sprawled around her. She took up a photograph and stared at those unknown faces.

He saw Divakaran, a neighbour of theirs. His father had once a serious fight with this man and got a bleeding mouth. He had hated him to the core. Even now he stared at him like a foe, least inclined to call out for help. After all, he was a true father's son. He had to prove loyalty to his father. In anger he even felt like throwing a pebble at the enemy but desisted somehow.

Bulldozers and tractors were mechanically laying bare the mud and wreckage to find bodies and bones. Bloated, purpled and smashed bodies were washed up on the neighbouring beach. Aah, with unstinted brutality the nature had devoured everything around. The very same ocean that was a source of livelihood had angrily snatched everything from them in one sudden surge.

Nearby, a cement and plaster statue of the local deity had been miraculously left unscathed amidst all the terrible ruination around. The male deity's softly feminine features appeared aloof from the physical world mercilessly swallowed up by the tidal waves. Some people were still standing with bowed heads before this symbol of unflinching faith, praying for the safety of their near and dear ones. A lone coconut frond, survivor, proudly swayed its tattered branches on this serene sunny morning.

At a short distance, people of all religious hues were digging up graves in the *dargah's* graveyard. The mighty sweep of death had removed all post-death distinctions among the corpses.

A boy suddenly went gaga over his find of a radio from the wreckage. His shrill, playful cry brought grimace on the faces of the gravediggers.

All around the cumulative fate had been catastrophically locked. The grey crest of seamlessly swelling waves had catapulted trees, boats, nets and concrete from near the shore into the rice fields two kilometres inland.

****

That was all that remained: The little boy with his younger sister. He had forgotten that he himself was a kid; he just realised that his little sister was too small and needed care. She was sleeping, her head in his lap. He stared into the chaos, to salvage some hope, to grab some more fragments of their past, to build a rope of better hope to reach their parents.

***

23. The Miracle Boy

In a sleepy mountain hamlet, there was an orphaned boy named—sorry nicknamed—Yamdoot, meaning the one who carries out the errands for the God of Death.

Within a couple of months of his birth, both his parents departed for the other world. One of her *buas*, his father's sister, lashed by a storm of pity for the infant, took him under her care. But then death seemed fond of this new arrival in the world. Within a couple of years, three deaths struck the thatched cottage by a gurgling water channel in the foothills.

Now whenever the little one cried, she thought the angel of death was singing a dirge. So her lullabies changed to cursing words and her fondling fingers adopted the shape of claws that seemed eager to smother him to death. Few of her goats and sheep entailed their masters, which was enough to convince her of the child's ill-omened presence.

Despite many protestations by one of the boy's *mausis*, mother's sister, she somehow managed to cast away his ill-omened shadow from her cottage. Now the onus was on this *mausi*, but she herself by now eyed him with suspicion. Nonetheless, any chance of kicking him away was belied by her husband who would laugh at her superstitious nature.

"Death has its own invisible, secret ways to pick up the targets. Why should we club up that thing with the presence of this little poor one?" he would laugh with his simple farmer's logic.

So the poor child got some semblance of love from the farmer who cultivated his narrow striped fields contouring along the hillside and took his herd to the pastures further upslope. The *mausi*, however, was a fussy lady, so to save the poor boy from the bombardment of her tantrums, the kind uncle often took him along while he worked in the fields or went up into the pastures with their small goat herd.

Thanks to the unrelenting hard work of the family patriarch in the coming years, they seemed to prosper from the parameters of a self-sustaining economy. However, the mysteriously unfolding canvas of happenings is ever under the risk of being bespattered with the callous colours of tragedy. So again the mildly glistening colours of normal luck were swiped away by the coal-black colour of tragedy.

He was around eight by that time and like so many occasions had gone with his kind and gentle uncle upslope with their goat herd. It was a windy afternoon. Bulbous heaps of white clouds were being carried over the peaks by sighing mountain winds. A goat calf tumbled down a precipice bordering the sharp turn of the goat-track along the hillside. Panic-stricken it bleated for life and got stuck up in thickets grown over a little ledge overlooking the sheer rock-fall which appeared almost vertical from above.

Taking enormous risk on his own life, the herder climbed down to the precarious projection along the slope-fall. But then there is a threadbare distinction between life and death. Death which is ever so near, always appears too far to our hopeful eyes. This time it struck both the master and the tiny animal. The poor fellow had unfortunately went down the steep cliff-face just to accompany the helpless animal in its journey to the other world. While the day was closing its shutters upon the tiny hamlet, the boy's profuse cries and endless tears carried the news to the village.

His status as the carrier of doom and destruction had been confirmed again.

"I always knew that you'll take our family up to the snares of death. But his senses were betrayed by your innocent looks. Hai, hai, see, whom have you carried to the dank cellars of death?" his *mausi* almost accused him of murder.

Further, she flatly declared that in order to lift the pall of death from her house, she was required to dispel his ominous shadow from her hut. Of course she did it summarily.

Where was he to go? His own village seemed to be the only choice. So a tired, hungry and wearing tattered clothes our Yamdoot approached his own village in the cradle of a tiny vale. In contrast to those around him with fair colours nurtured by the mountain climes, this poor orphan had dark colour. This coupled with his pitifully brooding features made him look almost synonymous with the nickname he carried on his poor head.

His grandfather still survived. However, he had long since handed over the baton of patriarchy to his only surviving son. The old man was thus ongoing like an old sack in a musty corner in the barn; ever trying to make himself handy in the scheme of things energetically devised by the younger lots. He failed very often nonetheless. So he could have had no role in helping his unfortunate grandson. Now, we draw out our conclusions from the blatant order of happenings and mishappenings—still priding ourselves for braininess?!—so his uncle and aunt flatly refused to give him shelter.

When nobody came forward with a helping hand, an old, childless, widower farmer came up with his lurching gait and hesitating proposal:

"I'm ready to keep him as a helper. Even if what is said about him is true, I need not worry much because the deadly eventuality is sure to strike sooner or later!"

The boy thus started to stay with the patron farmer. Despite his ill repute, which destiny had smeared him with, he grew fast and strong. Since old-age helplessness is weightier than mountains, the farmer's debilitating energies seemed to be soaked up by his young companion's strong limbs. People did criticise nonetheless. The prevalence of the rumour about the boy made them oblivious to the fact that their fellow peasant was really old and his lurching gait and sagging steps had in fact already, and naturally, accelerated his pace towards the final destination.

"This time Yamdoot will snare the old man. The death-attracting magnetism in him will focus Yamraj's deadly gaze on the old man's cottage!" the commonest among them refrained.

However, a surprise was waiting in the wings. Before the sowing season, with the boy's help, the old man had cleared his stone-infested plot of land. Their wheat turned out to be the best in the village. The goats too gave beautiful, healthy calves. The tiny flock of sheep had a thick wad of wool. The mulberry tree in their yard became almost a juicery with so much droppings that both of them could even choose to survive on mulberries only.

"Fattening the chicken before luring him to the God of Death!" they had plain vestiges of jealousy.

Yamdoot was twelve by now. It was perhaps the best season of his life enjoyed by the farmer; coming at a time when the sky had dusk purple curtain over the clouds and shadows were lengthening. Nonetheless, all is well that ends well. Basking in this late life glory, the farmer one day declared Yamdoot as his heir apparent.

First childless and then a widower at an age when his joints had started to complain, the farmer's tale had been that of dispirited work—just enough to earn him two meals a day—and unmotivated look at the sun of life, childless and wifeless as he was. Whenever he got serious over any matter concerning his well being, people got almost pinpricked and said:

"God has been kind enough to free you from the worries of rearing children and nurturing lineage. Nothing will be left of you after you die, so why do you take all this trouble?"

Now, but, all his sorrowfully sulking monologues got this happy stopover. All in all, his tragic tale ended on a happy note which lasted for three years. He died peacefully with the fifteen-year-old boy by his side.

The villagers had started the countdown for the old man's departure a long time back, expecting the event to happen sooner than later. Still they jibed:

"Didn't we tell you so!" thus adding one more mournful feather to the boy's nickname.

We almost make traditions of our attitudes. So without going much into the details, even the little ones who hadn't seen the tragedies themselves, smartly adopted the established view that he was called Yamdoot for good reasons. He thus remained an outcaste. However, he was a strong, healthy-limbed and handsome-featured dark boy, who could earn his morsels from what he had inherited from his foster father.

Robbed of any further chances that could exemplify his ill-omened image, bound by the tradition and myth about him, their eagerly suspicious eyes started connecting him to everyday mishaps. So, many a time, a lot many cursed themselves as unlucky if they happened to see his ill-fated face in the morning. But shackling all myths, if something good happened, it was ignored. It didn't qualify as something odd.

At any place, at any given time, problems and mishaps are bound to crop up naturally now and then. Whenever these happened, people mulled their heads, thinking whether they had been unlucky enough to see Yamdoot's face early in the morning that day. So it became a myth that if you see Yamdoot's face as the first object after getting up in the morning, the day will inevitably turn disastrous.

One day, the most influential person in the village started lamenting that it was Yamdoot who was responsible for his bad luck since he saw his face as the first thing in the morning. Later in the day, as the man claimed, his ox-wagon laden with farm produce fell into a precipice on its way to the sleepy town market beyond those ridges in the mazy distance. Inconsolable over his loss, and hell bent to find a scapegoat for the economic tragedy (since he couldn't find some other means to do it), he accused Yamdoot as the harbinger of doom and destruction for the village.

Following the tradition of hate against him, self-substantiated and biased on account of their own logic, on the testimony of now and then occurring chance mishaps, they managed to throw him out of the village. Accepting his fate as he had always, the young man set up his tiny hut upslope beyond the arable land of the village and shifted there with whatever possessions he had inherited from the old farmer.

Early youth can make or break one. If you find yourself and your capabilities positively related to the society around, you acquire some voluntary, involuntary guiding principles. He was but all alone, a tiny inconsequential speck in the mountainous terrain. All his memories related to that kind old farmer, whose visage anchored him and saved him from the dispassionately heaving waves drifting along in the bay of society.

Thus exiled, he had all his time to himself. That very loneliness and solitude seemed to make him, to wispily guide him along a forlorn path towards a vague destination. During those undisturbed, long, tranquil hours, the silently and broodingly flowing spirit gave its full energy to his occupation. He nurtured his few duties falling between his plot of land and the goat and sheep herd with such unflinching devotion that it became a happening world in itself.

His isolated days had a marvellous monotony. He was but immune to the vacillating, waxing and waning fortunes of the nature around. The striking dawns, beautiful clouds suffused with multiple colours at dusks, autumnal surrender, spring's rejuvenation, winter's frigidity, rain's mirth, storm's fury and breezy lullabies were just simple facts of life to him. He simply looked at these with his eyes only, while his mind slowly, unhurriedly mulled over his daily routine, which he was required to follow strictly in order to survive as a self-surviving entity. Over the years, his heart had been put behind the smoke-screen of his nickname.

His patch of cultivable land was away from the others. Working there he could see the silhouettes of farmers working in their striped fields along the ledges carved out of the gentler slopes. He never looked at them with the purpose of particularly watching or observing them. Only his chance eye-shots fell on their forms from a distance. It is however another matter that some eager pair of eyes watched his shadowy form from a socially safe distance. If we had a chance to have a close-up of those eyes, we would have seen a glint of sympathy and concern in those beautiful big eyes.

If we unrelate good looks from the fairness of colour—with white at the ruling acme—we could easily see traces of genuine handsomeness on his broad, squarish face. He was a strong-limbed lad of eighteen now. Perspiration drops on his body glinted like stars on the face of dark sky as he worked under the sun, clad only in a piece of linen cloth draped as a dhoti covering him down to lower thighs.

Fondness grew with changing seasons and the fleeting patterns of nature. There was a big bale of emotions and feelings buried safe in her bosom. Whenever she shaded her eyes with her hand to have a look at him, the agony of her pining heart touched a new high. The girl stole as many chances to steal as many glances at him as was permitted by her circumstances. Since the days were passing just like before, her eyes bore vestiges of desperation now.

She was the daughter of the very same person who was the chief mover of the scheme that dubbed the poor boy as the harbinger of doom for the village's common fate. The early adolescence of a girl, but, is not driven by such calculations, rather she looks at the world against the background of musically soft chanting by an exuberant, excited heart. Her heart looks at the world differently from behind her beautifully vaulting bosom.

When he was turned out of the village, there was a torrent of sympathy and love through the vast, spacious halls in the secret palace of her heart. With the passing time, and he completely immersed in his solitude defined by that disgraceful sobriquet, this love blossomed to the extent that she could no longer bear the situation's stagnation at the same point.

Love when ascents the acme of its graph, turns one bold and decisive for the leap of faith. So this mountain maiden, pining for her lover, set out of her house on a stormy night. It was an early winter sky laden with black clouds enjoying itself through lightning and thunder-clapping. Though dead afraid, she took hesitant but definite steps towards the alluring destination. Thoughts about him acted as a guide and torch.

His hutment made of logs, grass, reeds and mud was surrounded by a low stone fencing. On the right to the entrance was his cattle shelter made of roughly-hewn stones and a roof of uneven loggings. The low sloping thatch covering the sleepy air over his head was visible to her suddenly in a flash of lightning as she crossed the small fencing. Its dark bluish spark sent a rambling tremor through her heart.

Till now she had been drawn like a helpless, hooked fish by the cord of love through the delightful waters of youth; but now after coming so near to him, the fluidity of her flow was stuck up on the threshold of shyness and hesitation. After all, there was no formal prelude to love between them, holding onto which she could advance and declare her love straightway. Their eyes had never met which could have sent that secret message in the language of heart to arise feelings at his end. So the big mound of emotions for him which lay in her heart now seemed weightier than ever.

She got puzzled and scared, for he seemed standing unconcernedly, without having the slightest hint of the heaving sea of her emotions, at the farthest end of earth. Unable to think what to do next, she sat by the hard support of a cold stone and stared at the tiny, dark structure. Sitting there she gave the hardest of pulls to draw her out of the marshy, muddy waters; but the more she tried, the more distant, unconcerned and faded became his unmindfully busy dark silhouette.

Still younger, she had stolen sympathetic glances at him during his stay with the old farmer. But despite thousands of urgings by her heart, there was hardly any moment when she could claim that he looked at her with particular attention. And even that was almost three years ago. In the meantime, even that real life image had been taken over by his slowly, unhurriedly moving outline in his plot of land at a distance from the village. From a distance his outline was darker than the swathes of night. Darkness had claimed his identity completely now.

Sitting there, doubts and apprehensions clouded the crystal clear rays of genuine love and passion. 'How will he behave at her sight?' the thought sent a chill down her spine.

She now fully realised that it was totally out of control of her girlish heart's ability to further advance on the love-path so directly. With a pining heart she decided to leave. Still she couldn't persuade herself from not leaving behind something which the swipes of coincidence might arrange in a way that he may get some clue to her heart's agony. Her one-sided love was dying to spread its fragrance in the other half of the bond.

She had an unornamented plain brass bracelet on her fair wrist. Wincing with a bit of pleasant pain, she pulled it out. It being just a small article, she could not drop it anywhere. A plank served as the hut's door. It appeared a suitable point where she could be sure of it not missing his eyes in the morning. But his dog may bark! Her heart was racing with excitement. It had to be done nonetheless. In the heart of her hearts, she even wished that the dog barks, thus waking up the master and leaving both the strangers face to face.

With her heart in her mouth, she noiselessly stepped ahead. The dog was but sleeping soundly with the master inside. As she put the bracelet in front of the closed door, she felt a soothing sensation of victory; it being the first firm step on the path authoritatively charted out by her heart.

Next day, as he opened his door to a supposedly similar dawn, his eyes caught sight of the bracelet. He was quite surprised because the first instinct told him that it had been placed there deliberately to catch his attention. The oddity of this event struck him with some force. After all, he had been completely isolated from that mountain village and was living in his hutment like an outcaste.

It was a girl's bracelet. He knew it from the size and the make of it. Any other heart would have jumped with excitement after laying hands upon a bracelet purposely left at his threshold by some unknown but interested girl. However, his separation from the village had been complete and even in the wildest of his dreams, he could never have thought that any girl would dare or care to come this far to his place.

As far as he could remember, he was not in a position to recall even a single face that could have some interest in him. So his mind just explored other possibilities which could have resulted in its chance placing by his door. And after years he was imagining/thinking about something that didn't fall in the customary fold of his almost otherworldly—as far as the human society was concerned—pursuits.

Right from his birth, his imagination had been thrown into a ditch, so his reflections over the possibilities were rather few and, even these sounding totally extraneous, he struggled to think still further. After that the disinterestedly lurching wood cart of his imagery got stalled in the muck of uncertainty along the desolate path; and he left it there; and after a couple of day's drudgery of thoughts, gave up the pursuit altogether.

From a distance his silent lover now eyed him with more care, concern, worry and urgency. Her heart struck with sobbing pangs. There was no change or deviation from his earlier silently brooding and detached demeanour as it was visible from the distance which she somehow managed to steal on one pretext or the other during the day.

Already she had taken some hesitant but concrete and bold steps on the love-path. And further unable to bear the love-pangs and the situation's killing stagnancy, she once again decided to visit the place of her lover during the dark night. This time she was already aware of her inability to carry out the love mission and its message directly to the destination. So again she decided to leave behind something that might catch his attention, putting some serious reflections in his unconcerned mind. With an exciting, soft smile she decided the object must put some ripples in his heart. It must be something that will serve as a symbol of her undeclared, unknown love.

During a country fair held at the foothills, where she had gone visiting the previous year, she had purchased a little vial of cheap, strong perfume and a lipstick. With all the girlish dreams and desires of a lovely future, she had kept these safe and unused. Her slender fingers shaking with excitement, she took out the rickety trunk which her mother kept to store the bridal accessories for the occasion of her marriage. Taking out a beautiful embroidered and filigree-bordered handkerchief, she put it under her pillow along with the perfume vial and the lipstick.

The moon's first crescent had started shining in the misty vault of the sky even before dusk. With an amusing and solacing sigh, she ogled dreamily at it. The mist was rising; the light was fading; the stars were surfacing and the crescent's paleness was turning to a bright smile. Each moment appeared laced with hair-tickling possibilities and softly-sashaying loveable uncertainties.

Traversing across that dewily vaulting starry sky, the moon set before midnight. In a world that criminally sabotages the lovers' moments, the darkness becomes the perfect accomplice turning invaluable servicer for the love's cause. Stealthily availing this service, she set out like a cat taking every precaution with each step.

She held the perfume vial in the tiny pocket on the inner side of her bodice. It was just the size of her little finger. Strongly perfumed liquid in it felt the pleasantly stormy soufflés of her heart passing through her firm girlish breasts. Her breasts' soft tissues were in hilarious agitation against the hardness of the little perfume container. The hanky was tucked on the other side of her bodice. She held the lipstick in her hand as if to gather courage from her grip.

Her virgin love of yonder—which is hypothetical in the sense that the lover is just lost in the thoughts (almost metaphysical) of that sweet personage—was now silently, harmlessly heaving with passion and physical yearning. Her heartbeats went onto scale newer heights as each step took her nearer to the cottage of her lover.

She stopped at a distance from the enclosed hut. Its existence was indicated by a lone tree standing in the middle of his little courtyard. With still more furiously beating heart, she pulled out both things from her bodice and sprinkled a few drops of perfume on the hanky. This done she inhaled it deeply as if she was inhaling the whole essence of her lover.

Quickly she put on lipstick on her lips. It was a strong red colour. She wanted a thick layer, so grazed it quite roughly against her rosy lips. Then overpowered by the strongest of lovely desires, she carefully kissed the hanky, holding it on her straightened palm to leave an imprint of her love and desire for the lonesome creature. In the dark it seemed as if she was kissing his hard, weather-beaten, darkish cheek covered with fluffy, sparse locks of virgin beard.

The dog was, but, today in the tiny barn shelter. She heard its sleepy growl as if some goat had stepped onto its tail. She thus decided not to enter the yard. Taking as much precaution as she could manage under her fear, she approached the wooden cross-bar put across the opening in the fence. Then with nimble finger-work, she tied the kissed and perfumed hanky with so much slowness and scared ease as if she was afraid of arousing the littlest yawn by the sleepy fragrance layered upon the soft cloth.

A lover's smelling power is less than a dog's; for the faithful friend of man is known for this faculty only. The master found his pet sniffing the object in the morning. He ran to untie it. And he was right in running for it. It was no simple rag; rather beautiful, scented piece of cloth. The fragrance seemed to run the errand of love. He smelt it and a strange sensation hit him for the first time in life. He held it at full length and the earth almost shook under his feet. The imprint of love sent all his senses into a strange jumblement.

Overpowered by shock and surprise, he leaned against the stone fence. His finely modulated features against their swarthy background struck a note of awesome query. Holding its two corners by finger tips, he held it against the early morning freshness and stared like it was the eighth wonder in the world.

First the bracelet and now this one! No, it cannot simply be a coincidence. His mind seemed to vouchsafe and the pangs of strange excitement sent a tremor across his hardy, muscular body. Then, inevitably, the adolescent man's heart too sent the message that it was a female's ornate wipe-cloth...and...and the lips! His heart leapt to its highest octave.

He went inside and fetched out the bracelet casually put on a wooden chest. Now he reflected over these with more from heart. And as the heart's imagery is manifold diversified, colourful and exhilarating than the mind's, this time unscaled emotions and reflections entered his lonely being.

He was a forlorn young man, almost unrelated to the world. So these emotions subdued him with unusual weight and power. While stoically busy in his oft-usual chores, his mind now mulled over the secret of the bracelet and the handkerchief. Pulled by these anchoring thoughts, many a time now, he looked towards the village; but on the next thought turned his face with a force as the memories came hurtling upslope. How criminally they had mistreated him!

Till now he had been almost oblivious of their condemnation of him; mostly believing it to be his fate, for this is all he had seen while growing up. However, now the two objects had connected him—even though in an intriguing way—to the humans around. He felt the pangs of victimisation. And once this feeling of victimisation arose, he determined that he too would shut the door in society's face with as much force as it had been doing since he was born.

Since there was no other way for the redressal of the wrongs against him, he decided to vent out all his grievance on the night-gifts from that unknown human—and a female he was sure now—by throwing these into the mountain brook that gurgled nearby. As he raised his hand to throw the objects, his heart felt the weight of it. After all, he was a human being. Having failed to accomplish the task, he returned even more brooding, sulking with a heavy and uneasy heart.

Now however hard he might try, he just couldn't get rid of the thoughts about that unknown human being who intentionally—he was sure on this account also—left those things in his yard; thus, in the way, breaking all the taboos related to him. Tormented by such thoughts, many a time, he kept awake during the nights in the hope of busting the secret.

During those forlorn moments in the dark, as if lying on a watch-out to meet that person, he would feel a pleasant prick at his heart, 'What if it turns out to be a girl from the village!?' He tried to deny this possibility even though the things mathematically proved that it was sure to be a girl. The more he tried to shut out the thoughts, with more force these came striking at the closed doorway of his suffering heart.

His silent lover also knew that his position in the society forbade him from making any advancement on the queries put forth by the things left by her. She thus realised that she will further need to follow the commands of her suffering heart in order to reach some initial, feeble milestone on the love-path. As a girl should do under such circumstances, she gathered the tit-bits of his routine. She did it cleverly without arousing anybody's suspicion about the love fountain bursting inside her.

Many things being vague, one fact was assuredly known that he took his herd upslope for grazing. After those nocturnal forays, now was the time to let the love-crystal shine in the broad daylight. She was overpowered by a peculiar love-gripped admance against the furious whiplashings of doubts, fears and inhibitions arising out of her status as a young maiden on the path of making her love known to the pearl of her heart, the man whom the villagers had forsaken.

It was late autumn. The sun shone brilliantly over the wind-fallen canopies of trees. The sultry evenings were impregnated with the distant calls of winters. This morning was particularly calm and cool. The sun showed all the promise of a bright sunny day. Cool breeze struck the peaks and seemed singing a lullaby to the littlest of fluffy piece of cloud standing almost still in the vast cradle of blue sky.

It was a love adventure in broad daylight. Taking great care to avoid meeting anyone in the intended direction, she took a long and circuitous route and then turned in the targeted direction at a safe distance from the mountain village. Every step turned her bolder than earlier. However, it was a long walk and it was noon by the time she reached the place where she hoped to find him with his grazing herd.

Who can, but, properly estimate the exact twists and turns of a mountain clime? The day which seemed full of sunny prospects suddenly nose-dived on its early-morning promise. A huge dome of black cloud raised its foreboding appearance from behind a ridge. Its peal of thunder was particularly warning. Rising like a challenge against the sun, the force of lightning distinctly flashed even at the noontime. As any girl would, she shook with fear and nervousness. The soothing breeze soon turned into a storm.

Prompted by the weather's theatrics, the silently suffering doors of her heart were opened and like a drowning human clutching at saviour-sinews, she yelled out his nickname with the full force of her feminine vocal cords; though at the same time feeling the pangs of guilt because the name was almost a stigma which the poor boy carried on his lonesome existence. She was ashamed of it but there was no other way of addressing him to draw his attention. Her almost sobbing cry pattered against the rocks and vanished somewhere, while the fearsome cloud almost eclipsed the day to make it almost night-dark.

She shouted with more force and more urgency, moving her nimble steps in all directions. There was but no response. Now she shouted and cried in between and called him as if they knew each other from yore and had talked to each other many, many times. Against all these unexpected, fearful uncertainties he seemed the one acquainted since time's start and the only support to her. The peal of thunder was almost unbearable and lightning flashed—so near—with the propensity of burning everything.

Then the first big raindrops began to fall. There was a lull for a moment and with all the capacity of her throat, she shouted once again before being put to silence by the strike of a big drop on her head. There upslope at a distance, he had faintly heard one of her shouts. Now it was confirmed to him that somebody was calling out for him.

More importantly, it was a girl's voice. His heart's inner voice that was trying to convince him of the possibility of a girl leaving those two objects in his yard in the dark, now opened the floodgates of excitement. It was a completely new sensation, entirely unlike what he had experienced in life since his birth. And like the one who had been unrelated so far, but suddenly found the pole star of relatedness, he hurried down-slope almost beating his herd along the way.

The fury of the rainy storm was almost unprecedented in the region. Not knowing how to address the caller, he just kept on shouting, as he hurtled down:

"Yes! Yes! I'm coming!"

Fearing for life, she took shelter under a tree and kept on calling him as loudly as was allowed by her feminine force. Then he arrived along the goat trail; his arrival pronounced by the new high of thundering and lightning. Their eyes met for the first time! Time stopped. Rain, thunder and lightning fell into poor background. And all the untold stories were told; all questions answered in a moment; all secrecy was busted; and all mysteries were laid bare. The language of eyes is no slave to words and time. Both of them knew that they were lovers.

Like a sparrow escaping the claws of an eagle, she ran and took shelter in the safe confines of his muscular arms. New height of his love-struck heart was absorbed by the peal of thunder and a terrible flash of lightning. All melted, they looked into each other's eyes from so close. Distances had vanished. She had got him. Her locks wet, her fair colour over her delicate features shone with the vibrancy of a bright star against the background of night. His big eyes said all his tongue could not.

They were completely drenched in water. Still he tried to shelter her from the wetness, thunder and lightning. Taking her to the tree, he put his wet blanket on the muddied earth and made her sit on it. Then looking at her with utmost devotion like she was a Goddess, he rose and drove his herd under the tree around them as if to protect her from all the dangers in the world.

All the pent up emotions in his hitherto sealed heart now rained more stormily than the rain. Still he couldn't mutter a word. As a symbol of what went inside his heart, he just put forth the two prized possessions with him: the two little things which tortured and soothed his lonely being at the same time; the things whom he had so many times tried to throw into the pebbled brook, but after each such failed attempt clutched them to his heart with more love and passion.

His fingers shaking under the throes of his heart, he held both the night-gifts in his hands in front of her face. She was flushed with shyness. There was a look of both question and answer on his face. With a shy, feeble smile she nodded. All the stormy noise didn't exist for them now. It was perfect silence and loneliness for the love-whispers to hear each other even though the lovers didn't speak a word.

"I...I...had no other way of declaring...my..." she stopped, blushed and hid her face in his chest.

A gust of warmth sashayed over her cold, wet body and she slid herself still closer into his torso. Unprecedented tremors passed through his body. He the outcaste and now so close to humanity, so near to somebody's care and love. It was overpowering. He held her with such softness as if he was handling a butterfly.

"For nights...I...kept a watch..." he put up an effort to talk like a normal human being after almost endless loneliness in the world, "to...to find out."

There was again a tremendous peal of thunderclap and she sneaked into the safety of his bosom. "I entered your heart...rather intruded!" she muttered from behind the cosy secrecy his chest.

He ran his fingers through her wet locks. It was like he was caressing society; touching humanity. She could distinctly feel his heartbeats even against the background of thunderous events around. She put her soft palm on it to absorb and assuage his pains.

"Your heart beats faster...due to fear or love?" she pouted.

"It beats for both. Fear for us and love for you."

"So like a true lover, you wander with love-gifts in your pocket!" she whispered coquettishly.

"These and you are more of a dream to me. Hardly believable or even imaginable," he sighed.

"So you dream too. Have you ever dreamt of women?"

"Yes...but no...not that way," he hesitated, "society cannot rob one of dreaming!"

"I often dreamt of you. But even in dreams you appeared as distant as you look from far away in the village while working in your field," she sounded cosily complaining.

"So you watched me from a distance. Sometimes my heart leapt suddenly with joy. It must have mysteriously felt the touch of your eyes."

"As if!" she gave a little slap on his chest.

Their talk and whispers were beyond all natural and worldly storms now. However, the storm too wouldn't give in. It went on aggravating to disastrous limits in proportion to the sweetness of their heart to heart talk and soul-solacing deepest depths of love and passion. They, but, were now immune to all the noise around.

They were at the peak of their youth. He was beyond the pale of society and forlorn to the limits a human being can bear. She loved him with the passion of a fully ripe girl. The love-bond brought them nearer and nearer till all inhibitions melted and were washed away along with the rivulets let loose by the torrential rain. Deep rumblings of the clouds turned them deaf to all social admonishments. Flashing light made them turn their eyes from the judgemental society. Individualities melted and they became a unit catalysed by love.

As they tightly embraced each other, forgetting themselves, they were groping into the innermost depths of each other. They beat the storm in their kisses, caresses and fondling to reach the inmost recesses of each other's heart, soul and bodies. The herd, meanwhile, jutted around the tree with animalistic fear and strange detachment.

The peals of thunder looked capable enough to break the mountain. Lightning seemed eager to burn the wet forest. Many a time, the strokes of lightning reached almost to kiss the tree's foliage, followed by hellish noise. But they were oblivious to all this. In those precious moments, he was busy in removing that archaic separation which had kept him aloof and away from the normal human relations and emotions.

With each silently, pleasantly suffering grunt and esoteric moan, all that debris of fate and society was washed away. He forgot what he had been made out to be; leaving him just a human being burdened with the garbage of fate and its bearers on earth. Though he was making love to her; but his body over hers appeared more like protecting her from the treacherous weather.

The fate had played a sudden, decisive, unexpected role in his life. Today too it played its startling card. Like lightning it had struck those around him, sparing him unscathed and making him the scapegoat as the bearer of that nick-name, the carrier of ill-fate, a veritable agent of death, Yamdoot.

Today too the bolt hit mercilessly.

When both of them were in that mesmerising, forgetting state of oblivion, when all being is scattered to the vectors of infinite bliss and joy, the fate struck again. The lightning strike seared through the tree's foliage. However, this time he was lovefully arched over the loveliest thing for him in the world and bore the brunt of this bolt.

He convulsed with the last jerk of life that took her body and soul to the farthest end of oblivion and pleasure. The peak of exhilaration and ecstasy! Forgetfulness!

He indeed was a miracle boy.

The strike was so harsh that even the ring on her finger and the silver pendant around neck vaporised, being atomised. However, the stroke of pleasure was still bigger and overpowering. She felt no pain, just the lightening strike of pleasure. The calamity and ecstasy had coincided. There were burn marks in place of the ring and the pendant. And he had been freed from the cage of his ill-omened nickname.

The tree's foliage was intact, so was the herd which was now running, bleating in all directions. She with a few scars on her body was crying over the body of her lover in her arms.

She made no effort to bury the incident and thus escape from the clutches of a scandal. For the sake of her dead lover, she told the story with details to draw him out of the chains of that ill-omened name. And they laughed at her as the one with a fallen character and then having gone mad.

24. The Dust around Her Feet

Her beautiful bluish eyes were sparking with reflections from the swift torrents in the Ganges. Standing by the support posts of Ram Jhoola, the huge suspension bridge in Rishikesh, she took a deep view of the spiritual panorama like she had so many times since her arrival, believing the place to provide her spiritual succour, a food for her ruffled soul.

On the steps below an old *Sadhu* was washing a brass image of Nag Deva in the sediment laden waters of the spiritually ebullient Ganges in this rainy season. She marvelled at the way his frail fingers, charged with devotional fervour for his beloved god, were busy in creating a shinier visage for the Godly metal. He seemed to be lost in a musical prayer; the mystical ripples in the holy mother chanting songs for him. His frail body, long locks of hair and beard all ensconced in devotional fervour and cosmic unison. Swiftly flew *Ganga Maiya* with the crop of its erosion work in the Himalayas.

With the enthusiasm of a spiritually spellbound foreigner, she took a snap and the flash of light seemed to have disturbed the idol washer's prayer. He stood erect holding the rag with the help of which he was using the abrasive power of the sediments to make his faith shinier and fresher. The talisman of his faith was shining in the sun. The flashlight's sudden whisper distracted his devotional work.

In the distance a conch shell blared with devout urgency. He looked at her and a faint smile surfaced on his lips lost in the rag-tag beard. It then changed to laughter. The bearded laughter was a strange one and made her uneasy.

The people's voices, devotional music blaring in the temples, dull vehicle sounds from the other end of the holy river's holistic water sprawl, incense and the sacred fervour sashaying over the breeze riding the Ganges torrents all appeared to have stopped for a moment.

She was clad in an Indian way, *kameez* and *salwar*, and looked resplendent with her fine curves and angelic features. For a fraction of a second he stood like a hypnotised soul.

Uneasily she moved onto Ram Jhoola, the great suspension bridge, which spiritually swayed to the buffets of cool wind travelling down the valley. Vidhut followed her like a quadruped and taking a pity on the invalid she stopped. She knew the short summary of the long tale of his tragic, deprived life. The previous day, a local guide had translated the invalid's story for 50 rupees.

The crippled beggar was born with limbs that just allowed him to crawl on all fours. He was born at 'Pili Bheet' she tried to recall the name but missed. He was 20 years of age now and had left home a good seven years back to sustain himself on all fours, while the more important bipeds scampered over him across the narrow swinging bridge swaying over the majestic sprawl of the Ganges below. He spent his nights in the verandas of *dharamshalas*, making it a point to stick around as long as possible till he was kicked out along with the stray dogs. When his luck struck best, he even landed with 100 rupees at the end of the day.

After hearing the translated story, she had given a nice blue 100 rupee bill as she took a snap, and he had taken it as the modelling fee. After all he was special. As she walked up to him he expected another modelling assignment. But she passed with the best smile ever possible that took him off all his fours.

The devotional world on both sides of the Ganges carried on among the bathing steps, temples, rest houses, *dharamshalas*, ashrams and bazaars buzzing and crammed to the guts with religious items and souvenirs.

For a whole month the rain Gods had been dripping in their pleasant fury. Even though it was not cold, still after so much of water and dampness it is desirable to have sunrays.

"For the last one month so much water has fallen over us that I feel like a fish permanently relishing the sea!" a saffron-clad *babaji,* flaunting his English commented as he looked sideways while crossing her on the bridge.

She was tempted to look back but knew the risks a beautiful white woman carried in this part of the world, and quite contrary to her open nature she did not turn back. Such looks, simply born of curiosity, are misinterpreted very easily as *green signal* for a fling. She thus avoided the trouble.

The incense-drenched world on both sides of the great river appeared slowed down and subdued by the rains. Deep foggy clouds did endless rounds amidst the surrounding little vales and very easily found pretence to unburden themselves of whatever moisture they carried.

From the surrounding ridges, water was perpetually slipping down to copiously feed even the tiniest sub-tributaries of the small rivulets further feeding the moderately big rainy drainage and the latter finding their way to the big river: the vast convergence rushing with the gurgle and gusto of holy waters to quench the thirst of millions of hungry, restless souls.

She needed this type of small place solace, far away from New York where the big world had piled up enough restlessness in her to go footloose. A chain smoker, she had not smoked even once since she arrived here a week back. It was nothing sort of a miracle and she was looking forward to add many more such soothing wonders to her experience.

She loved this seemingly ancient world and more so in this antique shop. It was fragrant with anciently aesthetic fragrance. There were old paintings, saucers, sculptures, brass tortoise, frogs flat on their bellies, dogs, puppies, candle stand, carved silver vessels, a huge cone (God knows for what purpose), lizards, scales, compasses, trays, tumblers, beautiful vases, lamps, chimers, the oldest gramophone she had ever seen, horse riders, Gods and Goddesses, soldiers, crockery, Victorian trinkets, copper bronze and silver coins, a big painting by a Britisher, a Harappa type violinist sitting on a chair, lamps of various shades, a marble mermaid, horse bust, electroplated punch bowls, an old rusted gypsy pan, old time watches, and so forth.

She tried to observe each and everything. It was a pleasant mess. It was more exotic than her city-cramped senses could afford to see, forget about buying. She started taking pictures.

The attendant chided in her broken English, "If all take photos who buy!?"

She was embarrassed and to avoid further awkwardness bought an old replica of a boat. She also wanted to buy the British period copper bugle but found it too big and abandoned the idea.

As she came out, she met the gaze of that very same *Sadhu* whom she had seen washing the brass God in the sandy waters of the river. His face bore a strange look. She got the pin-prick of scare and lowered her eyes to sneak past into the jostling crowd in the narrow bazaar street. She was apprehensive, knowing very well the risks the foreigners may face in India. But possibly it was incidental and probably the woman in her was exaggerating the threat. She had many muddled thoughts in her mind as she again found herself lost and spread out in the unknown world of agonies and ecstasies.

****

Sitting by a small roadside tea stall, the old man in ascetic robes—but the real earthly self of worldly needs clearly visible through the charity-expectant look—was asking for a packet of biscuits. With a fistful of coins, he had purchased himself tea and retrieved a bit of honour. But to carry his will further, i.e., tea and biscuit both, he still needed the favourite aid of asceticism, i.e., asking for alms.

"Can't see, lost my specks, now who would take mercy on an old man like me?" he pleaded.

Oh thou holy place! So many disbanded, discarded and obsolete human beings take shelter in your teeming streets laden with religious fervour. Incense, chanting, charities, soul-salvaging rituals, flying locks, saffron robes—it's a world in itself catering to the needs of so many as they dump their poor selves here. In between mother Ganges washed away littler, muck and sins without any complaints.

Somebody bought him a biscuit packet and the religioner opened his worldly identity. "I'm from Pushkar in Rajasthan."

He was on a month's tour to some ashram here. However, arriving here he must have calculated his chances better at this place than home. Further, it simply won't raise any issue in his family if he didn't return at all. So he just added a number to the thousands of nameless and faceless humans milling around in the religious fervour.

"Let me see if there is a man of God who can get me specks!?" he quaked in beseeching fervour, trying to pull the strings of the devotee's salvage-seeking spirits.

"You are asking too much *maharaj*! It'll cost more than 100 bucks, so you should ask in instalments, collect your money and then buy new eyes to see this beautiful world!" a fat gentleman mused.

"There is a place but from where you can get a pair of specks in charity," another person wrote hastily an address on a chit of paper and the old *sanyasi* proffered a blessing over his head.

This world is a little merry-go-round thing. The very same person who had taken the pains to write the address of a charitable organisation found the old man trying to invoke further kindness in devotion-smitten souls walking over Ram Jhoola.

"O men and women of God, can't you spare something for my stomach treatment. It pains...day in and out. They say an operation is required. Please-please, I die daily of this pain! God will bless you with pleasures unimaginable if you help me relieve from this torture!" the sonorous notes of his insistent voice mixed into the cool breeze blowing over the waters of the kind, cleansing river.

The address giver moved towards him with a meaningful smile. The charity seeker but was unmoved and stood solid with his present version of need.

"It's not that I just survive for free. I work as well. I wash the utensils in that big temple over there!" before the gentleman could start with some lesson in morality and ethics of charity, the old man put up his defence guard.

"You had told me that you'll directly go to the charity shop, get your specks and leave for your home!" the gentleman seemed upto some jest with the old man.

"Yes I'm gathering fare to reach the spot you mentioned. And to get money here you have to have a good reason, so this stomach ailment," the old beggar was trying to salvage some respect.

The gentleman gave him 20 rupees and asked him to take a shared auto to reach the place before it closed for the day. Possibly he wanted to accomplish one pious deed in the day at any cost! He literally shoved him to the auto stand and hid himself around some corner to see the old man's chain of action.

The old *sanyasi* was suddenly spellbound and looked at her feminine majesty as she passed at a distance, unmindful of the gaze that was anchored on her with particular interest. The hiding gentleman could not hold it anymore and came angrily chiding, "Tricky old man, befooling people with the need of specks and here you have all the eyes for that beautiful white woman!"

****

Vidhut, the invalid from birth, had a sort of office on Ram Jhoola, crawling on all fours, wearing *chappals* in his hands and another pair tied on both knees of his malformed little stumps of legs. As the devotees came gazing into the majestic torrents of the holy river, he pulled at the strings of their conscience, coming as a means of their salvage, a mode of drawing God's blessings by being kind to him. Crawling like this on the spiritual path of the pilgrims he daily earned 80 to 100 rupees. These days he visited his family very rarely.

Pili Bheet in Uttar Pradesh was almost a forgotten place now. His family looked completely satisfied with God's verdict to have him at the holy site as an instrument of Godly blessings for the luckier chunk of humanity. Yesterday he had a strong sense of purpose in life and rented a room for rupees 400 a month. He felt like respecting himself more, and draw more respect from the *dharamshala* caretaker who had kicked him out the previous day.

Once again her curious ears were gathering all these interesting tit-bits about the invalid through another paid translator, a local street urchin who had picked up smatterings of English to get some pocket money in the bargain. The Ganges was creating stormy ripples below the mighty suspension bridge drawn from corporeal to the incorporeal. A man with puckered face watched with jealousy and interest.

“I have helped him many times, saved him from the policeman who try to drag him off the bridge. They in turn hit me with batons. I still carry the mark!” desperately he tugged at the local interpreter’s shirt to translate it for Madam and get some attention on him for being good to somebody whom she liked to talked to.

“It’s a fracture. You must have got it while stealing something,” the translating boy just snubbed him in rough Hindi and shoved him away.

Surely, Vidhut was in news among the beggar group on Ram Jhoola.

“These white people are so strange that she might even adopt you and take you as far as America, the heaven!” one of his fellow beggars was creating the celestial world of luck beyond imagination.

And of course Vidhut hated the particularly interested stare of the old beggar from Rajasthan whenever she passed along. Had he approached her like any other beggar then it would have been normal. But the old *Rajasthani* was principally drawn to her persona and still did not go for what is expected, i.e., alms or charity, but simply looked from a distance. It convinced him that the old man was drawn to her in a hateful way. And he cursed him for that.

****

If you are a foreigner and happen to be at some pilgrimage place, you are then supposed to enjoy the devotional and spiritual fervour of the place, however tedious the exercise might come to you. The experience is, however, recommended.

After the *Satsang* organised by Swami Ramsukhdev ji Maharaj, in which innumerable chants and hymns and preaching interventions passed over her bent head, she was putting on her shoes crouching on the ground. A well decorated *Sadhu*—we mean a hugely religious persona decked up in the articles of faith for the visual delight of it—hovered over her bent head. The priestly hand moved and was placed on her head with all the showers of this and the other world. She was awestruck looking up at his religious make up. It was amazing and impressive from all corners of this world.

"Are you from England?"

"No *Maharaj* I'm from America," she had learnt to address the people attired as such with this word.

"Need a place to stay? You can stay here at the ashram. A very nice room!" he pinched slightly at her arm, straightway driving a strange intimacy.

She got to the immediate fringe of some vaguely lurking danger. The ashrams vied with each other in having more and more white skins staying there for bigger impression and better gains in more than one form. It was a big industry to cater to money and even carnal desires. She was somehow perplexed beyond the calculation of her senses and found herself, as if hypnotised, going with the *Sadhu*. Now he was becoming more and more direct.

"This Godman is a ruffian...bastard...Has fun with girls staying at the ashram," again he pinched at her arm mischievously, his voice now shaking with some slippery, natural passion.

She was scared beyond all her limits, even scared to scream loudly, after all these people are revered even more than God. She had seen hundreds falling at their feet since her arrival.

"You know we as humans should love each other. Oh, you don't know how much I have liked you since I saw you. I'm blessed to have your company," he was becoming more direct taking her shell-shocked state to be her consent. Or had she been drawn into some trick of hypnotism?

By now she could feel the pangs of lust effulging from his holy robes. But she was scared even to say something, forget about shouting. Suddenly, Vidhut lunged forward in his dusted world, straying around like a puppy among the stampede of the bigger world above.

"*Maharaj, maharaj*...this life is wretched...I won't let you go of your holy feet, bless me...I'm a worm and die every minute, please, oh please..." he was squirming like in fits and howling so piteously that dozens of people stood around to have a look.

She regained her composure and just took the fraction of a moment to sneak out of the place, but not before looking into those dull dark eyes of the invalid, knowing fully well that he had done it deliberately to help her slip out of the difficulty.

****

As per the norms of the social set-up based on the appearances, we have to call him a lunatic. Her attention was drawn by the oddity of his forlorn situation. He was sitting on a heap of stones and a rimmed paramilitary hat perched safely on a towel wrapped around his 'lost somewhere' brain. To add more to his otherworldly attractiveness, he had wrapped a polythene sheet around him as if to guard his identity about which the bigger world wasn't concerned anymore.

Much to her surprise, he somewhat positively responded to her accost. The saggy beard around the jaw-line moved to some faint vestiges of smile on his face which appeared that of a Sikh. The smile seemed like an iota of reciprocation for the swathes of sympathy on her beautiful features. He was eating soybean seeds from a packet. Sandals picked out from somewhere; a little school-boy's tie; a sweater; a bag full of empty bottles and packets—it was all that remained to him in this world. In his pockets he had a torn diary and a pen.

"What is your name...name, name!" she treated him like a fellow human being, emphasising on 'name'.

It was like talking to a stone, to something, to some empty bottle in the garbage pit stinking with all the muck in the world. We are sure he had not been addressed so specifically with such particular attention for a long time. He even got scared, getting into that evasive action to avoid a hit on the face. But then the beauty on her face was too assuring. His petrified eyes groped into the depths of her blue eyes. Sanity lurked feebly from the unfathomable well of his miseries.

"M...M...Meer Singh!" his eyes closed under the impact of the push he gave to his crippled mind to draw sense for this beautiful creature from the outer world.

The way he had responded he seemed the case of someone who had lost human sympathy rather than his mind.

She could recall Vibhut so particularly emphasising the place he was born to the translator. People carry the place of their birth even more importantly than their names.

"Where are you from?" she was trying to make him understand the question more through gestures.

He kept on muttering some name again. Perhaps he was telling the name of the place. Since she was not aware of the local names any guesswork in that direction was of no use. He was trying to say the same word with a huge effort through his salivating mouth. Having failed to go any more, he gestured with his index finger towards his head and finally like the dreamy world of an opium-fed man, he circled his finger over his hand to indicate he was mentally crippled. He had conveyed his identity.

"Education, education, studies, studies, books, school, school..." she held onto the iota of sanity that the anchorage of her sympathy had caught onto from the unknown dark gloomy sea of his oblivion.

"Matric!" the effort found spittle dandling across the tufts of beard on his chin.

Again he circled his finger over the hat. Well, that was his identity now.

Possibly, drinking had something to do with his mental disorder for he picked up an empty cold drink bottle and muttered, "Bad, bad, hicc!!"

His eyes contorted with fear and he was looking now at something behind her back. Scared herself she looked back and was terrified beyond imagination. So it was not incidental. That smile by the riverside when he was washing that idol and that appearance by the trinkets shop, it wasn't just a simple coincidence.

The old man but seemed even more terrified than she herself was. Realising this, her fear turned more of a curiosity. The man stood there with folded hands. Before she could even react she saw Vidhut crawling up from behind and he straightway lunged into the old *Sadhu's* legs, misbalancing him and toppling him on all fours. He was shouting like anything, raising a scare, drawing people's attention, trying to save the princess from the danger that this old bad man—more beggary than anyone else in the semblance of saffron religiosity—presented.

Vidhut was crying as he hit the man and clawed his face. The lunatic man also got up and unnerved by a strange sense started stomping the ground like an angry ape. He too started beating the old man with his hat. It was a real melee and before the people got together to disentangle the three of them, Vidhut had shown enough crawling, clawing heroism to thoroughly roughen up the old man who was shaking and crying with convulsive sobs.

"All I wanted was a photo with her, *hai hai* send this rascal to jail, this crawling villain has shaken up my bones, police-police, is there any...is there a God-fearing man to take the side of this old *Sadhu* who has been unjustifiably beaten up, *hai hai*, look at this worm who wriggles around the *firangi* woman!" he pointed at Vidhut.

She had already left the scene. People saw them going together. She was walking at a moderate pace and he crawling as fast as he could manage. Many tourists clicked a picture of this beautiful moment. There was mud across the narrow path. She put all her strength to lift the invalid's mud-smeared body, getting herself soiled in the effort, and put him on the other side. People applauded.

Somebody cheered, "She might have even fallen in love with him, these are crazy people, white people, expect the most daring from them!"

***

25. A Long Walk to Freedom

1974, Mahuwa township in Rajasthan's Dausa district. Sandy summers bear-hugged the desolate landscape. The desert around the district lay sun-baked. Scattered thorn trees and bushes stood in pools of hot eddy. Prickly branches arrayed in battle-march column guarding their stony ramparts of leaves against the unrelenting sunrays ever eager to bring out more evaporation and thus more life out of the desert vegetation.

A lovely flower blossomed in a dusty alley in a lower-middle-class locality. It was, however, a doomed flower. The social and the caste soil under its soft, innocent petals did not blend, although its roots tried its flowery best to gather around a fistful of the two constituents.

The young couple's sin was laid open under the scorching scrutiny and hateful sandy sighs. The boy belonged to a relatively lower Bairwa caste; the girl to a comparatively higher one—Gujjar. They were minors. They knew the consequences. From skirmishes and slaps inside their own respective walls, it could flare up to engulf the two communities involved. Sarla was particularly scared. Couple of years ago, there had been an honour killing for the same crime as hers.

Caste panchayats pleasantly smirked at such on-the-spot judgments. During those days media hardly existed. There were no women's organisations, social activists and human rights groups as are safely patronised by the Women's Commission during the present times. Whatever we can imagine as a semblance of women's rights and their protection must have been in embryonic form.

The reactions against such inter-caste affairs were taken as acts of unavoidable desperation to keep the social fabric intact. So even police preferred to ignore such cases; sometimes they even covered up if it involved influential local families. So the scorching sands contained the unknown sand grains of those unfortunate lovers—mostly girls because the stigma was bigger on their faces—who, somehow, suddenly died during nights and hurriedly cremated during the late hours of a mutely, conniving night.

Hence, eloping was the only escape option. Thus one night, Ramesh, his life stuck in his throat, eloped to save his and his flower's life.

"My widow aunt Saraswati, who is a domestic help in a big house in Delhi will help us," he tried to calm Sarla as she shook with fear and wept.

Reaching Delhi was the longest journey of their lives. "We will somehow hide in this crowd and eke out a living," they sighed with relief looking at the capital crowd.

Saraswati lived in a filthy shanty neighbourhood. Ramesh's uncle had died five years ago after a struggling matrimony lasting the same number of years. Just after his marriage, the adventurous labourer in him had prompted him to seek greener pastures away from the barren land. These five years saw drunkenness, domestic violence, arrival of a bony girl, bone-breaking toil, loneliness and uprootedness in the merciless, uncaring crowd. Then from the path of misery he was swiftly plucked by death as he fell from some few-storey high scaffolding and died on the spot.

A young widow mother, and on top of it appearing exquisite in her Rajasthani rustic charms, she was very easily preyed upon by Imarti Lal. A pock-marked wretch, and an acquaintance of the diseased man, he hurriedly sneaked in with natural ease taking advantage of her helplessness. He arrived as a selfless sympathiser to begin with; got her the job of a domestic help; brought gifts for the sickly baby girl; raped her after a month feigning almost innocence and helplessness all the while; and proposed marriage after another month.

She reflected over this and found no other way out. There was no past or future to do calculations about. The sands of Rajasthan appeared too far and uninviting, even scornful. She thus consented, or rather gave in.

Then the real drama of villainy started. Addicted to visiting brothels he led the parallel life of a pimp, slowly acquiring mastership in his modus operandi. He arrived late, accompanied by hollow, consumed drunkards whom he introduced as his friends and partners in trade. After some days, she too was leading the gutted parallel life of a domestic help during the day and a paid woman during the night.

Soon afterwards the sickly girl child died. She too would have died of grief, if not for Rizwan, a young and handsome pimp under whose swarthy muscular physique her wheatish sweat-soaked body writhed in love, pleasure and painful groaning. He had sex with her not as a customer, but as a lover. She could feel it.

From among the many men who were intimate with her, she felt only Rizwan inside her, rest of them just extracted their money's worth from the impassive dummy. They even complained to her husband that she did not open the full treasure trove of her body to them and Imarti Lal had whacked her many times for this. But now she felt far less insulted, for she herself let out long chains of unbearable foul words, firstly with a bit of momentary hesitant tongue, and later with perfect ease—a thorough-bred sex-worker in the making.

Having served as a field worker in the industry, gaining valuable experience in striking deals, fixing up rooms in guest houses and hotels, her husband now thought of moving further in running a more lucrative prostitution racket. Saraswati helped him under the garb of many pretexts which continuously, invisibly kept on sending subtle sexual advertisements that were easily smelled by the brothel birds.

Ramesh was struck by the change in her manners. His first memory of hers stretched back to that diminutive, cowering, almost child-bride ten years back. He was seven then and thought she was only as old as him. The little bride was casting curious looks around. Next time he saw her five years back when they were in the hometown for a relative's marriage. Despite the trials and tribulations of the gripping urban struggle, she then appeared a fully blossomed female, who at least had the consolation of a husband and a child, if nothing more.

But now the change was striking. Once all the inhibitions are cast out, sex-workers take life head-on, without caring a damn about any social expectations based on norms and beliefs. Flesh trade is such an overpowering system that centuries-old female inhibitions and shyness are blown into society's hypocrite eyes. Words, behaviour and gestures acquire such grotesque, pugnacious tidings that it strikes the so-called cleaner society, shaking them up from their so-called better claims to status. Dress, make-up, hair do's and language make them super-females who can beat any man in wanton display of aggression and domination.

Once she started carrying that typical air around her, she had to quit her job meant for a more decent society. She carried her identity too strongly now, so the entry in the so-called good houses was not welcome. It happened just a month before the eloped couple landed there. Rizwan, Imarti Lal and Saraswati were on the threshold of a more enterprising trade. Their eyes said that they were more than happy in receiving the eloped couple.

Ramesh was confused and surprised when a wealthy-looking gentleman addressed his aunt as Sarika and she responded in an unheard of coquettish way, in a peculiarly flattering manner overarched with Rajasthani-accented Hindi. It was her new brand name. Her over-coloured, over-done lipstick and bright silky red *salwar kameez* appeared to tell him many stories on the very evening of their arrival, but then greenish traditional tattoos on her wheatish forearms and around the corner of her eyes dispelled the uneasy thoughts and the minor couple fell into a fatigued sleep.

Asharfi Lal, a notorious pimp from Mumbai's red light district visited them after a couple of days. Surely, some significant upswing in the hosts' business was in the air. His middle-aged decimated, tobacco chewing face—his persona lost in the illegal trappings of helpless, fleeced, ignorant, sold and cheated females across India—glowed as he saw the wild, fair, sharp-featured, glowing with the peak of youth countryside beauty.

Sarla looked really beautiful. Her supple body shone with abundance of fresh youth. A fountain of pure water in the land muddled with impure rivulets carrying social sewage. In the obnoxious, dimly lit corridors of flesh trade, the people involved took pride in counting 'the buds violated for the first time'. Though the male in Asharfi Lal was almost satiated—or it had been broken like a criminally overworked pack mule—it still hissed in its full hunger when it saw the opportunity to register a fresh name in the dark book of prostitution.

In the lewd language of the trade he conveyed his dirty intention to his beetle-nut-chewing hostess, her lips curved with coquetry to appease this important cog who could help them in rising further in the illicit trade. The trade was rapidly growing in the areas along the highways. The booming transport industry with its over-strained, overworked, frustrated, tired, and fatigued truck drivers, helpers, cleaners, hotel and restaurant servants were being swiftly sucked into the momentary dives of forgetfulness in the pool of paid sex.

Taking a full bright rose from the hair knot at the back of her head, Sarika threw it at his greedy lips watching the girl passing out of the tiny door of her dingy best room. He in turn took the gold chain off his neck and gently held the bait before her greedy eyes.

"Full purchase! She will serve better than here," he gloated and explored the possibility of striking a deal.

"You want to open the cork, drink the wine, and sell the bottle to cheap mother-fuckers! For this pittance I'll just allow you to open the bottle, have a few hasty swigs and leave the rest with me," she mocked at the uncontrollable urge in the greying pimp.

The deal was struck. The fate of this new entrant was sealed. At night Rizwan took Ramesh out on the pretext of attending a marriage function.

"It'll ease your spirits," he slapped his shoulder in a friendly manner.

Immediately after they departed, Sarika laid the snare. First she cajoled, used all fleecing tricks to get her consent, but when the dumbfounded girl did not budge, she and the old pimp dragged her into the dark, dimly lit cellar where her helpless screams had no effect on the crowded, noisy, unconcerned world outside.

Old Asharfi Lal was drunk and raped her with the fury of a young body. She was just fifteen when she was raped.

She and Ramesh had made love during their courtship back in the home town. They had taken the risk of their lives to satiate the love, lust and curiosity born storm clouded with infatuation of the age. These were the moments they had stolen from the unforgiving society around. However, the ratty society has a special knack to smell out such lovers' rendezvous moments. And the minor couple's natural, innocent curiosity into each other's anatomy entailed a painful rumble in the bowls of the social cloud unleashing a storm. They somehow saved themselves from the torrential fury by eloping but landed here into a bigger trouble.

The world is never sufficient to accommodate the love-cooing of hearts in conservative societies.

It was a night of nasty parallels for the couple. Rizwan got Ramesh drunk. When his suspicions, hesitancy, fears and cautions were untied to let loose into the zone of meaninglessness by the fuming spools of alcohol, he introduced two semi-naked middle-aged whores (who were not left with much of business) in the sphere of his boozed up spirits and closed the door behind him.

Even tipsy to the core, Ramesh resisted, as a love-bound man, committedly tethered to the peg of faithfulness.

"What will Sarla say?!" it flashed in his mind as the expert sex-worker tore through his clothing.

The huntresses were too insistent. The prey was just left with a portion of his physical and mental strength. They succeeded in seducing him. He vented out the full fury of his youth in wrathful convulsions as a punishment to them as well as himself.

Next day, the couple's dead cast eyes stared at each other. Without speaking they sulked indoors for a couple of days, almost in mourning. They had lost a significant part of their respective identities and were well aware of the gravity of their loss. One is most often forced to accept the circumstances. The rarest of the rare have the strength of breaking the circumstantial shackles. Like a game of dice we accept the favourable throw as well as the worst one in utter humility. We might shout with both joy and sorrows. We might sulk. But we accept and reconcile nonetheless.

Once initiated into the tribe, the love and affection of those around doubled. During this period of reconciliation and coming to terms with reality, they shut themselves in the cellar she had been raped, first wept over their bitter position, and when the tears had dried up, they embraced and kissed each other softly as a souvenir of their innocent love when they exchanged pleasant glances, whisked away letters, blew flying kisses, and thought about each other almost 24 hours a day; when a smile, a soft word appeared the most valuable thing in the world.

And when the shattered glass pieces of their dream palace pinched their young bodies with desire and lust, their fatigued and defeated selves ran to take shelter in each other's flesh with a beastly urge. They made love as many times as their bodies allowed. It went on for a week in the damp and dank light in the initiation cellar.

"Want to sap all the juice of each other before seeking greener pastures!" Rizwan winked at Sarika.

She in turn pouted her reddened lips and gave a lusty pinch into the groins of her paramour, "Hope it will not be the case with us!"

As it happens in the free-wheeling corridors of the sex bazaar, the parasitic undergrowth of desire, love, lust, survival, pleasures and pains get embaled in a wenchy heap covered with a slutty, stained rag. Time being a great healer, Ramesh made love to his aunt, saying it was the price she had to pay for getting them this nice job. Rizwan enjoyed with Sarla prattling she was the most beautiful among all the women he had slept with. Even old Imarti Lal encroached in sometimes mischievously. Ramesh and Rizwan both enjoyed with the new ones. Sarika too engaged with new customers sometimes. Imarti Lal would pay both Sarla and Sarika to arouse him.

In those days, sex trade faced little hindrance except for the bitter pill of social ostracism. But who cared—those who poked their disgusting noses at them, their own linen lay scattered on the brothel floors. There was no scarecrow of the police. Police? Yes, they troubled them sometimes but it was basically meant to increase the local police's share in the profits. And the trade and its profits just boomed unprecedentedly.

Deeply foraging into the society from their pathetic positions at the social fringe, forgotten in their native lands, they facelessly encroached into the estranged morals. After a decade and half's struggle, Sarika ran a posh brothel in the red light district at GB Road in Delhi. Imarti Lal died at the cusp of his glory. His frail heart overcome and over-shoved by the deeply rumbling pangs of lust, alcohol and performance-enhancing drugs as he desperately tried to make up for the money paid to a foreigner lady of the trade in a cheap guesthouse in Paharganj.

"Tried to drink from a dead, dry well and thirsted himself to death," his 42-year-old brothel-owner wife just evinced the littlest of interest in the tragedy and gave a rare cold sigh.

Her face tried to contort and put up a wifely show of sorrow. The heavy mask of cheap cosmetics got a strain, opening a few lines and cracks to allow the reality sneak out a bit. In quick desperation, she overpowered the urge to be a mourning wife. With pangs of jealousy, she stared at the far fresher face of a decade younger Sarla.

"Perhaps they do not nibble at her face, as they have done to me over the years," she felt the unavoidable feminine pang of jealousy.

It was an instinctive female reaction, otherwise they shared a cordial relationship, almost that of a mother and daughter. As a rule, Sarika treated her girls very well.

They moved through the first half of the nineties smoothly. In the drunken haze of loose morals, wanton gestures, lewd stares, illicit relationships and rawest humour that gripped the naked flesh on GB Road, Rizwan and Sarika's brothel dangerously came close to being the best in the business. Even after the 'standard deductions', their girls and pimps were left with decent money.

Sarika's paramour moved in a car now; was treated with respect in society for money gets you respect and more importantly he maintained a second rung of high society girls, educated, smart and sophisticated, to cater to top-class clients. It included a failed heroine, some struggling models, a couple of ladies from the theatre scene in Delhi, three college girls, and two over-flying airhostesses. Here, costliest deals were struck in the lobbies of posh hotels.

You cannot hope to rise forever. Fortunes fluctuate. Rizwan's rival brothel owners got him murdered. Profits were going too far and too deep one-sidedly. Throat slit, his rotting body was fished out of the dark polluted waters of Yamuna. With him died the pale glow of the hopelessly burning candle of Sarika's life. In the buzzing merciless dehumanised sex bazaar one still catches at the strands of love and relationships, even if these are available in strained, grotesque form. In her case it meant Rizwan. She was now cast into the open sea of loneliness, her anchor gone; life became purposeless. She just could not come out of the pit this time.

As if nursing some inexplicable hate towards the brothel owner, a new arrival sighed, “Now she’ll go mad. I saw it. She depended too much on him. He meant everything to her.”

Sarika just sulked silently, never wept, stopped painting her face to pretend youth and went further and further into the pit of doom.

Sarla did her best. She was more of a manager of affairs and allowed only ‘important for the trade people’ to touch her. She was no longer just a body of flesh rolling in stained bed sheets.

There is a thread of relation management between a brothel and the clientele. The chance arrivals of some frustrated outstation male, with almost finished pockets cannot put a brothel on the speedy track of prosperity. Well-pampered regulars having fat pockets do the job. With Rizwan it was gone, and so did their dark prestige and prosperity.

Moreover, the second half of the decade arrived with all the wrong messages for the sex trade. A reformative horde of Bharatiya Nari Sudhar Sabha was frequently making acrimonious inroads into the sex-workers’ dungeons along the ill-famed road in the national capital. Most of the time, they preached safe sex and sex-workers’ rights. The utmost un-conservative sex trade was deaf to the clarion call. Their preaching was sometimes interlaced with talks of rehabilitation and alternative professions. They distributed some sewing machines and parroted many a word to the girls regarding the necessity to get education.

How can a huge ship carrying socio-economic filth be stopped from drifting into the abyss by such light, flippant anchorage! Nonetheless, subdued by such a mighty clean voice from the first-rate society, the sex-workers too felt duty bound to do something for the society. Rubbing shoulders with such clean folks, who were there for higher purposes, Sarla after a long time realised she too was a human being like anyone else. She had come to feel like a totally different species, something grotesquely dehumanised and caricatured.

AIDS was becoming a huge scarecrow. Hellish talks of the afflictions born of the deadly virus were sending goose-bumps down the spine of even the most confident and regular brothel hunters.

Feeling like a normal human being in the company of activists, much obliged Sarla presented their leader a fat cheque meant to help them in their charity work. It was her moment of glory when she presented the cheque to the cleanest *khadi*-clad gentleman she had ever met so closely. It was a momentary flash of dignity, pride, cleanliness and being human like anyone else around.

Driven by its pleasant repercussions, she even arranged a supper for the workers, which they were forced to accept, not being able to say no and make the inherent repulsion evident to stand as a contradiction to what they preached.

Stretching each and every sinew of her stigmatised self to make the function as socially clean as possible, she had chicken soup, chicken *biryani* and fish cuisines in the non-veg section and sweets, *parathas*, coffee, chocolates and *kulfi* in the veg section, completely forgetting in her zeal that these clean idealists are not supposed to touch meat.

With some hesitant mouthfuls, they formalised the occasion by taking some items from the cleaner section. Their embarrassed looks dividing the chasm more and more. Eating with prostitutes! Even the hardened idealist in the leader could not ignore the buzzing scarecrow: AIDS...HIV...these heavy words struck at his rattled senses. During those days, the disease was more maligned than the causes. There were huge misconceptions like the rumour that one can get it even while eating with the afflicted person.

The sex industry got a mighty shove by the rumours and talks of a pandemic. A team sponsored by United Nations Funds for Women went scurrying. They spread hair-raising information about the most lethal disease, dumped condoms at every nook corner to save the clean world from these living forms of death.

"HIV is a virus that causes AIDS...spreads through unprotected sex...females are 2.5 times more susceptible to the disease...no vaccine to secure life...drug abuse...sharing needles...etc...etc..."

Sarla's courage gave in. She was hesitating in going to be tested at the first referral unit-cum-antenatal clinic sponsored by AIDS Prevention Society and a foreign NGO. Many in the locality had been tested positive. A redder alert had been blown in the red light district. Prevalence rate was dangerous.

Her head was dizzy with fear. When life is at risk, all other tensions of this world do not mean anything. All we want is just life, nothing else. Spectres of death in all its wanton forms loomed in her head. A group of work-broken farmers, their faces weather beaten, lustfully came begging at their doorstep. They had sold the harvest in the grain market and had plenty of money in their pockets. She knew they had money but turned them away. She had decided to take all her crew to the clinic.

"The sluts, the whores...even they have the choice of choosing by looks!" one rowdy farmer spat.

The results came. They felt like celebrating. Only the latest arrival—who had been least in the trade—was tested positive. The poor girl fainted after hearing the sure-shot chimes of death right in her ears.

"Strange...but it's just luck...ours! Just lucky so far not to have a virus-ridden customer. This poor one unlucky to have one," one was heard sighing in a mixed cauldron of emotions.

Ramesh? Haven't we forgotten him? Well, nothing to tell much either. The glory of his days ended before it could really start. He had spent most of the days as majority of the inside men of the trade do. He never showed the promise to rise high in the profession. Just remained there like a pet dog. He and Sarla had come too far from each other, even though they shared the same place. Pathetic in shape, decimated physically, tobacco chewing and drinking, their relationship had come to be that of almost mere acquaintances since long.

The unfortunate new girl continuously mourned her fate, while her colleagues consoled her with some unease from a distance. A thick wall now separated them. Circumstances had forced her into that ghetto just three months back. From a village in Uttar Pradesh, she had gone intimate with at least a dozen boys and men by the time she turned sixteen. However, the pining won't go away. Her helpless nymphomania was well diagnosed by a widow from the village who led the double life of a nurse (in the eyes of the villagers) and a lady of trade in the city. No need to elaborate further how the poor girl's journey was facilitated to this end.

“Oh the filthy scum...only he has given it to me! All my lovers in the village and customers here were in pink of health,” she arrived at her desperate conclusions.

“It can only be he. He injected me with the foul grease!” she ran towards to the top-storey cubicle assigned to Ramesh.

She came out dragging the weakling. “A dying proof of what can this disease do. Oh, only if I had the guts to refuse this skeleton!” she roared and could not control the fits again and fainted.

Fully convinced of the truth of her charges, the other girls felt relieved for they felt a strange repugnance to him and could not remember having done it with him.

“So the dog sometimes went outside. Oh we hardly thought him to be capable of walking even. Got his blood spoilt with some sick bitch and then fouled this young filly!” one was heard commenting.

“What is this noise about?” the lady of the house muttered in a strangely resigned tone.

Each passing day brought new strands of grey hair, more wrinkles, and further debilitation of Sarika’s brain resulting in lesser control on what she said, heard and did.

A shocked Sarla dropped back into her chair, the memories of that night more than two decades back flashed across her memory vividly. A terrible pang of pity, even for herself, gripped her. She silently cried and sobbed watching his weak body cowered in a corner. He appeared so poor and helpless.

Later they took him to the clinic. Yes, he was positive! HIV-positive people are the unfortunate lepers of the new age. The information of every new case shook the still remaining frail foundations of their loose self.

The grief-stricken girl almost went insane. She thought of committing suicide. But her boiling guts, vigour and anguish blunted her instinct to do so. She was burning with anger and agony.

"The bitch in me will kill as many dogs as possible before I die," she was rapidly losing control of her senses and ran away from the brothel.

"Throw the sick dog out," most of the girls were adamant.

Just then a spent middle-aged man barged in. "Will have to use a condom," the lady of the house announced even before he could say anything.

"Why that would be even worse than masturbation. Scared of AIDS, eh! Why worry about your wretched life if I do not care about mine that is far better," he was fully drunk.

They threw him out. The business was suffering. The crowd in the ill-famed quarters had distinctly thinned of late. Delhi was a bustling metropolis crazily spellbound by the Western values for inspiration. To have a sexually consenting girl or boyfriend was becoming the norm. It too must have hit the industry.

There was no need to throw the sick man out. The pandemic was in its initial stage. Overzealous support organisations, government agencies and NGOs condescendingly accepted the slowly emerging cases to test the efficacy of their drugs and management of the patients. The world was lost in the myth of this new challenge to the medical science and everybody appeared puzzled and scared.

The man with imperilled longevity and suffering with almost every step was picked by understanding volunteers and shifted to the newly created AIDS patient ward of a charitable hospital. There he got the sweet-sour company of fellow sufferers and consoling, sympathising doctors. When they spoke to him in a normal, unchanging, un-mocking tone, the old man in this middle-aged dying body looked at them with the bright eyes of a child. And there he lived believing in the generosity of God and success of doctors. Ignorant of the biology of his disease that was eating his immunity like termite eat dead wood, he had every right to believe in curability till his senses were struck too weak to think and feel anymore.

With some little moisture in her eyes, Sarla wrote him letters, and sent him gifts sometimes. She still occasionally remembered those old times. She was now being helplessly carried by the current of sex trade in the endless sea of life.

Some inner glow was still burning in a clean corner of her conscience many layers below the frivolous make-up of a wench. Subconsciously driven by this semblance of truth, she started to spend much of her time in serving the old lady of the house who was rapidly losing and surrendering to premature ageing. She had virtually no control over her thoughts, words and memories.

Their business went downhill. Girls arrived hesitantly and once surefooted left quickly for greener pastures. From the past savings they had enough to survive. Sarla had attended school till the eighth standard before she eloped. She now scribbled words with a huge effort but with the eagerness of a child.

Their house was losing its sheen. What else can happen to a whore house where instead of cheap, sleazy sex magazines and books, you have works on AIDS comprising all the information and prevention of the deadly virus and the disease; the owner of the house ill; and the second in command going out of the ways and means of a paid woman?

She took the old patient to a neurologist. Pondering over the brain scan, he evaluated:

"Don't call her a bit mad! Please! She is mentally ill. It is an illness like any other, with the difference that in her case it affects her brain. We call it dementia," he tried to explain.

He prescribed anti-dementia drugs; requested the far younger looking woman to make the mentally ill lady take care of her daily needs so that it might muscle up her neurons. Even their conversation became an exercise module in which Sarla repeatedly put questions, providing multiple clues while the invalid fidgeted with every movement and word she spoke. Her sympathetic touches, drugs and exercises showed few distinct results and it was proven that the old lady was not completely mad after all. Struggling with her jumbled thoughts, memories and activities, she raked up some clues to her identity.

"Who are you and why do you constantly nag me?!" she would grind her teeth one moment.

Later, staring in the kind eyes of Sarla, she would suddenly remember her as the eloped girl who had been helplessly tossed at her threshold.

"O the poor girl! So they won't let you remain in your village!" she would hold her against her bosom, totally oblivious to the story further on.

Sarla was now in the whore house to help her see such moments, haphazardly, disarranged, but at least belonging to the old lady's life. On very rare occasions when Sarika called her by name, she thought she had been rewarded.

Why was she so sincerely serving the old lady? Well, some basic things are too deep to be ruffled by the superfluous rut of life however sleazy it might be. These may lie dormant but spring forth whenever the chance is ripe. Sarla too possessed such natural lotus that sprouted forth through the muddy waters of prostitution. She accepted whatever ray of light was filtering through the gutted by-lane of the sex bazaar.

Despite her best efforts, the old lady forgot her name completely, lost her ability to speak in a couple of years, and then further survived for another two like in a coma. They were not serving as a brothel now. She decided to serve till her death. However, problems galore, as they naturally should when you live mis-fittedly in a sex bazaar, not leading a life like those around you. But once the body has been cut, bruised, making one lesser scared of situations, then it becomes immune to further cuts. She thus braved these challenges, like a lady of her trade should. She knew that the good thing she was doing should not turn her into a cowering female, so her tongue snapped like a rattle snake to ward off any endeavour to take advantage of their changed situation.

As was inevitable, the old lady died leaving her almost all alone in the once bustling whore house. Her mourning tears for the diseased, whom she had literally served like her mother, further polished that goodness under her stigmatised skin.

Around this time elections for Delhi Assembly were announced. The Election Commission ordered that even the sex workers are to be registered as voters for the upcoming elections. The Electoral Registration Officer of the Paharganj area, accompanied by a much amused staff and committed band of social activists, toured the area. For a fortnight she toiled with the field staff to get the sex workers enrolled as voters.

The process however faced a nagging problem. Most of the brothel owners had no lease agreement with the girls. Some had not even the ownership proof of the place. So they were apprehensive of getting their girls' voter identity card, giving the place as their address. Sarla decided to get as many girls enlisted on her address as possible. She held the papers of ownership, inherited from the old lady.

However, the missionary zeal was met with an opposition and boycott. She was living like an outcaste now and she and others knew that their ways had parted on the ill-famed road. They warned her of dire consequences if she did not move out of the place—not because of the fear that she had a choice now and break free of the shackles, but because she could decide not to be a whore now.

In her early forties now, she sold the property and moved out of the filth with a decent purse and walked in a restrained, shy, unresolved manner. It was like walking on an alien planet. It was like she was learning to walk as a woman with a new identity. Almost three decades of fleecing, flattering coquetry had seeped into her skin and she knew the challenge of forcing herself to change her ways of dressing, looking, gestures and words to fit in the clean society outside.

Taking a two room set on rent in a respectable neighbourhood, she optimistically looked at the new dawn from her balcony. She was pondering over her future. But the fatigue and drudgery of three decades yawned within and she went inside to lie restfully on her clean bed again.

"It's another start for me. But this time I won't slip!" a wave of determination swathed her in a fold of contended sleep...after so many nights. After three decades in fact.

***